The Lit
Christmas
Teashop
of
Second Chances

ALSO BY DONNA ASHCROFT

Summer at the Castle Cafe

Donna Ashcroft

The Little, Christmas Teashop of Second Chances

An utterly perfect feel-good
Christmas romance

Bookouture

Published by Bookouture in 2018

An imprint of StoryFire Ltd.

Carmelite House
50 Victoria Embankment
London EC4Y 0DZ

www.bookouture.com

ISBN: 978-1-78681-601-6
eBook ISBN: 978-1-78681-600-9

For Chris, Erren and Charlie – my amazing family –
I'm so lucky to have you xxx

Chapter One

She was late, so very late! And Lily King was never late. As Lily trotted down Beach Road, she pulled her coat tighter and watched snow settle on the pavement and her nose.

Lily's eyes scanned Castle Cove promenade as she continued hurrying along the high street. On her left the pavement dipped down to a small beach which led to the sea. It was the coldest November she could remember and the waves looked dark and choppy. In the distance, a couple of boats bobbed up and down, completing the scene.

Lily checked her watch again and sped up. She shouldn't have spent so long searching for her mobile this morning, but where had she put it? Lily cast her mind back to the night before. She'd worked in the Castle Teashop until after closing time. Her phone had been in her handbag and she'd taken it out a couple of times to check for messages, expecting to hear from her best friend Emily Campbell. But her boyfriend had called instead – after that she couldn't remember anything. Pain stabbed her chest at the memory of their break-up and she shook her head, trying to forget their conversation. Perhaps she'd left the mobile on the counter in the kitchen?

On Lily's right was The Flower Pot, Castle Cove's florist, a jewellery shop and then a hair salon. The council had begun to put up Christmas decorations in preparation for the start of December and silvery-white lights twinkled along the shopfronts, lighting her way.

Lily sped up. She was really late now and still had to pop into the teashop to check for her phone before heading to the Castle Cove Restaurant, where she worked as a waitress three days a week.

Would Luc Bonnay – the restaurant's temperamental French Head Chef – sack her for tardiness before she'd even plucked up the courage to ask for a job in his kitchen? Damn, she hoped not.

As Lily passed the Anglers – the town's popular beachfront pub – the owner, Shaun Wright, flew out and came to a stop in front of her.

'Are you late?' His green eyes widened. Shaun was over six-foot and seemed to tower over her. 'Lily King the rebel. I never thought I'd see the day.'

'I've lost my mobile.' Lily fiddled with her coat, feeling jittery. 'I thought it was at home but it's probably at the teashop. Why are you up so early?'

'Heading to the brewery. We've run out of King Newt – think your dad will have opened up yet?' Lily's family owned and ran King's Brewery, which was situated at the edge of town near where she lived.

'If he hasn't, my brother will have.'

Lily's eyes darted towards the castle. 'I'm sorry Shaun, I've got to go or Luc's going to skin me alive.'

Shaun nodded, grinning. 'Blow my gorgeous fiancée a kiss when you see her.'

'Will do,' Lily said as she crossed the road to walk up the incline towards the castle. Her spirits dipped – could anyone ever love her the way Shaun loved her friend Cath? After Rogan Kelly had unceremoniously dumped her last night, there was no chance of becoming Mrs Kelly. Not that she'd particularly wanted that, but it was hard being rejected again. Lily was unlucky in love and her heart had been broken a few times now – so many that she wondered if it was even worth giving romance another try.

Cove Castle came into view as Lily broke into a jog. The castle could have been in 'Sleeping Beauty'; it had all the classic fairy-tale elements, from the four grey stone turrets at each corner to the sweeping staircase that curved up to the large oak front door. The building dated back to the seventeenth century and had been partly renovated in the last few years by the owner, making it a perfect haven for the many visitors who flooded to Castle Cove. There was a great hall, library, chapel, various living quarters and offices on the second and third floors and of course the restaurant, which catered for locals and tourists at lunchtimes and in the evenings. If you walked around the castle to the second front turret you'd find the cosy teashop, and Lily hurried towards it now, taking in the pink, blue and green Christmas lights that had already been hung in twinkling waves across the roof. As the castle was so big, it took three weeks to put up the outside decorations, so the staff always started early.

Lily got to the little teashop. It hadn't opened but was already a hive of activity as Cath Lacey – the manager and Shaun's fiancée – and Alice Appleton, the other waitress, whizzed around the welcoming room getting it ready for the steady stream of customers who'd be arriving later.

Cath's eyebrows drew together as she spotted Lily. 'You do know you're not working here today?'

'I've lost my mobile and Shaun asked me to do this.' Lily kissed her palm and blew in her friend's direction, making Cath's green eyes light up.

'Oh, I do love that man! Alice found a phone on the counter this morning. I was going to pop up to the restaurant later to see if it was yours.'

'Here it is.' Alice appeared from the kitchen. Her blonde hair was styled in a perfect ponytail and, as always, her uniform had been ironed with military precision. 'The battery's dead.'

'I'll charge it at the restaurant, I've got a spare cable.' Lily grabbed the phone, relieved. 'Thanks guys. I'll see you later.'

'I know it's pointless saying this but don't work too hard,' Cath sang as Lily headed out of the door. 'And for goodness sake, ask Luc about an interview for a job in his kitchen!'

Lily nodded, knowing Cath was just looking out for her, because while she loved working in the Castle Teashop, she was doing extra shifts at the restaurant to try to achieve her dream of becoming a chef. The Castle Teashop was like a home from home for her. It was where she felt comfortable and Cath had opened her eyes to so many things – but lately Lily had realised she needed to take a risk and follow her dreams. The time had come for new challenges and second chances if she was ever going to be happy.

Much like the kind of challenges Cath had grabbed for herself. After getting a second chance with Shaun after a messy breakup, Cath had recently shaken up her life and career by taking on even more responsibility for the running of Castle Teashop. Her first bold step had been to rebrand from café to teashop, which seemed more in keeping with the castle setting. So far, the change had gone down well with the locals and tourists and everyone was getting used to the new name. But watching Cath make changes had left Lily feeling both terrified and inspired.

Lily waved a hand as she trotted out of the front door, heading for the castle restaurant, her stomach in knots. Would today be the day she'd finally pluck up the courage to take a chance and change the lonely path she seemed to have settled on? Lily let out a deep sigh as she headed up the long staircase towards Castle Cove's entrance. Or was she destined to spend the rest of her life as she had until now – alone and too afraid to grab onto her dreams?

Chapter Two

'This soup has something floating in it and it's hot,' the woman in the red dress with the matching face complained as Lily smiled down at her. 'And you can wipe that ingratiating look off your face – waitresses should learn to keep their emotions to themselves.'

'I'm sorry.' Lily straightened the frills on her white apron as she glanced around Castle Cove Restaurant, trying to work out what to say to the customer without causing offence. 'I can see if it's possible to cool the soup if you like?'

'You should never have brought it to me like this in the first place,' the woman criticized. 'Everyone knows French soup is supposed to be served cold.'

'Of course,' Lily agreed, swiping a hand across her brown wavy hair and wishing the floor would just swallow her whole. 'Have you tried it hot though? It's really very good.'

The woman swiped a napkin across her mouth, leaving a trail of red lipstick on the starched white cotton. 'I have no intention of eating this muck. And what is that lump? It looks like someone accidently dropped their cheese on toast into my starter.'

'It's a crouton.' Lily nibbled her lip, wondering what Luc would say if he heard someone referring to his famous crouton as a mistake.

'It's typical of the dish, but if you'd prefer, I can get you a different appetizer.' Lily coloured as a couple sitting at the next table whispered and looked over, probably wondering what all the commotion was about.

'I don't want a different dish.' The customer folded her arms across her ample chest. 'I want this one, except I want you to serve it properly – cold and without any of those bread things.'

'I'm sorry, of course. You're quite right.' Lily ducked her head, picked up the bowl and headed to the kitchen, wondering how to tell Luc the customer wanted cold French onion soup. As she walked, Lily passed five of the restaurant's fifteen tables, all laid out with traditional white tablecloths, silver cutlery and shiny candelabras. The restaurant was busy this lunchtime, and she knew they were fully booked this evening.

Lily took a deep breath before entering the kitchen. As she walked into the square room, her eyes strayed to the stone fireplace at the far end. A large clock sat above the mantle, telling her there were at least another two hours before lunchtime ended, after which she'd help to lay the tables ready for her next shift.

Three walls of the kitchen were lined with modern metal cupboards, under which a mix of stainless steel industrial hobs, ovens, sinks and cooling racks sat. At the edge of the room was a servery counter, where Lily put the offending soup.

'Again, Lily? You do know you're supposed to give the food to the customers, not bring it back?' Suze Baker, one of the restaurant's sous chefs, joked. Her chocolate-brown hair was knotted on her head and she'd pulled a white cap over it. That and her white overalls contrasted with the wild smattering of dark freckles across her cheekbones and nose. 'What happened this time?' Suze asked patiently.

'The customer said it was too hot.' Lily chewed her lip as her eyes darted around the kitchen, looking for Luc. If he saw she'd returned with the soup, she'd probably kiss any dream of a job in the kitchen goodbye. He hadn't been in when she'd rocked up late this morning so she'd already dodged one bullet today. 'She wasn't so keen on the crouton either.'

Anya Jenkins, a five-foot-nothing blonde-haired waitress, whizzed into the kitchen and skidded to a stop. 'Honestly Lily, I don't know how you kept your temper. Why didn't you tell her that soup isn't meant to be served cold?'

'Because she'd have been furious. Besides, I thought the customer was always right?' Lily screwed up her nose.

'She wasn't. I love how agreeable you are, but you must be more assertive – learn to say no. No one's going to blame you for disagreeing every now and then. What are you going to do about the soup? You can't exactly freeze it.' Anya asked, running a hand through her short pixie-cut.

'I've no idea.' Lily squashed down the panic in her chest as Luc appeared from the back of the kitchen, barking orders at one of the kitchen porters. Lily's legs juddered and she picked up the soup, ready to scurry into the restaurant again just as Nate Miller, one of the other waiters, approached.

'Your customer is asking for you.' Nate gave Lily a pointed look – his cheeky dimples and surfer-dude hairstyle meant he never looked like he took anything seriously, which drove Luc nuts.

'What are you doing here, boy?' Luc glared at Nate. The chef was dressed in stripy blue and white trousers with a starched white jacket pulled tight across his rotund chest. A white hat hid his balding hairline and his permanent expression was annoyed.

'Picking up a ticket.' Nate pointed to the plates on the servery. Around them the kitchen buzzed with voices until someone dropped a dish that let off a klaxon-worthy crash and the whole room went quiet.

Luc's cheeks reddened. 'Get on with it then,' he snapped, turning on his heels and heading for the back of the kitchen. 'And sort out Lily's tables, one of you, she's coming with me.'

Lily went cold as she put the soup down again and mouthed a quick 'sorry' to Anya and Nate. Then she followed Luc through the kitchen with her head bowed. Luc stopped to scream at the kitchen porter who'd dropped the dish and to admonish a chef de partie for chopping carrots incorrectly before opening the door to the manager's office and waiting for Lily to step inside.

He sat behind the small grey desk in the centre of the office and moved his laptop to the side so he could see her. 'Sit.' He clicked a finger, pointing to a chair.

Lily's legs wobbled, but she straightened her apron and did as she was told.

Luc stared at her for a full minute before speaking. 'Simon Wolf says you wish to work as a commis?'

Lily whispered, 'Yes' and stared at the floor. There had been talk of a job coming up in the kitchen for a few weeks. The commis were the lowest rung in the kitchen, above only the porters, but it was the first step to becoming a chef and she'd been dying to talk to Luc about it but hadn't worked up the courage. She wound her fingers together nervously.

'Did you think speaking with the castle's owner instead of me would get you a job in my kitchen?' Luc's voice was low and Lily felt herself shrink.

'I honestly didn't talk to him,' she whispered. 'He overhead a conversation I had with Cath Lacey in the Castle Teashop. I'd never go behind your back.' Lily worked as a waitress in the teashop as well as the restaurant. It had been a quiet day and she'd been chatting with Cath behind the counter. Lily knew Simon had been listening but hadn't expected him to act on it.

'You didn't think of telling *me* you'd like the job?'

'I… I was working my way up to it,' Lily stammered.

'And were you planning on doing this before or after you retired?' Luc asked, before sighing deeply. 'There may be a position coming up, it's true. Honestly – Simon wants me to consider you, but I'm not sure you're the right fit.'

Lily lifted her head so their eyes met. Luc was about fifty with huge lips and a large nose that made him look terrifying. 'Why?' she squeaked, knowing her face had turned crimson.

'I have no room in my kitchen for a mouse, Lily King. I need people who work hard but say what they think, people with a brave heart.' Luc thumped a hand on his chest theatrically.

'I have a heart,' Lily peeped.

'I'm not sure if you're more scared of the customers or me.'

'You.' The word shot from Lily's mouth before she could stop it and she knew her face was probably burning even before Luc spoke – when he did, she was surprised.

'Okay.' He perked up. 'So maybe there is a brave heart buried somewhere deep. But you'll need more than that to work in my kitchen.'

'You want a flair for cooking,' Lily declared, as Luc scowled. 'Your mother told you to only ever hire people who are passionate about food, who can create magic on a plate. It doesn't matter what level they are, they need to prove they're worthy.'

Luc looked put out. 'You know this how?'

Lily looked at the floor again. 'You may have mentioned it.' *About ten thousand times.*

'*Bon.*' He bowed his head. 'And can you create magic, Lily King?'

'I make a good shepherd's pie.' Lily wanted to kick herself as Luc's frown deepened. 'And I'm quite good at… some other things.' None of which she could think of at the moment.

The chef tapped a finger on his desk. 'You will cook for me tomorrow morning, at six a.m. sharp. If it's good enough I will consider giving you a chance. If it isn't' – he waved a hand dismissively – 'you will remain a waitress. Now…' Luc pointed at the door. 'Get back to work. And Lily?' His voice hardened. 'If anyone complains about my soup again – or dares to suggest one of my masterpieces is served cold – you will tell them they are wrong, *non?*'

'*Non,*' Lily stammered. 'I mean, yes, of course. Sorry.' She stood quickly, her legs wobbling, and was out of the office and back into the kitchen again before realising that after all this time, she finally had a shot at her dream.

Chapter Three

The Beast, Lily's old car, rattled and groaned as she thumped it into first gear to ensure that this time they would get to the top of Princes Avenue, Castle Cove's steepest hill, without embarrassing themselves. On the passenger seat, the large portion of Veal Saltimbocco with prosciutto and butter sage sauce wobbled through the cling film, scenting the car and making Lily's stomach rumble.

'Almost at the top,' she sang as her ancient Nissan Micra rumbled to a stop outside a small cottage that had already been decked out prematurely in Christmas malarkey. It was only mid-November but lights flashed from the thatched roof, bejewelled reindeers dipped their heads into imaginary snow and Father Christmas waved a sack of inflated parcels in her direction.

Lily trudged through the glittering darkness to the front door.

'You're here.' Ted Abbott, a sphere-shaped man who Lily had only ever seen wearing shorts and a red fleece – and today was no exception – beamed at her from the porch. Ted was the local postman who'd been Lily dad's best friend for almost thirty years and was like family.

'What are you doing up?' Lily admonished. Ted had been ill for a few weeks and she'd been keeping an eye on him.

Ted whipped out a hanky and caught a sneeze before stepping back from the doorway. 'Waiting for you, I'm starved.'

'Sorry.' Lily checked her watch. 'I know I said I'd get here just after closing, but someone left their coat in the restaurant tonight so Simon Wolf asked me to drop it off on my way home. And I had to pick up the Beast first because I walked to work.'

'Couldn't someone else do it?'

Lily shrugged, presenting the wrapped plate with a flourish. 'You were lucky – this was the only one left.' She considered the veal. 'I added some peas because we ran out of blistered haricot verts, but I think it goes just as well.'

'One of your creations?' Ted eyed the plate suspiciously.

'No.' Lily sighed. 'I didn't have time to cook so Suze said I could have it. It's leftover from the restaurant.'

'It'll be good to try something new – your shepherd's pie the other day did taste a bit bland.' Ted followed Lily as she made her way around his small kitchen, popping the food onto a plate and sliding it into the microwave. Ted lived alone, but his kitchen was pristine and his yellow cupboards and oak worktops had recently been wiped down.

Lily laid a place at the small wooden table in the corner of the kitchen and poured out a couple of glasses of water.

'That shepherd's pie is one of my specials. I make it all the time at home.' Lily remembered the conversation with Luc earlier and scowled, wondering what on earth she'd cook in the morning. The delicate scent from the microwave filled the air and her stomach rumbled again.

'Any news on the job?' Ted asked, sliding his girth onto one of the spindly wooden chairs. The microwave beeped and Lily put the plate in front of him, ignoring the ache in her feet. How long had she been up? She checked her watch and grimaced.

'Luc's letting me cook for him tomorrow to see if I'm up to it.' Lily swirled the water in the glass in front of her, ignoring the knot in her chest.

Ted patted her hand. 'If he doesn't think so, I'll misdirect all of Cove Castle's mail.'

Lily snorted. 'You'd better not, but thanks.'

'How's it going at the teashop?'

'Alice is working there now she's staying permanently in Castle Cove.' Alice had moved to the area from London over six months earlier and had fallen head over heels with one of the local lifeboat volunteers, Jay O'Donnell. She had started working at the teashop part-time, while Lily had been covering one of the waitresses on maternity leave, but had decided to stay. 'There's still a job for me there. I'm working at least three shifts a week, and three in the restaurant, but you know I really want to get a job in the kitchen.'

Lily smoothed a finger over the crease on her forehead as Ted forked veal into his mouth. He closed his eyes and hummed. 'Wow, that's good.' He shovelled another large forkful, barely giving himself time to swallow. 'Really, really good.'

Lily nibbled her thumbnail. 'You don't think it's a bit over the top?'

'Nope,' Ted said, polishing off the rest of it with a gusto she'd never seen before.

'I guess I could try using a bit more seasoning in my shepherd's pie.' Lily thought about her treasured recipe.

'Or perhaps a different dish from time to time?' Ted coughed into his hanky which set off a melody of larger coughs. Lily started to get up but he waved her away. The hacking subsided and Lily poured Ted another glass of water and picked up his empty plate and put it in the dishwasher.

'Shouldn't you be in bed?'

'I guess.' Ted groaned. 'I feel like I've been stuck inside for weeks and the postman they brought in to cover me has been delivering things to all the wrong places.' His face brightened. 'That reminds me.' Ted heaved himself off the chair and shuffled into the front room. Lily thought about following, but her feet ached so much and she knew he'd be back in a minute, most likely forgetting why he'd gone into the front room in the first place.

'Here it is.' Ted returned and waved a pink envelope in Lily's direction, then sniffed it. 'I think the paper's scented. Postmark is London – looks like it was sent at least a week ago. My cover delivered it to the tattoo parlour in town.' He exhaled heavily as he sat.

'I don't know anyone from London.' Lily's stomach contracted.

'Isn't your fella Rogan from there?'

'His parents have a house in town.' Lily swallowed. 'And he's not my fella any more. He decided we should take a break.'

'Ah.' Ted's face said it all. 'Never trust a man who drives a Porsche. I didn't want to say while you two were courting, but it's a known fact.'

'Right.' Lily examined the envelope, wondering how many other known facts Ted had been keeping from her.

'You going to read it?' Ted leaned forwards, rocking the small table with his stomach. 'I thought about steaming it open and checking it for you, but Ben Campbell from Little Treasures popped in and I forgot.' Ben was Lily's best friend Emily Campbell's father and ran the local antique's shop in Castle Cove. Ben, Ted and Lily's dad were all friends from way back.

Lily slid a finger along the seal. Wasn't interfering with the mail illegal?

'Come on girl, the suspense is killing me.' Ted choked so she tore the envelope open and slid out the expensive sheet of folded pink paper, pulling it towards her before he could snatch it out her hands. As she read, Lily's body began to freeze, starting with her stomach and working its way outwards, until nothing seemed to want to move aside from her eyeballs.

Dearest Lily,

I thought a letter was probably the best way of getting in touch after all this time. I expected you to track me down, but recently I realised your father may not have told you anything about me. Since my maiden name is on your birth certificate, and I've remarried a couple of times, you might have found it difficult to find me.

I think you're twenty-five now? It's hard to keep up and the years have gone so fast. I'm aware I've missed out on a lot and I'd love to have the chance to make it up to you. There are so many things I'd like to share. If you feel the same, please get in touch. I enclose a business card with my contact details.
Yours truly,

Your mother

Lily opened the envelope and picked out the simple gold embossed business card which stated her mum's name – Aubrey Dean – and a profession: model. There were two phone numbers and an email account along with all of her social media accounts, followed by an expensive-sounding Knightsbridge address. Lily flinched as Ted plucked the letter from her hand.

'Oh,' he muttered a few times under his breath before finally putting the paper on the kitchen table, wafting Chanel No 5 in Lily's direction. 'That's a turn-up. I remember her leaving when you were in the hospital with pneumonia. What were you, eighteen months?'

'Almost two,' Lily whispered. 'And I haven't seen her since.'

'What are you going to do?'

Lily shook her head, still unable to move. She'd always wondered what had happened to her mother but had given up hope, years ago, of ever seeing her again. Having her get in touch after all these years was confusing. 'I have absolutely no idea.'

Chapter Four

Lily's hands quivered as she negotiated the Beast back down Ted's hill twenty minutes later. Her mother's perfume had penetrated the whole car and Lily opened a window, wincing as icy air blasted onto her face, doing the same job as two double espressos. Her mobile rang in her bag. She needed to check who'd called but there wasn't a good place to pull over – besides, she didn't trust the brakes on hills, especially steep ones.

Maybe if she sped up? That way she'd be able to find somewhere safe to pull over before the caller stopped trying. Lily put her foot on the accelerator, mildly distracted by the ringing.

The moon wasn't out tonight and the road seemed darker than usual, and even the few houses with their lights on didn't make much difference to visibility.

Lily squinted as she turned a corner, fighting the droop in her shoulders. It had been such a long day and she wasn't supposed to have worked the evening shift in the restaurant as well as lunch, but Simon Wolf had asked and she hadn't felt comfortable saying no.

Bright lights flashed suddenly, confusing Lily, and she momentarily straddled the white lines in the centre of the road. Should she go left, or right? Her heart hammered as she slammed on the brakes and pulled over to the right, swerving as a black car appeared from nowhere, filling the road.

The Beast groaned as it bounced off the edge of the pavement, bumping back onto the tarmac and then across the left-hand lane with a screech. The brakes complained loudly as Lily rammed her aching feet onto them. But instead of coming to a stop, the car seemed to spin in slow motion, sliding slowly to a standstill by the side of the road with a few worrying pings and a bump. As it did, her shoulder crashed against the edge of her door.

Lily stayed put as the car settled. She could hear steam, the kind that came from the slow cooker when you were boiling rice, but she couldn't see any damage from where she was sitting.

A face appeared at her window suddenly, then her door jerked open and she almost fell out.

'Are you okay?' Lily couldn't see the man's face in the darkness, but his gravelly voice was filled with concern.

'I'm not sure.' Lily swiped her tongue across her suddenly dry lips and wriggled her body. 'My shoulder's a bit achy.'

'You should probably try standing,' the voice muttered and she heard the crunch of shoes on tarmac as the man moved backwards, giving her space to get out. She took it slowly, and her feet complained as they hit the ground.

'Drat,' Lily whispered, taking in the Beast's front tyre, which was now flat. She wandered round to the front of the car and it took a few seconds for her eyes to adjust in the darkness. 'Is he wonky?'

Lily felt the man move beside her. 'I think you might have done something to your suspension.'

'Me?' Cross words caught in Lily's throat as she bit back the burst of irritation. She turned to look at his car, immaculately parked on the other side of the road. 'That's yours?'

'Yes.'

'You drive a Porsche?'

The stranger paused before answering, making her wonder if her words had come out all bitter and twisted.

'Only when the Lamborghini's having a tune up.' The man's tone was dry.

Lily turned. The lights from her car lit his face and she almost stepped backwards to get a better look – this man's DNA probably spelled H.O.T. because just a mere glance had her hormones dancing the Argentine tango. She couldn't see the colour of his eyes in this light, but they were large and almond-shaped and totally fixed on her, which made her stomach flutter. His jaw looked chiselled and was dusted with a five-o'clock shadow that acted like a rustic frame for a set of lips *GQ* would probably like to patent. Lily's heart hammered unhelpfully.

'I'm Josh Havellin-Scott,' the man introduced himself, his forehead creasing as she continued to stare. He held out a large hand and Lily looked at it.

'Lily King.' She squeezed the words from between her lips as her mobile started ringing again, making her turn back towards the car. 'You broke the Beast.' Tears pricked her eyes.

'Looks more like a Mavis than a Beast.' Lily raised an eyebrow at that and Josh cleared his throat, withdrawing the arm. 'And strictly speaking, you were the one swerving off the road.'

'If I hadn't I might have hit you,' Lily said politely, steeling her stupid hormones against his beauty. Ted was right, she really should have learned her lesson about hot Porsche drivers by now.

'I think we should probably leave our insurance companies to thrash out the details since I've just moved to Castle Cove – I assume you're from around here?'

'You're local?' Lily's words ended in an unattractive squeak.

'Moved in today – temporarily.' Josh's eyes tracked Lily up and down, making her feel vulnerable. She inexplicably wished she'd taken the time to freshen up her make-up before leaving Ted's house. 'Have you lived here long?'

'All my life.' Lily waited for the sneer.

'I'm from London.' Josh cocked his head, studying her before moving his eyes to the Beast. 'That's a magnificent car.'

'Thank you.' Lily blushed. 'Not many people see beyond the paintwork.'

'Oh, it's the rust.' Josh took a step backwards to admire it. 'Do we need to call someone to pick it up? I'm not sure you're going to get very far without help.'

'My brother will tow it for me in the morning. He's got a tractor…'

'I'll give you a ride home if you like? I'm not an axe murderer,' Josh added when Lily looked unsure.

'Is that because you've decided to specialise in executing cars?' she joked.

Josh's lips curved but Lily couldn't tell if he was smiling. 'Or you could get someone else to pick you up?'

Lily thought about calling her dad or one of her brothers at this hour. 'I'll take the lift, thanks.'

'Do you mind if I take some pictures before we leave?' Josh trotted to his car without waiting for Lily's answer and pulled a large camera from the boot before striding back. Then he knelt down and took a few shots of the Beast's bumper, angling the camera to the left and right. 'Incredible colours,' Josh murmured as it whirred and clicked.

'He's not rusty,' Lily croaked to herself. 'He's old and well-loved. Not that I'd expect someone like you to understand.' She picked up her handbag and locked her car, stroking a hand over the wing mirror as she waited for Josh to finish.

After what felt like hours, Josh headed for the Porsche and put his camera in the boot before climbing into the driver's seat and firing the engine. Lily got in beside him. The car smelled of leather and coffee, unlike Rogan's which had always smelled of aftershave. Lily gripped her handbag, hoping Josh was telling the truth about not being an axe murderer.

'I live on Victoria Street.' She grabbed the handle on the door in case he drove too fast. 'If you head for the hospital I'll show you where to stop, or I can give you directions from here?'

'I've been to the hospital.' Josh took a right and waited as a couple crossed the road.

'I thought you moved to Castle Cove today.'

He laughed. 'I used to holiday here when I was a kid, and a friend lives in town, so I've visited recently. I tried to take a photo of a puffin once and fell off a cliff – broke my arm in two places.'

'That was unlucky.'

'I probably shouldn't have ignored the keep-off signs,' Josh admitted.

'Oh...' Lily trailed off, unsure of how to respond. She was relieved when Josh pulled into Victoria Street. At least he hadn't broken any speed limits on their drive. 'It's up here, on the right. If you stop there I'll be close enough.'

Josh pulled up outside a row of Victorian terraced houses. They were all red-brick maisonettes built in the early nineteen-hundreds. Each had wooden sash windows and multi-coloured glass front doors – a couple of Lily's neighbours had already put Christmas wreaths up, adding even more colour.

'You live in one of those?' Josh eyed the houses.

'Upstairs, on the right, number five.' She shouldn't have told him that. Her brothers would go mental.

'Pretty glasswork on those doors. You should probably give me your number before you go,' he said suddenly, pulling his phone from his pocket.

'Oh.' Lily went crimson. Was he planning to ask her out? 'That's really nice,' she stammered, wondering how to politely decline. She wasn't ready for a new boyfriend.

Josh grinned. 'So we can swap insurance details?'

'Of course.' Mortified, Lily opened the car door and stumbled backwards towards the houses as she talked. 'Don't be silly, it's fine really. It was obviously all my fault, not yours at all. Good luck in your... um... new home, Mr Havellin-Scott, and thanks for the lift.'

'It was my pleasure. I haven't had so much fun in a while.' Josh grinned, making Lily's legs wobble and her blush deepen. She continued to back away as he watched.

'I… well. That's great,' Lily lied, feeling like ping-pong balls were bouncing off her skin it was tingling so much.

'Perhaps we'll run into each other again. I'll make sure I'm extra careful at corners from now on,' Josh teased.

Lily opened her front door in a rush, aware Josh was still watching her from the car, and closed it quickly before running upstairs to her sitting room. Then she stood by the window and watched the Porsche drive away, feeling a mix of relief that Josh had left and an odd desire to see the reckless stranger again.

Chapter Five

The tractor coughed and spluttered as Lily's brother, Scott King, steered it into King's Brewery car park before grinding to a stop and putting on the handbrake.

'It's a good job Andrew could lend me his tractor because I'm pretty sure you've buggered the suspension,' Scott moaned as he jumped out and stared at the Beast. Lily's Micra had been hooked onto the towing ring so the tyres hung in mid-air and she had an unexpected urge to hug it. 'Tell me again how it happened?' Her brother slung an arm over her shoulder. At six-foot-three Scott stood head and shoulders above Lily and she found herself leaning in to him.

'Row with a Porsche.'

'So the weasel's back?' Scott tightened his grip around her shoulders.

'Nope, another Porsche.' Lily thought about the man with the jaw-dropping looks and took a step towards her car, shaking Scott off. She turned as her brother narrowed his brown eyes. 'Rogan's still in Edinburgh – and we're no longer dating.'

Scott's full lips curved into a half smile but the sentiment didn't reach the rest of his face. 'You finally saw sense?'

Lily ignored him and headed across the gravel car park towards the brewery. The building was large and had a set of concrete steps leading up to the glass double doors, which had King's Brewery on them, painted in red, gold and black. She pushed them open and entered. They rarely felt the need to lock up, even when the shop wasn't open.

The entrance to King's Brewery was a combination of tasting room, pub and shop. The tasting room was rectangular and, while there were windows at the front, the heart of the brewery operation sat behind it, so there wasn't a lot of natural light. The floors were dark matt wood and dusty, something that didn't seem to bother Lily's brother, dad or their customers.

The wall to the left of the room had barrels of different King beers piled up against it – including Castling, King Newt and their recent award-winner, Queens IPA. There were barrels along the right edge, seating for those who wanted to linger and a long bar filled with taps advertising the craft beers Lily's family brewed. The whole place smelled of hops and beer and she took a deep breath, feeling herself settle. Her dad, Tom King, stood behind the bar sorting change into the till.

'Lily.' Her dad's face brightened and he lifted the hatch so he could give her a hug. He was almost six foot with a broad boxer's body that reminded Lily of a bear. 'I heard about the Beast. Don't worry, I'll take a look at it later. We'll get it fixed up.'

'We were talking about how it happened.' Scott's voice was dry. He'd followed Lily into the brewery and she watched him enter the small bar area so he could take over from their dad and continue to count change into the till. 'Some Porsche driver. Not Rogan,'

Scott added quickly as their father's expression turned murderous. 'Apparently Lily and Rogan are no longer seeing each other.'

Scott dropped the change, popped the hatch closed and leaned onto it, a slight curve playing on his full lips. Her brother had let his hair grow out recently so the brown locks curled around his neck and Lily had a sudden urge to pull them like she had when they were younger. Instead she smiled.

'Were you busy yesterday?' Lily asked, desperate to change the subject. She picked up a couple of dirty glasses from one of the barrel tables and put them on the bar in front of her brother. He tussled her hair.

'No longer seeing each other?' Her dad scratched his chin. 'Whose decision was that?'

'It was mutual.' Lily crossed her fingers behind her back.

'And did this split occur before or after we transferred the brewery's insurance policy to his company?' Tom looked irritated.

'Really, I've no idea.' She flashed her brightest smile as a combination of humiliation and hurt stabbed her chest. 'Do you really think you can fix the Beast?' She changed the subject.

'If I can't, I know a man who can.' Her dad's frown disappeared as he smiled indulgently at his daughter. 'How did the interview go this morning? Weren't you meant to be creating magic for Luc – did you cook your shepherd's pie?'

Lily grimaced. 'Luc got called away to France last night because his mother fell ill. Suze said I can do the interview when he gets back. She's going to help me practice.' She wasn't sure whether to feel disappointed or relieved. After receiving the letter from her mother the night before, the interview had paled into insignificance.

'Might not be a bad thing,' Scott mumbled, but Lily ignored him.

Lily paced the store, feeling her shoulders tense as she worked herself up. 'Speaking of the restaurant, someone came in called Aubrey yesterday,' Lily lied. Out of the corner of her eye she saw her brother straighten his back. 'It's funny because I've been thinking about our mother recently.'

'She's not my mother,' Scott shot back, looking annoyed. 'She was my stepmother for less than three years. I was six and you weren't even two when she left while you were in the hospital with pneumonia. I've barely thought of her during the twenty-three years since.'

'She's *my* mother.' Lily heard her voice wobble and planted a fake smile on her face. 'I'm sorry Scott, I was just wondering if she ever got in touch?'

Tom King jerked his head from side to side as his eyes darkened. 'Aside from asking for the divorce, I'm afraid not, love…' He turned away and busied himself pressing buttons on the till. 'Do you fancy a cup of tea?'

Lily shook her head and opened her mouth to ask another question.

'Isn't your Emily supposed to be flying back from Nepal today with that fiancée of hers?' her father asked, making it clear he didn't want to talk about Aubrey. 'Ben mentioned something to me last night, said you'd offered to pick them up from the airport.'

'Yes.' Lily picked up her handbag. 'She's not called yet, so I'm not sure what time to expect them.' She looked out of the double doors at the front of the brewery, at her poor broken Beast. 'I might have to borrow your car.'

☆

The Castle Teashop was busy. Alice, the newest member of the team, Cath the teashop manager and Lily almost sprinted around the counter situated to the left of the cosy tea room. The cream tables were packed and the room buzzed with the sound of laughter above the low hum of Frank Sinatra on the record player.

'Four slices of Death by Chocolate,' Alice sang as she rushed towards the kitchen with a full tray of dirty plates and cups.

'How's your dad?' Olive Simms, the wrinkled but spritely receptionist from the Castle Cove veterinary surgery, tugged on Lily's white apron as she tried to pass.

'Great.' Lily smiled, darting a worried look at the couple who were sitting at the end of the teashop underneath a colourful Cuban painting, waiting to be served. 'How are you?' Impatient, she hopped from foot to foot.

'Good.' Olive's large green jumper slid to the right of her shoulder and she tugged at it. 'It's been busy at the vets. How's the restaurant?' Before Lily could answer, Olive continued. 'I've been meaning to come up one lunchtime to try one of Luc's specials.'

Lily's smile froze. 'You don't need to eat at the restaurant. You always used to come to my house with Ted for shepherd's pie so I could try out my recipe.'

'I know, love.' Olive patted her hand. 'But a change is as good as a rest. When are you going to put up your Christmas decorations? It's looking a bit bland in here.'

'Table four's waiting.' Cath came up behind Lily, her red curls bouncing on her shoulders. 'Olive, you know I won't have decorations in the teashop before the first of December.'

'I've got to take an order,' Lily said to Olive. 'I'll come for a chat when I'm on my break.'

As Lily headed for table four, Alice appeared out of the kitchen and grabbed her. Alice's blonde hair was knotted on the top of her head and her black and white uniform looked immaculate, even though she'd probably done twice the work of everyone else since this morning. The woman was a machine.

'Your mobile's ringing in the kitchen. I know you're waiting for a call from your friend Emily, do you want to get it?'

Lily winced. 'I can't.' She indicated to the couple waiting to be served.

'I'll take their order.' Alice didn't wait for her answer.

The mobile was still ringing when Lily entered the kitchen. The room was small and dark even though they'd painted the walls bright yellow, so she switched on the overhead lights. Tall oak cabinets loomed over black marble counters and a butler sink sat to the left of a large fridge freezer. Next to that was Lily's brown leather bag – she scrambled inside it until she located the phone.

'Emily.' Lily grinned as she picked it up, but her friend had rung off. She quickly tapped redial and held her breath.

'Lily.' Emily answered immediately. 'Thank goodness I've caught you!'

'Are you at the airport already? When did you fly?' Lily's dad had dropped her at work so she'd have to walk back to the brewery to pick up his car.

'Not exactly. I'm sorry Lil…'

Lily's stomach dropped. 'What's happened? You okay?'

'We're fine, but there's been a small earthquake overnight.' The line buzzed for a second and then cleared.

'You're not in England?'

'I'm still in Nepal. The earthquake was a few miles from where we've been living. A few people have been hurt, thankfully not badly, but the school and local hospital are shut.'

'You can't fly today?' Lily pulled a chair out from the table in the middle of the room and sat.

'I'm not sure we're going to be able to fly for a couple of weeks. The airport's closed, there's a crack in the runway and the replacement doctor and nurse from Doctors Without Borders who were coming to take over from us can't get here. Even if they do, there's too much to do for us to leave straight away.'

Lily leaned on the table, pushing the phone against her ear. 'What about your wedding?' Her stomach contracted. 'It's in six weeks.'

Emily went quiet. 'I don't want to postpone. I've got my heart set on this Christmas. Rita Thomas, Simon Wolf's new PA, only squeezed us in at the castle because someone cancelled. If we change it I might not get another date for at least a year and I know it's already booked solid next December.'

'Can you organise things from there? Maybe on Skype.'

Alice burst into the kitchen to pick up a cloth, then waved at Lily on her way out.

'There's too much to do here, Lil. Besides, I'm on the only working phone and the internet's been up and down all day. I might get cut off any minute. I wondered…' Emily paused. 'Paul and I wondered…'

'What?' Lily tapped her fingers on the table. She already knew what Emily was going to ask.

'Would you organise the rest of the wedding for us?' Emily's voice came out in a rush. 'It's just a case of arranging the car, cake, shoes, food, flowers, that kind of thing. I've chosen the wedding dress. It should be okay but I need you to try it – I'm so glad we're the same size – and you can make sure your bridesmaid dress fits at the same time. The venue and vicar are booked. So is the entertainment for the evening.'

Lily choked. 'I've never organised a wedding.' She'd barely had a boyfriend for more than a few months, let alone found someone who wanted to marry her.

'Lily, you're brilliant at everything. I wouldn't ask if I wasn't desperate. Oh, and Paul's brother has just moved to the area temporarily for work so we've asked him to help out.'

'Paul's brother?'

'I've never met him. I know he's younger than Paul, and he's been living in London until recently. He'll do the wedding photos so you don't need to worry about that. Paul says he's got a good eye and he'll know what Paul likes. The two of you organising the wedding is the next best thing to us doing it.'

'Emily, I'm not sure I can.'

'Please Lil – Rita knows exactly what needs doing. I've already called and she can see you both tomorrow morning at eleven o'clock. There are only a few of the smaller things to do. I know you'll be brilliant. Please?'

Lily felt her resolve crack. 'Of course I'll do it, Emily.' Lily closed her eyes, wishing she were the kind of person who could say no. But she couldn't let her best friend down – and at the rate her love life was going, this might be the only wedding she ever got to organise.

Chapter Six

Josh parked his Porsche on the road running along the edge of a grass verge adjacent to the Castle Cove cliffs. It was a cold morning, and it looked like it would be cold all day, but he didn't mind because the sky looked especially blue which would create some good contrasts if he found the right shot. He pulled on a jacket before picking up his beloved camera from the front seat.

Josh's mobile rang as he locked the door. He hadn't managed to find a proper parking space, so the car sat partly on the road, but he wouldn't be long. He was meant to be at a meeting – he checked the clock on his dashboard – in twenty minutes.

Besides, the crazy brunette with the beautiful rust bucket was unlikely to be back on the road just yet, and hopefully not all the residents of Castle Cove drove like her.

Josh's mobile rang off, then started up again, so he pulled it out of his back pocket and answered. 'Marta.' The word was clipped but Josh's tone was warm. Marta West ran Picture Perfect, Castle Cove's art gallery. They'd been friends for almost five years, ever since they'd run into each other at a photography exhibition in Soho one Friday afternoon and had united over a dislike of the art. Now they were working on an exhibition of Josh's work to be held at Marta's gallery.

'*The Castle Cove Gazette* has offered to do a feature on your show.' Marta launched into an animated explanation, ignoring any niceties.

'Marta, how are you?' Josh's voice held a hint of sarcasm. He picked his way over a fence with a large sign on it reading *Danger, Keep Out* and headed for the edge of the cliff.

'Sorry,' Marta gushed. 'I'm excited. They're offering to do an interview, to feature pictures of the gallery and even some of your photos. This is huge, Josh.'

Josh stood at the edge of the cliff for a few seconds weighing up the shot. The air was crisp and the sea looked dark and choppy. A strong breeze cooled his face as he figured out the best angles.

'I know you hate this kind of thing, but will you at least talk to the journalist?' Marta's voice took on a pleading quality.

Josh exhaled noisily. 'I told you when we agreed on this exhibition: I don't do interviews.'

'It's *The Gazette*, Josh.'

'You talk to them then.' Josh moved further left for a better view.

'They want to talk to you.' Marta's tone was curt and Josh knew her well enough to know she was irritated.

'So do it with a deep voice.' Josh slid his feet closer to the edge of the cliff and looked down. Now that was a shot. Waves crashed against dark rocks, spurting white foam into the air; above them seagulls circled, searching for food. If he wasn't on the damn mobile he'd be able to capture it. His fingers stroked the camera.

'Fine,' Marta sniped. 'I've already told them you're unsociable and difficult so they won't be surprised. Will you at least give me a quote and I'll fill in the rest?'

Josh smiled. 'How about "if people wasted less time on the phone there would be more art"?'

The phone went quiet. 'Or, "I'm delighted to be able to display my photographs at one of the most prestigious galleries outside of London and I can't wait to see how it's received"? It's almost the same.' Josh heard the smile in Marta's voice.

'Sure. But don't expect me to speak to anyone on opening night.'

Marta huffed. 'If I feed you enough whisky, will you crack a smile for at least part of the evening?'

'Depends on how good the whisky is.' A large wave crashed on the rocks, sending an incredible arc of spray into the air. 'I've got to go Marta; my muse is calling.'

'Bullshit, Josh. Make sure you take some good pictures. I'm relying on you to wow my clients. If you're not going to talk to anyone, at least make sure you knock their socks off.'

'Always,' Josh said, and he hung up the phone and stuffed it into his back pocket. He moved even closer to the edge of the cliff. If he slipped and fell, his work would probably triple in value, which would make a few of his customers very happy. Marta would hate him, though, and he cared enough to keep his friend happy. He grabbed the camera and began to click.

Chapter Seven

'Would you like a cup of tea?' Rita smiled at Lily from behind her large desk. Her hair had been cut short and styled in spiky grey wisps and she wore chunky amber earrings and a large necklace with what looked like a dinner plate hanging on the end of it.

'I'm fine.' Lily blew out a breath and checked her watch again, trying to bank her irritation. Emily's almost brother-in-law was already late and she had to be at the restaurant for her shift in less than thirty minutes.

'I'm sure the groom's brother will be along soon.' The dark black eyeliner framing Rita's eyes gave her expression an intense edge which made Lily nervous.

'What exactly is left to plan?' Lily pulled out a notepad and pencil and laid it on Rita's desk. The pink envelope containing her mother's letter poked out from inside the notepad. She'd put it there after her visit to Ted and hadn't read it since, still undecided about what to do.

Lily caught a waft of Chanel No 5, so picked the envelope up and stuffed it back into her bag, then glanced around the large office, distracting herself. The room had been modernised, so there was a radiator next to the fireplace on the right wall and instead of exposed stone walls – like in the restaurant and chapel on the floor below – they were plastered and painted white. A framed print of Cove Castle hung on the wall behind Rita's desk. To the right of it, a small window looked out over the castle grounds. Lily could see a field of grass and beyond it lay cliffs and the sea. The sun was out and the day looked cold and crisp, but the addition of modern double glazing on the windows meant the room felt warm.

'Flowers, wine, cake, cars, shoes… and the wedding dress has been taken up so the length needs checking.' Rita read from a half-ticked list in a diary on her desk. 'You're the only bridesmaid – you need to try on your dress. Emily is on top of most things so it's just about finishing touches.' Rita smiled. 'The fun bits, really. She's definitely going to make it home in time for the wedding on Christmas Eve?'

'Definitely.' Lily checked her watch. 'Paul's brother knew what time we had to meet?'

'I spoke to him last night. Do you need to head off? Because I can run through what we need to do with both of you separately.'

'That would be way too much bother for you. It's fine.' Lily used her brightest voice and tried not to think about the expression on Suze's face if she rocked up to work late.

The door to the office opened suddenly and a man walked in without knocking. Rita began to rise and Lily stood too. She'd been half wondering if the hot Porsche driver could be Paul's brother, but it wasn't until she saw him standing in front of her, underneath the spotlights in Rita's office, that Lily realised how much she'd been hoping to see him again.

The man was even more gorgeous in the daylight than he'd been in the evening and that was saying something. Lily's stomach did an inappropriate washing-machine spin. His clothes were ruffled and he'd clearly been outside because his sandy-brown hair was windswept. Josh fixed Lily with those dark amused eyes she hadn't quite forgotten, and his full mouth tried to ease itself into an agreeable smile but didn't quite manage it.

'Josh Havellin-Scott.' He held out a hand – had he already forgotten who she was? Lily felt ridiculously disappointed.

'I remember.'

'How's Mavis?' Josh asked, his eyes scanning her face.

'The Beast is doing well,' Lily lied. In truth, her dad hadn't been able to fix the car and Scott had towed it to a garage, but she didn't want to make Josh feel guilty.

Lily watched as Josh introduced himself to Rita. He had a large camera slung over his shoulder and a black jacket that was half undone. His canvas trousers looked thick and he had grass on his boots. Josh took the chair next to Lily and put his camera on the floor and she waited for him to apologise for being late.

'So, the wedding's in…?' Josh looked at them expectantly.

'Five weeks, two days.' Rita's voice was cool but she kept her professional smile fixed firmly on her face. 'As I explained to Lily here, there are still a few things to sort out. I believe your brother wanted you to be involved?'

Josh got up so he could look out of the window. 'Great view.'

Rita looked perturbed. 'Perhaps if you leave me an email address I'll send you a list of exactly what there is to do. For starters, I've organised you an appointment with Pat Tennant for the day after tomorrow at eleven in the morning. She owns Patty Cakes, the bakery in town – Pat creates most of the cakes in Castle Cove, even the ones served in the teashop downstairs. She's been booked to create the wedding cake.'

Both Lily and Rita watched Josh's back as he continued to stare out of the window. Lily found her eyes dropping from his jacket to the back of his legs. They were long and even though his canvas trousers were loose, you could see he was muscular and probably athletic. Rita made a noise in her throat and Lily faced forwards, her face flaming.

'I think I'm meant to be setting up for lunch then,' she admitted, focusing on her hands so she didn't look at Josh again.

'I know,' Rita agreed. 'Pat's going to bring samples of cake up to the restaurant for you both to try. It's directly down the stairs when you come out of this room, then turn right,' she explained to Josh. 'You can start your shift an hour late, Lily, at midday. Simon's already cleared it with Suze who's filling in for Luc while he's away.'

'I might be late,' Josh said.

'That's fine,' Lily interjected. 'Honestly, I'm happy to choose the cake myself. I cook, so I know what I'm looking for and I know exactly what Emily would like.'

Josh studied Lily for a few seconds before turning his brown eyes on Rita. 'Is she a good baker, this Pat?'

'Exceptional.' Rita's tone was clipped.

Josh dipped his head. 'Then I'll get there for eleven, or there-abouts.' He turned to Lily. 'I eat a lot of cake so I know what I'm looking for too. Just make sure you don't eat all the samples before I arrive.'

Lily kept the smile on her face as Josh gestured goodbye before disappearing through the door.

'Well,' Rita said after a moment of stunned silence, her earrings jangling as she nodded. 'This could be interesting.'

'Indeed.' Lily grimaced, wondering what the hell Emily had got her into.

Chapter Eight

'Table three needs a fork,' Cath sang at Lily from across the teashop, her red curls shining in the sunlight that streamed in from the large floor-to-ceiling windows at the front.

Lily headed for the kitchen, almost bumping into Alice as she headed out balancing a tray of plates. 'Is it me, or is it busier today?' Alice asked as she passed.

'Definitely busier,' Lily replied.

The bell on the front door rang, signalling a new customer and, after dropping off the fork, Lily went to greet them. A woman with a young girl, aged somewhere between eleven and fourteen, entered. The girl wore a red and white school uniform and her hair had been plaited into long blonde bunches.

'Table for my daughter and I please.' The woman beamed.

'Window okay?' Lily asked, heading for a small table, empty except for a blue vase with a yellow rose in it. The woman sat and the girl glared out of the window as Lily tried to hand them menus.

'It's fine.' The woman waved them away. 'I've heard about your Death by Chocolate. Let's have two slices and hot chocolate for both of us please. Okay, Molly?'

Her daughter didn't turn her head but Lily detected a slight nod.

At the counter, as Cath sliced into a carrot cake, a large diamond sparkled on her left hand.

'Every time I see that ring it reminds me of how Shaun proposed,' Lily said wistfully, joining Cath behind the counter.

Cath's green eyes shone at the happy memory. 'It's true. It's not every day someone serenades you in a teashop on a Sunday afternoon. I can't wait to become Mrs Wright.'

'It was so romantic.' Lily blinked as her eyes welled up unexpectedly. 'It must be incredible knowing someone loves you that much.'

Cath handed her a tray with cakes and drinks piled on. 'Remember, it wasn't all plain sailing. A couple of months ago Shaun and I weren't even talking. I've got to say you deserve someone far better than Rogan – your prince will come.'

'I'm fine. I'm happy with my life,' Lily lied in her perkiest voice. 'Which table?'

'Nine. Marta West is here with Simon Wolf again.' Cath looked confused. 'I don't get those two. They spend a lot of time together for a couple of people who supposedly hate each other.'

As Lily approached the table she could see Simon and Marta were arguing. Their voices weren't raised but there was something about the expression on their faces. Lily watched Marta say something – the woman always looked immaculate and today was no exception. She wore an elegant forest-green dress with small black boots that set off her long legs. On the other side of the table, Simon clenched his jaw.

'If you continue to grind your teeth at me like that, Simon, you'll have none left,' Marta grumbled without looking at him. She flicked through a pile of papers and tapped a page with her pen. 'Ten per cent commission on sales for just displaying my art in your buildings is too much. I've told you that before, and I thought we'd agreed on two per cent?'

'I thought it was four.' Simon folded his arms and leaned back in the teashop chair. His black suit was Armani or something equally expensive, but it only succeeded in making him look like a funeral director. His blonde hair had been cut short and – while his eyes were generally a cold grey – Lily thought she saw a flash of something hot as he glared at Marta.

'Here are your drinks and cakes.' Lily placed them on the table and began to back away.

'You working at the restaurant later?' Simon asked, his mouth set in a grim line.

'I'm doing the evening shift. There's a party–'

'I know,' Simon interrupted, and Marta gave him a sharp look before picking up her cappuccino.

'Is he working you too hard, Lily? Lunchtime in here, dinner in the restaurant. Surely you need some downtime?'

Simon narrowed his eyes.

'I'm fine.' Lily flushed. 'I love working at the restaurant.'

'But what about your social life?' Marta's lipstick was bright red and made her lips look full.

'Not everyone needs to be out every night,' Simon argued. 'Some people like to take their life and business' – he looked at the papers Marta was reading – 'seriously.'

Marta's eyes sparked and Lily began to back away.

'I've got to serve a customer…' She trailed off, heading to the counter where Cath had already made the hot chocolate and sliced the cakes.

No one was talking at table two. The woman looked desperately at her daughter, who was still staring out of the window as Lily approached from behind.

'I know you liked the red bra, Molly, it's just not suitable for school.'

'Erren has one – her mother says it's fine.'

Even from where she was standing Lily could see the woman's shoulders stiffen. Lily had to hand it to her, she was doing a good job of holding onto her temper.

'How about I get you one for Christmas, for when you go out? I understand what it's like. When I was young my mother didn't let me have what I liked either, and it was frustrating.'

'I just feel a bit left out,' Molly explained, her expression softening.

'How about we drink our hot chocolates and get some energy back for more shopping? Maybe we could choose something together?'

Molly's mouth curved and she dipped her chin in agreement as Lily approached and put the drinks and cake on the table. The mum winked at Lily as Molly picked up her fork to dig in.

Lily wandered through the teashop towards the till. When she'd needed a bra she'd had to go to her dad. Her face flushed as she remembered. Tom King had sent her oldest brother Andrew to the shops with her. He'd taken her to a huge department store and she'd made him look at men's clothes while she'd tried on different training bras. None of them had thought about booking an appointment with a proper fitter or asking a woman to take her along. Asking for help wasn't the way the King family rolled.

No one had been there to police the colours, but Lily would never have chosen anything other than regulation white *sans* lace. She might have done her own washing from the age of twelve, but she'd never have risked her father, or either of her brothers, seeing the kind of underwear that stood out. Even now, Lily kept to muted colours. What had Rogan once said? *Mary Poppins could give your underwear a run for its money.* Lily had laughed at the time. Now she wasn't so sure it had been a joke.

If her mum had been around surely things would have been different. Lily's stomach warmed, imagining how lovely it would have been to go for a hot chocolate and cake with Aubrey. Her mum would be fashionable – that much was obvious from the Knightsbridge address and job. She'd know all about correct colours and dressing right. Someone tapped Lily on the shoulder and she turned.

Ted pointed at one of the tables in the middle of the teashop. 'That one okay?' He looked better than he had a few days before. He was wearing his regulation shorts and a red fleece again.

'You back at work?' Lily asked. She wouldn't need to take the order – he always had the same thing.

'Not yet. Still got a bit of a cough.' Ted tapped a hand against his chest.

'I'll get your drink.'

'You contacted that woman yet?'

'No.' Cath waved from the counter and Lily mouthed, 'Chocolate cake, please.'

'Probably for the best.' Ted pulled out a chair and made a huge performance of sitting. Even though he was meant to be resting and hadn't delivered any mail for over three weeks, he still carried his post bag. He dug inside it and pulled out some paper. 'I was doing a little digging earlier, online.' He unfolded the paper and placed it on the table. 'Your mother married a couple of times after she left your dad.' Ted tapped a finger on the piece of A4 on the top of the pile. 'She is a model, so that wasn't a lie. When I saw her on Wikipedia, I recognised her face and found this ad.' The picture showed a woman who looked about forty, sitting on a sofa with a kitten curled up beside her. Lily leaned closer. The woman was pretty, her hair was blonde and even from a distance you could see her eyes were striking.

'It's a bit fuzzy – my printer's old – but you can see you've got the same cheekbones. Her eyes are blue.' Ted studied Lily. 'Yours are brown. You got your dad's eyes and hair but you've got Aubrey's height and looks. I remember her being a looker.' He looked gloomy. 'Your dad lost his head when he met her, I remember that too. Andrew and Scott's mum, Shirley, had died eighteen months before and he was still grieving.'

'Dad doesn't talk about Aubrey.'

Cath brought Ted's hot chocolate over, her eyes scanning the papers on the table. 'Why don't you take your break, Lil, catch up with Ted? It's calmed down in here.'

Lily pulled out the chair opposite Ted.

'The whole thing was a bit of a whirlwind.' Ted looked miserable. 'I always said it would end in tears. When Shirley was killed in the car accident, the boys were only three and five. Tom had a rubbish year, then he met Aubrey at a Christmas dance over in Portsmouth and fell head over heels. She was gorgeous, but only nineteen. Tom thought she was too young. I guess eight years is a fair age difference, but a lot don't think so. Aubrey didn't give up until Tom agreed to a date. They went out and got on. The boys didn't seem to bother her – at first it all seemed like a fairy-tale.' Ted glared at the printout on the table. 'But she wasn't so keen on the boys after they married, then you came along and—'

'I know she wasn't happy,' Lily admitted. 'I was a difficult baby.'

Ted looked thoughtful. 'No more than some. Aubrey found motherhood difficult. Your dad ended up looking after you and the boys most of the time. I think he thought she'd get there in the end, but the older you got, the less she coped. Then you got pneumonia, poor mite.' He grimaced. 'You were so poorly.'

'Yet she left.' Lily felt the pain of the truth in her stomach. If she'd been easier, if she hadn't got ill, maybe she would have had the chance to go bra shopping with her mother?

'I thought you could both do with a treat.' Cath served Ted his chocolate cake, putting a slice in front of Lily along with a drink before disappearing back to the counter. Lily picked up a fork.

'I'm pretty sure she was never fully committed. You all seemed better off when she left. Tom didn't want to talk about her and he got on fine as a single father.'

'Aubrey definitely never got in touch? I asked Dad but he doesn't want to talk about her.'

'If she did, your dad didn't mention it and I don't see why he'd have kept it from you.'

Lily had a bite of the cake. It slid down her throat and seemed to stick so she took a sip of hot chocolate to wash it down. 'But she wants to see me now. Maybe she's changed?' She could hear the desperation in her voice and ate another piece of cake to hide it.

Ted grimaced. 'She might have. But remember what they say about leopards and spots, Lily.'

'I remember.' Lily just wasn't sure she wanted to believe it.

Chapter Nine

Lily's flat was situated in an upstairs maisonette located just a street away from her dad's house. She'd moved in a year before in an attempt to assert her independence, although her family checked up on her so regularly she probably should have stayed home. She paced the small living room and looked out of the window. At ten a.m. it was still grey outside and she only had an hour until she had to be at the restaurant to meet Pat and Josh. She slumped on her cream sofa and pulled her legs underneath her before picking up her mobile and staring at the screen.

The pink envelope containing her mother's letter lay on the coffee table in front of Lily. Like her car, the whole flat seemed to smell of it, like her world had been scented with Chanel No 5. Maybe it was a sign?

Lily tapped the screen of her phone and picked up her mother's business card and stared at it. If her dad or brothers found out she'd called Aubrey they'd be hurt. If she didn't call, she'd never know why her mother had left.

Was it because she hadn't been a good enough daughter? Had the cold she'd picked up one Sunday afternoon at the park that had ultimately led to pneumonia been the final straw in a long list of smaller ones? Had her mother ever loved her? Could she love her now?

She had to know.

Biting her lip, Lily dialled.

'Hello?' The woman who answered had a cool voice, *sophisticated* you might call it. Lily took a second to absorb the moment. For the first time since she was eighteen months old she was in contact with her mother. Her hand quivered. 'Hello?' the woman said again. Words hovered in Lily's brain. What would her dad say? He'd be furious and hurt. Would her brothers ever forgive her? Lily hung up.

The room felt instantly smaller, like Lily had somehow shut a part of the world out. She stood and looked out of the window at the street outside. She had a great view of Victoria Street which ran along the middle of Castle Cove and passed the entrance to the local hospital. The same hospital Audrey had walked out of twenty-three years earlier before packing her bags and leaving for good.

Tears pricked Lily's eyes. What had she done wrong? Hadn't she been a pretty enough baby? Maybe the illness had made her ugly and fractious? Too demanding for her mother – a girl of only twenty-one – who'd been destined for greater things than motherhood.

Lily picked up the mobile again and stared. Was she brave enough to find out? She jumped as it began to ring.

Lily picked up. 'Um, hello?'

'Hello.' It was the same cultured voice from before. 'Were you trying to get hold of me?'

'Y-yes.' Lily plonked herself onto the sofa, feeling lightheaded.

The woman paused. 'Is this Lily King?'

'Yes,' Lily whispered. 'How did you know?'

'I wrote to you a week or so ago. I've been expecting your call. It's the reason I called back.'

'Right.' Lily licked her lips and looked around the room, lost for words. On the mantelpiece above a small open fire sat a framed picture of her and her two brothers. It had been taken on her twenty-first birthday. They'd bought her the Beast and she'd fallen instantly in love, more for the car's imperfections than its ability to get her from A to B.

'So, Lily,' her mother continued on the other end of the line. 'I've been thinking about you recently.'

'Okay.' Lily went cold. Only recently? Aubrey hadn't been out of her mind since her father had sat her down when she was six and told her the mother she kept asking about wasn't worth having. That he, Andrew and Scott would give her more love than she'd need in a lifetime. When she'd started to protest, her dad had looked so sad Lily hadn't had the heart to push it. She'd tried to find out a little more about her mother as she was growing up, but her dad never wanted to talk about her.

'Would you like to meet up?' Aubrey continued, oblivious to the guilt gnawing at Lily's gut.

'Oh, I hadn't really thought about it…' Lily lied, twisting a finger through her hair and winding it into a brown ringlet. 'We could.' She knew she sounded unsure.

'Good,' Aubrey said swiftly. 'I'm free next Thursday. You can come to my house. It's easy to get there. I'm not far from Knightsbridge tube, on the Piccadilly line.'

'Oh right.' Somehow Lily had been expecting Aubrey to visit her in Castle Cove. Then again, if they met in London there would be far less risk of her dad or brothers finding out. She'd have to tell them eventually, but not yet. 'Okay. What time?'

'Three o'clock if you can make that? I've got a hair appointment in the morning and a meeting with my manager at five. It will be good to see you after all this time.'

'Yes.' Lily gnawed her thumbnail, feeling out of her depth. 'I'm meant to be working but I'll see if I can change my shift.' Cath would be flexible and Alice might swap shifts with her. Thankfully, Thursday was her day off at the restaurant.

'Good.' Lily heard the scratch of a pen. 'It's in my diary. I assume this is your mobile number?'

'Yes.'

'I'll text you the details before Thursday,' her mother said.

'Okay,' Lily said, wondering if she'd just made the biggest mistake of her life.

☆

Pat Tennant, owner of Patty Cakes, had set up a table in the restaurant and filled it with an assortment of cakes. Pat was tall and slender, despite her excellent cookery skills, but her most striking feature was the permanent smile that seemed to wrap itself around her face. Lily couldn't match it today – instead she checked her watch.

'Josh should have been here twenty minutes ago,' Lily observed, feeling jittery. She only had forty minutes until her shift started, and with Luc away she didn't want to make life difficult for Suze by being late.

'Do you want to try some cake?' Pat asked, her smile broadening as Anya delivered a large pot of tea with three bone-china cups and saucers and began to unload the tea service onto the starched white tablecloth.

'I always need a cuppa with cake,' Anya shared, her eyes widening as she surveyed the spread. 'Is that your famous Death by Chocolate, the one they serve in the teashop?'

'The very one.' Pat beamed. 'I should have brought more. There's a Red Velvet too, Battenberg, Vanilla & Lemon, Carrot and Fruit – all my specials, but I can do anything you fancy.'

'Let me just say yum. Is whatshisname not here yet?' Anya checked out the restaurant, but there was no point. They didn't open until twelve, so while all the tables were laid with starched white tablecloths and sparkling cutlery and glass, there was no one there to enjoy them.

'Not yet.' Lily brightened her smile. 'I guess he's running late.'

'He can't like cake, or he'd have been queuing outside before we opened. If you need any help…' Anya trailed off.

'I'll save you some, don't worry.' Lily checked the time again. Did Josh even own a watch?

'Thanks, Lily.' Anya beamed and collected the tray so she could disappear back into the kitchen.

'Did you want to try one?' Pat asked, pouring tea into the white bone-china cup.

Lily bit her lip. 'It doesn't feel right starting without Paul's brother.' Even if said brother had an almost pathological aversion to punctuality.

Pat shrugged. 'Did Emily give you any ideas about the type of wedding cake they wanted?'

'I think we should go with traditional.' It was the only option that made sense – they wouldn't offend anyone and everyone liked fruit.

'Traditional is not a word I like to hear used unless it's describing my next malt whisky,' a deep voice rumbled behind Lily, making her hormones perk up in sync with her irritation. She began to turn, but Josh pulled out the chair next to her and grabbed a slice of chocolate cake before she could stop him.

'Help yourself,' Pat said. A slight smile formed on her lips as she watched Josh devour it with an animated sigh. He wore the same coat, with jeans today, and a black t-shirt that stretched across his chest. The camera was slung over his shoulder again – the man had pounced on the cake so quickly he hadn't even stopped to put it down.

'That's good.' Josh reached for another slice but Lily grabbed his arm.

'We're meant to be comparing notes.' Lily pulled a pad and pencil from her handbag and put it on the table.

Josh stared at them. 'I'd rather eat than make notes. Life's about doing.' He picked up her pencil and pad and put them in his pocket before Lily could stop him. 'How about you try some? You've got to have been waiting for…' He checked his phone. Lily noted he had one of those. 'Ten minutes already – you could have started.'

'It was twenty,' Lily murmured. 'And *we* didn't want to be rude.'

Josh ignored the barb. 'May I?' He waved a hand in the direction of the carrot cake.

'Yes.' Pat's smile broadened as he bit into it.

Irritated and itching to reclaim her pencil, Lily picked up a piece of Death by Chocolate with the cake slice and placed it onto her plate, then she cut it in half so she could save some for Anya. She forked a little up and tried it, letting the flavours dance on her tongue.

'As always, that's really good,' Lily said. 'And you're right, I don't need to make notes because while this does taste incredible, chocolate isn't very traditional for a wedding cake. I think we should stick with fruit.'

'Paul's not keen on Fruit Cake.' Josh shovelled down the rest of the carrot cake and turned to Pat. 'Do you have anything with Smarties?'

Lily sucked in a breath.

'I could.' Pat looked intrigued. 'I've also done cakes with Maltesers or Aero, whatever you want.'

'No.' Lily put down her fork, feeling tension in the dip between her shoulder blades. 'That's something you'd expect at a children's party, not a wedding.' Her tone was sharper than she'd intended.

Josh cocked his head and studied her, his brown eyes dancing with amusement. 'Says who – *Good Housekeeping* or *Brides Magazine*?'

Lily smiled at him sweetly. 'Have you ever been to a wedding?'

Josh chuckled. 'One or two of my friends have tied the knot and I've never been one to turn down a glass of free champagne.'

Lily couldn't help herself, she huffed. 'Did you try their wedding cake?'

Josh winced. 'I share the same deep hatred of Fruit Cake as my brother. Bad childhood experience – we don't like to talk about it.'

'Why?' Lily leaned back in her chair and folded her arms. 'Did someone make you a Fruit Cake in the shape of a clock?' She flushed, feeling a sudden urge to apologise, but before she could, Josh laughed, a deep belly laugh that lit his entire face.

'Funny, very funny.' The corners of Josh's eyes crinkled as he studied her. 'What have you got against Smarties?'

'Nothing. But wedding cakes need to last until the first baby. Smarties aren't known for their longevity.'

Josh snorted. 'We can always get another cake made for the christening.'

'It's traditional,' Lily pleaded. Didn't the man understand anything?

'So is tea, but you won't catch me drinking the stuff.' Josh shuddered theatrically. 'Do you think I could get a cup of coffee?' He looked around the room.

'Once we've agreed on the cake,' Lily said firmly, surprising herself. What had got into her today? She wasn't normally so bossy or rude.

Josh didn't argue. Instead he looked at the display on the table again. 'How about we get two cakes? One to satisfy decorum and the other to actually eat.'

'We have a budget.' Lily pouted, wanting to tap her pencil on her notepad to punctuate the point – except they were still in Josh's pocket and she wasn't brave enough to rescue them.

'I'll buy the alternative cake – chocolate and Smarties.' Josh smiled at Pat. 'Lily here can choose the boring one that no one will want to eat.' He reached across and grabbed a piece of Red Velvet cake and practically inhaled it. 'Perhaps some of this on the top – I'd like three tiers too.'

'But they'll have to cut two cakes.' Uneasiness bubbled in Lily's chest. Would Emily hate it, and hate her for letting Paul's brother get away with it? She thought about her sweet-natured friend. Probably not.

'I can't imagine that'll be a problem for either of them. It's only a cake. Let's just hope we can agree on their shoes…'

'Oh.' Lily stifled the desire to pull a face. They'd have to decide on so many things, working together to create the perfect wedding for Emily, but they couldn't even compromise on dessert.

'Is that the way to the kitchen?' Josh asked, suddenly getting up.

'Sorry?' Lily watched him head to the back of the restaurant. Josh began to try the kitchen door and Lily darted a worried look in Pat's direction. 'Are you okay to wait for a second?'

'Yes.' Pat nodded.

'That's private.' Lily said tentatively, trotting so she could catch up with him. 'It's not for members of the public.'

Lily found Josh just inside the kitchen door with his camera out. He followed the room round, clicking pictures of counters and worktops, a half-cut onion, a pot bubbling on top of the stove. The kitchen team were busy chopping and prepping and hardly looked in his direction.

'I'm not a member of the public, I'm a photographer.' Josh turned, pointing the lens of his camera at Lily, and she stepped back, feeling exposed. As she did so, she heard a click.

'That's—' Lily held a hand in front of her face. 'I don't want you to take a picture of me.' She'd only applied a light layer of make-up because she'd known she'd be working today. She backed away towards the kitchen door, beckoning that Josh should follow.

Josh dropped the camera from his face. 'I'm sorry. I'm not used to my models running away.' He looked thoughtful. 'Although there was that sheep I took a photo of yesterday – she wasn't that keen either.'

'Are you comparing me to livestock?' Lily put her hands on her hips, feeling indignant, and Josh grinned.

'Not on your life. You're way prettier.' He glanced around the room. 'There are loads of great photo opportunities in here. I'd love to come back and set up a proper shoot.'

'You'll have to talk to the owner, Simon Wolf.' Lily opened the kitchen door and gestured to Josh to go through it. He paused for a second, making Lily's heart stop, then walked back into the restaurant.

Pat had started packing up, although she'd left the rest of the samples on a couple of plates. Anya was already there, clearing up the cups and saucers and eating chocolate cake.

'This is amazing,' Anya gushed as she finished the piece Lily had saved for her. 'I've left you the fruit.' She pointed to a lone slice sitting on one of the plates. 'I'm not so keen. Are you a photographer?' Anya pointed to Josh's camera.

'How did you guess?' Josh teased.

'Is that why you're in Castle Cove?' Lily blurted, her face turning crimson. 'I'm sorry, it's none of my business.'

'It's fine.' Josh's full lips curved into a half smile. 'Yes, I'm here to take photographs. Which is good news for you, because I'll be around to help you plan the wedding.'

'Super,' Lily murmured, as her heart sank.

Chapter Ten

Lily wandered down the street in Knightsbridge and checked the address on her mobile again. She straightened her skirt, wishing she'd worn something shorter, or more fashionable. Instead she'd opted for the blue suit she'd bought four years before when she'd first been job hunting. While the cut flattered her, it felt boring, especially considering she was about to meet her mother for the first time in twenty-three years.

The houses here were huge. As it was London, they were attached, but each had a set of deep marble steps running up to a black front door. Every house had the same polished silver door knocker, white shutters and a CCTV camera trained on the street. Shiny BMWs and Audis lined the pavements outside, and Lily tried to imagine what the local residents would think if she'd driven here in the Beast.

Lily came to a stop outside the gate of number forty and checked the address on her phone again, feeling her stomach churn. This was it. It was only after she'd knocked on the silver door knocker a couple of times that Lily wondered if she should be here at all.

She didn't have time to change her mind because after a few seconds the door opened and a short man dressed in a forest-green suit stood in front of her.

'Lily King?' he asked, flashing perfect white teeth.

'Yes.' Lily looked behind him, but the hall was empty.

'Ms Dean is expecting you, come in.' The man stood to one side and Lily dropped her eyes to take in his polished black shoes – definitely designer, but she couldn't tell which. She followed as the man walked to the end of the large hallway, and took in her surroundings. There was a huge oak staircase that had been buffed to a shine; a white carpet runner led up to the second floor. Above them hung a sparkling chandelier that wouldn't have looked out of place in Cove Castle. The rest of the room looked relatively empty, aside from an oak sideboard and vase with a bouquet of white lilies on it. Perhaps a visual welcome especially for her? The man came to an abrupt stop and knocked on a door to the left of the hall before entering.

Lily's mother sat on a purple chaise longue by a large fireplace that already crackled with flames. It looked like a scene from a movie. It was the last week of November but there were already Christmas stockings hanging from the mantle and a silver candelabra filled with three white candles sitting on the top. To the right, a tall Christmas tree had already been dressed in coordinating purple and silver baubles and tiny white Christmas lights winked in between the branches.

'Lily.' Aubrey rose to greet her – she looked as beautiful as she had in the photograph Ted had found. Her blonde hair was a similar length and stopped at her chin, her blue eyes were sharp and her skin looked perfect.

Aubrey's fingernails were red, the same shade as Lily's, and she wore a pair of tight black-leather trousers and a cream silk shirt. The combination made Lily feel frumpy.

'Aren't you pretty?' Aubrey flashed her white teeth before taking Lily's hand and kissing her on both cheeks. Lily was hit by a waft of Chanel No 5 and tried not to sneeze.

'You've got your father's eyes.' Aubrey studied her. 'But you're as tall as me and you've got a fantastic figure – well done.' The comment made Lily feel like a racehorse but she smiled anyway. 'Do you want a drink?' Aubrey asked.

'Water please.'

Aubrey nodded, making Lily feel like she'd passed her first test. 'Albert.' Her mother pronounced it *Al-bear*. 'Can you get us some water and bring in the clothes?'

'Clothes?' Lily asked, as Aubrey indicated that she should take the matching purple chair on the other side of the fireplace.

'A small gift,' Aubrey said, still studying her. 'I thought I'd buy you an outfit from my favourite designer. It's a little late in the season but he dropped off his winter collection earlier. I wasn't sure of your size, but I assumed you'd be slender like me, and I've missed quite a few Christmases.'

'Oh,' Lily said. Aubrey's gesture was sweet but odd. They'd never met and she was a little old to be dressed by her mother.

Albert knocked again and wheeled in a rail packed with clothes. Even from where she was sitting Lily could see the material looked expensive. The colours were muted and fashionable – dark blues, greys, silvers and, of course, black. Albert placed a couple of glasses and a bottle of water on the table before disappearing into the hall again.

'So Lily.' Aubrey poured them both a drink. 'Tell me about yourself. I know how old you are, and that you're pretty – of course

– but what do you do with your time? Have you got a boyfriend? Where do you live?'

Lily put down her glass. 'I'm a cook and a waitress.' She ignored the pinch of Aubrey's lips. 'I'm between boyfriends at the moment.' No point in going there. 'And I live in Castle Cove.'

'Ever fancied London?'

Lily swallowed. 'Not really. I love Castle Cove.'

'Ever thought of modelling?' At Lily's frown Aubrey quickly added, 'I expect Tom wouldn't have allowed it.'

Her dad probably wouldn't have said no, but Lily didn't argue.

'Are there things you'd like to know about me?' Aubrey leaned back in the chair and crossed her long legs. She had a beautiful figure and no wrinkles – the result of good genes or medical intervention? Lily wondered.

'I look after myself.' Aubrey read her mind. 'I'm forty-five, in case you were wondering. No other children.' Her lips curved downwards. 'Work always got in the way.'

'You're a model?'

Aubrey smiled at that. 'I still get plenty of work. My ex-husband, Leigh, is my manager. We managed to stay friends.'

'Ah. Good.' Lily glanced around the room. There were a couple of pictures on the wall near the fireplace. One watercolour of a boat on an empty beach and one of a half-dressed woman – it could have been a painting of Aubrey – but there were no family photos. Lily darted her eyes back to the Christmas tree. 'You've got a very nice house.' She bit her lip, feeling uncomfortable. She'd been expecting the conversation to be smoother, for them to fall into an easy pattern – then again, they were practically strangers.

'I worked hard for it. Had to give up a lot.'

A daughter, for one, but Lily wasn't going to call her mother on it.

'Do you want to try something on?' Aubrey asked suddenly.

'Oh, um, now?'

'Go on, it'll be fun.' Aubrey sprang to her feet and went to flick through the rail of clothes. 'You look good in blue.' She winced at Lily's suit. 'But if we want to make an impact I'd say silver.'

Aubrey pulled a body-con dress from the rail and held it up in front of herself. The colour set off her skin and Lily shrank. It was an attention-grabbing design, one that screamed *hey, look at me*. This dress wasn't designed for a woman who never demanded anything, let alone attention.

'Don't you think it'll be a little small?' Lily asked in her most reasonable voice.

'Nonsense. You'll look fantastic. Slip it on.' Aubrey slid the dress off the hanger and handed it to Lily. 'If you go back into the hall and take the door opposite, you'll find a bathroom.'

The cloakroom looked bigger than the entire bathroom in Lily's flat. The sink was the size of a small bath and the designers had managed to fit in a bidet as well as a loo. The radiator almost reached the ceiling; next to it sat a floor-to-ceiling mirror and a basket filled with all kinds of toiletries. Lily studied herself in the mirror before pulling off her suit and slipping on the dress. It wasn't as tight as she'd been expecting but it hugged her figure like pastry on a sausage roll. Thankfully it flattered her and Lily studied herself critically, pulling the neckline up so it covered as much of her cleavage as she could. Luckily, the silver worked with her skin tone; she'd been expecting it to make her look pale. Lily brushed her hair with her fingers until the light brown curls sat just right on her shoulders. Perhaps if she'd been wearing this the last time she'd seen Rogan he wouldn't have been so keen to break it off?

'Are you ready?' Aubrey knocked.

'Yes.' Lily checked herself out on the way to the door. When she opened it, her mother studied her for a few moments.

'You look good.' Aubrey finally smiled. 'Great, actually. You remind me of myself at your age. You'll need some different shoes. What size?'

'Five,' Lily croaked. 'It's not necessary. I have shoes at home.'

'Same size as me.' Aubrey backed away from the door, looking pleased. 'Let's go back into the sitting room. I've got boxes of shoes given to me by designers. It's great PR if I agree to wear them at parties. I don't always manage it. Albert,' she shouted. The man in the forest-green suit appeared almost instantly. 'Can you go through my wardrobe and find those silver Manolo Blahniks I was given last year? They're still in the box.'

He nodded and disappeared.

Aubrey sat and indicated that Lily should do the same. Lily dropped into the chair, finding it hard to bend, the dress was so tight. The price tag flickered into her eyeline and she read it. Fifteen hundred pounds? Lily stood. 'I can't accept this, it's too much. I mean, thank you, it's a generous gesture, but it's so expensive.' She walked towards the bathroom.

'Nonsense.' Aubrey rose smoothly and came to stand beside her. 'I get a hefty discount. I'm a very good customer and really, I'd be so offended if you said no. I feel so guilty about leaving the way

I did. Let me do a little something for you. I know it won't make up for all those lost years.' Aubrey swiped a finger underneath her eye, looking tearful. 'But it's my way of saying sorry. My first step. I know you'll find it hard to forgive me but I'll do whatever I can to put it right.'

She looked so distraught Lily patted her arm, feeling awful. 'It's fine. I'm sorry too. I just – it's a lot of money and I don't want to take advantage.' Also, she'd never wear it. There wasn't much call for silver designer dresses in Castle Cove, but Lily didn't think her mother would want to hear that. 'Perhaps we could find a cheaper one?' Her voice trailed off as Aubrey lips tightened.

'It should be this dress. You look amazing. When you come out with me you can wear it so I can properly show you off.'

'You want to show me off?' It was everything she'd wished for. Her mother wanted to go out with her, to introduce her to her friends. How many years had she been waiting for that?

'Of course. All my friends want to meet you. They'll be so excited when they see how gorgeous you are,' Aubrey exclaimed. 'And I've got lots of contacts in the modelling business so we can talk about opportunities in London.'

'I've got the chance to move up in my current job,' Lily shared quietly, but Aubrey carried on chatting about modelling opportunities as she led them back to the chairs by the fireplace. Lily knew she'd have to come clean eventually, but after all these years of waiting to have a relationship with her mother, she wasn't about to rock the boat now.

Chapter Eleven

'You're late.' Marta didn't look up from the computer when Josh entered Picture Perfect, instead she continued to tap the keyboard, looking grumpy.

'I brought cake,' Josh grunted, putting the box of chocolate cake slices from Patty Cakes on Marta's desk, along with the cup of Earl Grey she insisted on drinking. He made a face as the smell wafted towards him and glanced around.

Picture Perfect was Castle Cove's prestigious art gallery. It had a rectangular showroom, about forty-foot by twenty-five, with white paintwork and fashionable silver lights that glared at the customers from the ceiling, probably checking for flaws. The walls were filled with a mixture of art in all mediums – watercolours, oils, pastels and what could have passed for poster paints. Dotted around the space, tall display units showed off pottery, sculptures and the odd bit of hand-crafted jewellery. The whole place felt modern and trendy. On slow days, like today, Marta played hard rock on the state-of-the-art music system; when it was busier she favoured Beethoven.

Josh paced the floor, feeling irritated and scratchy. He hadn't taken a decent photo of anything for over a week, not since he'd caught Lily King in the kitchen at Castle Cove and had compared her to a sheep. His lips curved as he remembered her expression. Feisty with a hint of vulnerability – if it wasn't for the latter he'd already have asked her on a date.

'This is ugly.' Josh pointed to a red and yellow oil painting on the wall, before removing the lid on his black coffee and taking a sip. 'Reminds me of a muddy puddle.'

He heard Marta's heels tap across the long room and felt her stop behind him. 'That puddle is worth over forty thousand pounds, and it's one of the artist's cheaper works. Some of his larger paintings fetch six figures. He's very popular.'

'So is this music?' Josh winced as the drummer on the sound system performed a particularly loud solo. 'Doesn't mean it's any good.'

Marta narrowed her eyes as she turned to face Josh. 'How is *your* masterpiece shaping up for the show?'

'I'm not feeling very inspired,' Josh teased, fighting a grin when Marta looked irritated.

'You promised me a crowd pleaser.'

'If I don't deliver I'll get Picture Perfect tattooed across my chest and dance naked on the Castle Cove promenade.'

Marta laughed softly. 'I'm sure that would draw a crowd but I'd prefer a good show. A lot of people are looking forward to coming and I've persuaded more press to turn up too.'

Josh opened his mouth to complain.

'Before you tell me you're not going to talk to anyone and your work should advertise itself – I know because I've heard it all before. Besides, as you prefer actions to words, I'd like to remind you that you're supposed to be photographing me for that profile piece in *The Castle Cove Gazette*. Or are you only here to be annoying?'

Josh picked up his camera. 'I still don't understand why you couldn't get a professional to do this.'

'You are a professional, Josh,' Marta snapped. 'Besides, you're free, and with Simon Wolf demanding I pay commission on everything sold up at Cove Castle I'm a bit more strapped for cash than I'd like. But your show should change that.' Marta's face brightened and then darkened again. 'If you actually create anything to sell.'

Josh lifted his camera and peered through it. 'It's under control. Did you want the muddy puddle in the background or the more interesting white wall?'

'They're already featuring the work in the article, so wall, please.' Marta pursed her lips and went to stand in front of it, adjusting her hair. Josh took a couple of shots.

'Are your parents planning on coming to the opening?' Marta asked.

'They might accidently walk past the gallery on their way to Paul's wedding, otherwise I doubt it,' Josh said, as irritation burned his chest. He pushed it aside and took another photo. 'I'll email these to you later. Was there anything else?'

'Yes.' Marta headed for her desk. 'You mentioned you wanted fifty per cent of the commission from the sales of your work to go to which art college?' She picked up a pencil and scribbled something onto a pad, reminding Josh of the fascinating Lily King and her love of notepads.

'St Georges.' Josh cleared his mind, pushing Lily away. 'Why?'

'I thought I'd mention it to the press.' At his scowl Marta added, 'It's good publicity for St Georges and makes you sound vaguely human. Perhaps if people know about the cause they'll donate.'

'That's stupid.'

'It's called being commercial. Besides, it's not about you.'

'Jeez. Fine.' Josh went to check out a photo of a piece of drift-wood on the beach and angled his head. The light was okay, but he'd have framed the shot differently. Maybe he'd go walking again later, see if he could find anything interesting to photograph. 'You've heard of St Georges?'

'Of course.' Marta sounded frustrated. 'Best art college in the UK. What's the money for?'

Josh knew he'd have to explain it, knew Marta wouldn't leave it alone until she'd uncovered the truth. 'A bursary for students who get a place but whose parents can't afford to send them.'

Marta's hazel eyes darkened and she looked unhappy. 'Like you?'

'Oh, my parents could afford it,' Josh said, feeling a hot flash of anger. 'It's just they decided it wasn't the right course. Too busy trying to make me into a doctor like Paul.'

'You'd be a rubbish doctor.' Marta watched Josh carefully. 'You have no bedside manner at all.'

'Thank you for understanding.' Josh smiled wryly. 'It's a shame you're not my mother because she really never has.'

'Has she ever *seen* one of your photos?'

Josh closed his eyes. It had taken him a long time not to care what his parents thought about his photos and he wasn't about to start again now. 'Not recently.'

'Then she's as much of a philistine as Simon Wolf.'

Marta sat in her chair and began to make notes in her diary, and Josh watched her affectionately. For all their playful banter, Marta was his best friend. She got him and totally understood what his photography meant – would go to bat for him in any situation.

Aside from his brother Paul, Marta was the closest thing to family Josh had. While he'd always appreciated her good looks, he'd never found his friend remotely attractive and Marta felt the same about him – which had saved them from any awkward complications while working together.

The large door opened at the front of the gallery and Marta looked up and scowled.

'Speak of the devil,' she said as Simon Wolf strode in. He was dressed in a dark blue suit today – it was well cut and expensive and he looked good in it, but somehow Simon always looked uncomfortable. He watched Marta on his way to her desk, and he frowned, but Josh was sure his eyes lit up as he got closer.

'We had a meeting at two p.m., Ms West.' Simon checked his Rolex. 'It's twenty to three.'

'Sorry.' Marta glanced up from the diary and blinked. 'I had an unexpected meeting with my client. You've heard of Josh Havellin-Scott, I presume?' Marta's tone suggested Simon hadn't and she rose to her feet.

'You've mentioned him before.' Simon offered Josh his hand and he took it. 'We've got a couple of your photos at the castle. Are you here on business?' His voice sharpened.

Josh laughed at Simon's possessive tone. 'Marta's been harassing me to do a show here for a while. The timing coincided with my brother Paul's wedding and he's been delayed in Nepal so I'm helping Lily King with the plans.'

'Ah.' As Simon grinned his face transformed from suspicious to handsome. 'Emily Campbell's do. Rita filled me in. I trust everything's going well?'

'Sure.'

'At some point, you should check out the wedding cars. There's a choice of a vintage Rolls Royce or Mercedes. I hire them for events or short breaks.'

'Did you want to have this meeting, Simon?' Marta interrupted. 'Because Josh has got a show to produce.'

Simon chuckled. 'Of course, Marta, I didn't realise you were so impatient to get me alone. Josh, I hope to see you again.' He pulled out the chair opposite Marta and sat. 'So, Ms West. Shall we pick up where we left off the other day?'

Chapter Twelve

Lily waited outside of Castle Cove's florist, The Flower Pot, and peered into the window at the blooms of roses, veronicas, lilies, pine cones and berries. Sparkly white lights, silver tinsel and holly lined the room, making everything look festive and inviting. Outside the store Christmas trees of various heights were wrapped in white nets and piled against the window, a large red bow on each, providing a flash of colour. Lily rubbed her hands together. It was getting cold and had started to snow. She checked her watch even though she knew it was pointless. Josh had no sense of time, but at least she wasn't working this afternoon so didn't need to stress about being late.

A hand gripped her shoulder suddenly and Lily shrieked and spun round. Josh grinned. His hair sat in tufts and his cheeks looked red and cold, but his eyes were bright. The camera was slung across his shoulder and Lily eyed it suspiciously.

'You're late.' Lily knew the observation was pointless.

'Am I?' Josh grinned, making Lily's wayward stomach launch into a happy dance. 'I've been on the beach. No clocks there. Have you chosen?' He darted a look inside the florist.

'I thought I'd better wait. I wasn't sure if you or your brother would have an irrational dislike of any of the flowers.'

Josh chuckled as Lily blushed. She wasn't used to being rude to people, but it didn't seem to bother Josh so she didn't apologise.

'Unless you're planning on making me eat one, I'll let you take the lead today. Shall we?' Josh pointed to the door.

Entering the shop felt like walking into a treasure trove of fragrances. Lily smelled pinecones, peppermint, roses, berries and the unexpected scent of rosemary. The bell tinkled above the door as Josh closed it and a woman appeared from the back room. She had long red hair that had been plaited down her back.

'Are you here about the wedding flowers?' the woman asked, scanning both of them, letting her eyes rest on Josh. Lily wasn't surprised. The man was a walking daydream if you liked that sort of thing – she ignored the voice in her head that said she did.

'That's right.' Josh's voice seemed to have dropped in pitch, making him sound sexy and mysterious. If he kept that up the florist wouldn't be able to form another sentence. 'Nice place,' he added.

'Thanks. I'm Kirstie Davis – this is my shop.' The woman smiled, revealing perfect white teeth. 'Rita told me you're choosing the flowers for Emily's wedding?'

Josh darted a look at Lily. 'Ms King here's in control. I know nothing about flowers. I like thistles, but I'm not sure they'd work at a wedding,' he added.

Kirstie nodded. 'It's become a surprisingly popular choice for winter weddings.'

'I love thistles but they are a bit prickly,' Lily said carefully. 'Do you have other suggestions?' She checked the buckets of red, yellow and white blooms stood on the floor.

'I like working with roses,' Kirstie admitted. 'Emily and I emailed a couple of weeks ago and she said she liked them too. As the wedding is on Christmas Eve you could add some sparkle. I've got pictures out back with some examples. I'll pop and get them.' Kirstie disappeared through an archway and a black cloak of material slid across it like a door.

'Do you think sparkle is a bit untraditional for a wedding?' Lily asked Josh, nibbling her thumb, but when she turned he was photographing a sprig of mistletoe hanging from the ceiling.

'It's good to add contrast to bouquets.' Kirstie returned and answered for him. 'Reds from berries, perhaps pinecones sprayed with silver. I've got pictures here to show you what I mean.' She put a book on the counter and opened it.

'I like that.' Josh pointed to a red bouquet with sprigs of silver foliage spraying outwards. What looked like pearls had been cleverly stuck in between the flowers. 'What are they?'

'Silver beads.'

'I… I thought I was choosing,' Lily said, flicking the page over to a white bouquet. Even she could see the whole thing looked boring. She flipped the page back to the red bouquet and exhaled. 'Okay, I like it too, and the men can all have a rose with a little sprig of silver to match.'

'Are you agreeing with me?' Josh spun Lily round. 'Or am I hallucinating? Do I need to take a photo to record this momentous event?' He picked up the camera before she could answer and clicked.

'Ha ha.' Lily hid a grin, finding Josh's enthusiasm disarming. 'Don't get too excited. We haven't chosen the shoes, remember.'

'Good point. At least let's go for a drink at the teashop to celebrate.' Josh's eyes sparkled.

'Why do I think you've got an ulterior motive?'

'You got me! I've heard they serve Pat's famous Death by Chocolate cake – thought you might buy me a slice?'

'Ha.' Lily felt her cheeks heat. 'I'll take you to the door, but you're buying.' She nibbled her lip, wondering if she was being too forward, but Josh just nodded. He hung back as Lily filled in the relevant paperwork for the wedding flowers, then they headed down the promenade, past the Anglers where Shaun stood outside chatting to a couple of customers. He waved hello before disappearing into the pub.

'It's pretty here.' Josh stopped to take in the view of the beach and the sea beyond it. The snow had stopped falling but there was a smattering of white on the pavement. The sky was blue, with a few white fluffy clouds. It made the air cooler but the sunlight still sparkled on the waves and white foam. Josh lifted the camera and took a couple of shots.

'Have you always been interested in photography?' Lily asked, watching as Josh adjusted some knobs before taking a couple more pictures.

'I started when I was fifteen,' Josh answered. 'My grandmother gave me an old camera. I was a bit of a rebel and she thought it might calm me down.' Josh kept the camera fixed firmly on the view.

'Did it work?' Lily asked, moving so they were side by side. Wind blew from the sea, giving them a blast of cold, and she shivered, wishing she'd worn a bigger coat.

'Not really.' Josh snorted. 'First pictures I took were of the girls' changing room at my boarding school and I got expelled.'

'Ah.' Lily choked, unsure of what to say. At fifteen she'd been a straight-A student, working in the brewery in her spare time. She'd never have dreamed of breaking a rule or doing anything wrong. 'Did your parents take your camera away?'

'Yes. But my grandmother bought me another one. She was a bit of a rebel too.' Josh dropped the camera from his face. 'Shall we get that cake?'

'Sure,' Lily agreed. As they made their way along the promenade a black Land Rover beeped and slowed.

'Lily.' Scott poked his head out of his car, scanning both of them. 'Not working today?'

'Wedding planning,' Lily said. 'Scott, this is Josh Havellin-Scott – he's the brother of Emily's fiancée. Josh, this is *my* brother.'

Scott didn't smile but he did nod. 'What do you drive?'

'A Porsche.'

Scott's lips thinned.

'Is that a problem?' Josh looked amused.

'Depends. Do you sell insurance?'

Josh choked on the laugh. 'I barely *have* insurance. I'm a photographer.' He pointed at the camera dangling from his hip. 'Landscapes mainly, if you were about to ask.' He smiled at Lily. 'I haven't progressed to nudes. *Yet.*'

'For goodness sake,' Lily muttered as her brother's expression darkened. 'He's joking, Scott. Josh is helping me plan Emily's wedding. We're going to get a drink at the teashop. I'll catch up with you later.'

Lily heaved a sigh as she continued to walk across the promenade, ignoring her brother as he sped off. He'd be on the phone later or paying her a visit with her dad.

'You enjoy winding people up?' Lily asked, puzzled.

'Sometimes.' Josh took his time, thinking about his answer. 'You're a grown-up. I guess I thought your brother interrogating me in front of you was uncalled for.'

Lily said nothing, taken aback because Josh hadn't been deliberately annoying – he'd been standing up for her. 'My brothers are overprotective. Dad too,' she explained.

'How does your mother deal with that?'

'She isn't exactly on the scene.'

Josh didn't ask more, perhaps sensing it was an awkward subject, which Lily was thankful for. They continued up the hill and approached the castle grounds, walking around to the second front turret where the teashop was. Castle Teashop had been built inside the basement of Cove Castle and a small extension provided plenty of places for tourists and locals to sit. They served cake from Patty Cakes, sandwiches and drinks in the mornings and at lunchtimes. The teashop had a patio outside with tables and chairs so customers could take in the incredible views of the coastline and sea beyond it. No one was sitting outside today, it was too cold, but through the windows Lily could see the place was busy. Alice whirled past carrying a tray of hot chocolates and Lily paused at the doorway to wait for Josh, who kept stopping to take photos.

'It's pretty here,' he said.

'Wasn't it pretty where you were in London?' She held the door open so he could enter.

'Yes, but it's different here. I like watching the sea and the coast is incredible. Most of my photos are of nature and there's a lot to be inspired by.'

'Do you photograph people?' Lily studied him.

'Not as a rule.' Josh's eyes scanned Lily's face before he walked into the teashop.

He'd taken a photo of Lily at the restaurant, had taken one in the florist too. Did that mean Josh found her as fascinating as she found him?

Chapter Thirteen

The teashop sparkled. There was no other word for it. As it was now the first of December, Cath had lifted her moratorium on Christmas decorations and every inch of the room glittered or flashed. A small tree crammed with gold and silver baubles sat in the back corner of the teashop next to the kitchen door. Multiple strings of lights hung above them – a mass of twinkling reds, pinks, blues and whites. On the counter displaying cakes, someone had added tinsel and an animated snowman. Lily knew from last year that the snowman would sing and dance if you pressed its arm. Last year they'd had to hide it in the kitchen after a particularly precocious three-year-old had got hold of it and continued to press the button repeatedly for almost an hour.

From the record player, which also sat on the counter, a selection of Christmas songs rang out.

Cath came to greet them. Her eyes widened as she saw Josh and she waggled her eyebrows at Lily. 'It's full in here at the moment but the couple on table three are leaving in a sec, so you could sit by the window.' She pointed to a table for two. 'Want a menu?'

Josh's lips curved and Lily's stomach sparked, joining the flashing Christmas lights. 'I've already tasted the famous chocolate cake, so two slices of that, a cup of coffee and whatever Lily here's having please. Shall we sit outside?'

'You can.' Cath looked uncertain. 'But it's been snowing.'

'I don't mind,' Lily soothed her. The walk here had warmed her and there were patio heaters if they needed heat. Besides, Josh looked uncomfortable in the busy room squashed with people. 'I'll just have a cup of coffee please.'

When they got outside they saw Ted had also arrived. He'd tied a black Labrador Lily didn't recognise to the legs of one of the tables and filled a bowl with water which the dog lapped up.

Lily kissed her friend on both cheeks.

'New beau?' Ted asked. He probably thought he was whispering but since he was slightly deaf his voice carried. Josh grinned as he sat.

'No,' Lily said firmly. 'New dog?'

'No. I picked it up on my round this morning, hanging around on Cove Road. The couple there moved to somewhere in Norfolk a few days ago. I think they left the dog.' Ted patted its head. 'I gave him some food and went to see Olive at the vets. He's not chipped. They'll put posters up in the surgery in case anyone comes looking, but he needs to go somewhere in the meantime. Only thing to do is take him to the dog rescue centre – if I take him back to the vet Olive said she'd drive him there. I can't keep him, I'm allergic to pet hair, but I feel bad so I brought him out for a walk.'

'Where's the rescue centre?' Josh knelt to pat the Labrador's head.

'Ten miles away. It's a shame, he's a great dog. He was as good as gold joining me on my round this morning and didn't even jump up when I fed him.'

Cath came outside with their cakes and drinks and put them on the table. 'I brought your usual too, Ted.' She smiled and disappeared back into the teashop.

'Are you sure he doesn't belong to anyone?' Josh asked suddenly.

Ted shook his head. 'I saw him with the couple who lived on Cove Road a few times. Always wondered if they looked after him properly – he didn't look happy.' Lily didn't ask Ted how he knew if the dog was happy or not. Her friend had a good heart and would know.

'I can take him.' Josh stood suddenly.

'What do you mean?' Ted asked.

'I'll take him home. I've been walking a lot recently. It'll be nice to have company. I might even put him in a picture – he's handsome enough.'

Lily's temper flared, the vehemence of it surprising her. 'A dog isn't just for Christmas. You can't take him on.'

'Why not?' Josh turned to face her. He picked up a piece of chocolate cake and wolfed it down. The dog barked and wagged its tail.

'Because he needs a long-term home. He needs someone to love him who isn't going to walk out the minute he's too much trouble.' Lily banked the emotion building in her chest.

Josh picked up another piece of cake as he considered her.

'Who says I'm going to do that?'

Lily went crimson. 'You can't decide to adopt a dog on a whim. Earlier today we were in a florist, last week you weren't even in Castle Cove. What happens if tomorrow you want to go clubbing in London?'

'Lily,' Ted admonished.

'It's true.' Tears welled up in her eyes. 'Not everyone's cut out to own a pet. He'll need walking and feeding. What happens if he gets sick? What happens if you get a sudden desire to photograph something in Morocco and having a dog isn't convenient?' Lily's voice rose at the end and she tried to squash down her emotions for fear of embarrassing herself.

'I'll take care of him.' Josh folded his arms. The amiable grin had gone – now he just looked annoyed. 'What qualifies you to know whether I'll take care of him or not?'

'I don't know you.' Lily used her calm voice, burying the anger in her chest. 'But what I've seen tells me you aren't very reliable.'

'Why?' A dimple appeared on Josh's cheek, signalling that his anger had turned to amusement. 'Because I don't own a watch?'

'You're here temporarily, at least that's what you said. Who knows where you'll live next? You told me you fell off a cliff ignoring a danger sign, and you ran me off the road the other night so I know you're reckless,' Lily snapped, knowing she was being rude, knowing in an hour when she replayed this conversation in her head she'd be mortified.

Josh laughed. 'On the up side, I have a job that pays, which means I can afford a dog and enough flexibility that I'll have the time to walk it.' He stepped forwards and Lily felt her legs wobble but forced herself to stay put. 'I don't commit to much, Lily King, and I'll admit it's rare, but when I do, when it's something I want, I stick and I certainly don't believe in abandoning things that need me just because they suddenly become inconvenient.' The edges of his eyes crinkled as he studied her. Then Josh turned back to Ted. 'He got a name?'

'This isn't a good idea.' The emotion in Lily's throat made her voice weak.

'Chester.' Ted watched Josh lean down to stroke the dog's head again. 'I'm not sure.' Ted looked conflicted. 'I don't know you and Lily's not keen.' His eyes darted across to her.

'You'll know where I live.' Josh stood again and looked towards town. 'I'm in one of the beach houses, two doors along from Jay O'Donnell.'

'I know it.' Ted's chin bobbed. 'You signed a six-month lease and they allow pets. I know that for a fact because the last lot who lived there had cats and a rabbit. You can afford him?' Ted still looked unsure but Lily could tell he was tempted.

'I do okay,' Josh murmured. 'I can certainly feed a dog. If you want a reference you could ask Marta West in Picture Perfect, we've been friends for a long time. She'll be able to tell you if I have a reputation for turning dogs into Chinese food or abandoning pets by the side of the road when I'm going to a party.'

Ted still looked doubtful.

'I can see you're not sure. That's okay. If you want to take him to the rescue centre, go ahead.' Josh picked up his camera from the table and quickly drank his coffee before nodding to them both. He was heading towards the promenade when Ted called him back.

'I'll talk to Marta. If she says you're okay, will you come with me to the vet and meet Olive so we can register you as the temporary owner, just in case anyone turns up to claim him?'

'Sure,' Josh said.

Ted walked up to look steadily into his eyes for a few moments before nodding too. 'I have a good feeling about you. I think Chester will be fine.'

Emotion clogged Lily's throat. Ted didn't understand. Nobody understood. She'd have to watch Josh closely now, check up on him regularly to make sure he didn't abandon the dog. She pulled the bag onto her shoulder and marched off, leaving her undrunk coffee behind as she headed home feeling upset and angry with herself and Josh – because for a brief unguarded moment, she'd begun to like him.

Chapter Fourteen

'You need to put emotion into your dishes.' Suze reached across Lily and added a couple of sprigs of rosemary into the lamb already laid out on the wooden kitchen counter. Lily had been working on the dish for almost an hour and tried not to wince.

'But the recipe doesn't have rosemary in it.' Lily heard the whine in her voice and tried to brighten her expression. Suze was doing her a big favour training her – she'd given up her own time to meet Lily at her house on their day off. Even though Lily knew that Suze was currently between boyfriends and had little else to do at the moment, she needed to appreciate it and concentrate.

'Do you ever just close your eyes and imagine how you want your food to taste?'

Lily bit her lip. 'No.'

'Food is an experience, an emotion. Cooking should flow through you like the *force* in *Star Wars*, talk to you like Yoda.'

'The recipe says—' Lily began, but Suze interrupted.

'I don't give a stuff.' Her friend shut the book, her cookery bible. 'You could be great, Lily, but you have to feel your food here.' Suze hammered a fist on her chest.

'You sound like a dog whisperer.'

'Ha. I like that.' Her friend snorted. 'A food whisperer. I'll try that on Luc when he's back from France.'

'How is his mother?' Lily asked, chopping more garlic, enjoying the way it fragranced the air.

'Better. The doctors think it could just be heartburn but he's going to stay another week or two just to make sure.' Suze pointed at the ingredients on the counter. 'Which gives us a bit more time to get you ready for this interview. As I was saying, this food should talk to you. You need to get to the point where you instinctively know how it should taste, which flavours go with which. Luc won't give you a second chance to try out for a job in the kitchen if you serve him shepherd's pie.'

Lily screwed up her face. 'This is stuffed lamb breast with lemon, ricotta and oregano. I'm trying to push my boundaries.'

'Push them more. You've seasoned the lamb, now create the stuffing without the recipe. You know the ingredients – decide the quantities for yourself.'

Lily gulped as she perused the garlic, egg, pecorino cheese, ricotta and five other ingredients laid out in front of her. 'I work better to a recipe.' She could already feel the fear building inside her. What if she made it and did it all wrong? What if Luc hated it and refused to hire her?

'What's the worst that could happen?' Suze asked gently.

'I could fail. It could taste awful.' *Everyone might hate her.*

'So, you chalk it up to experience, a failed experiment, and try again. I'm pretty sure Ted will eat whatever you take him,' Suze insisted.

'He likes your cooking best.' Lily pouted.

'Perhaps because I feel it rather than following this bloody book.' Suze picked it up. 'I'm going to take this to work and put it in my locker in the staff room until further notice. We'll make a cook of you yet, Lily King. You'll be feeling this soon, cooking from the heart, and when you do, you're going to be spectacular!'

Lily watched Suze put the book in her bag. She turned back to her kitchen counter and looked at the ingredients. She couldn't do this. It felt like she'd been told to turn water into wine without a method to follow. She picked up more garlic and began to peel the skin off. Suze didn't understand anything – this was going to be a disaster. Lily's mind drifted as she worked. She was heading to London later to meet her mother in a fashionable bar somewhere in Soho. Her stomach was already in knots imagining meeting Aubrey's friends. What if she wasn't good enough? What if they hated her? She'd have to be on her best behaviour and put on her brightest smile to ensure she won them all round.

Later that morning Suze took a bite of the lamb and winced. 'There's not enough garlic, Lily. How much did you add?'

'One clove. I chopped loads, but then I put in too much salt and I thought if I added lots of garlic it would be too strong and everyone would hate it.'

Suze pursed her lips. 'I think there's a little too much salt but it's a good first attempt.' They both regarded the offerings and Lily made a face. It looked underdone and messy. She'd used too many peppercorns and too much salt and not enough of the garlic or ricotta. Suze was just being nice – the meal was a complete disaster. Even Ted wouldn't eat it. Somehow the cooking *force* Suze had talked about had passed her by.

☆

The bar in Soho was buzzing. Lily pulled the silver body-con dress further up her body, hiding her cleavage. What had possessed her to wear this in the first place? Her eyes scanned the large room. She'd had to walk downstairs into the basement where the bar was located in the heels Aubrey had given her, practically falling on each step. And that was after a particularly precarious ride on the tube where everyone had been staring – most likely thinking she looked ridiculous.

The bar buzzed with people and Lily scanned the room. It was dim, with lamps in the shape of triangles that threw white light upwards to the ceiling. There was a large square bar in the centre of the room that you could walk around, with optics on the walls and a counter built in the middle. A couple of trendy waiters dressed in DJs created colourful cocktails and poured beer from bottles into long glasses decorated with limes. It felt a long way from the Anglers, her local pub in Castle Cove, and Lily looked around for a friendly face to talk to.

Aubrey had been introducing her to people all night. Lily couldn't remember any of the names and doubted many would remember hers. Most had scanned her up and down with fixed smiles and said hello before turning back to Aubrey to ask about her latest holiday. One man from a modelling agency had handed Lily a card and asked her to call him.

Lily checked her watch. The last train home left in three quarters of an hour. If she didn't leave in the next ten minutes she'd miss it. She picked up her glass of champagne, the one her mother had handed her when she'd arrived. She hadn't wanted to drink, aware all the time that she'd have the journey back, so had nursed it to the point where it felt warm on her lips and the bubbles had all but disappeared.

Where was Aubrey?

As Lily scanned the room again, her eyes caught on a man across the bar, watching her. He had brown eyes, the same colour as Josh's. The man tried to smile but Lily skidded her eyes further round the room, searching for her mother, pushing thoughts of Josh and Chester from her head, but they crept back.

Had Josh got bored of his four-legged friend yet? Was Chester already languishing at the rescue centre? Perhaps the playful Labrador had chewed Josh's camera, or expected to be fed at a certain time which had resulted in him being ejected. Her heart squeezed as she scanned the room.

Aubrey had disappeared twenty minutes earlier, saying she was going to say *ciao* to someone important, and hadn't come back. Lily checked her watch again, feeling her pulse climb. She didn't want to leave without saying goodbye, but if Aubrey didn't turn up in the next minute she'd have to.

'Hello darling.' Suddenly Aubrey slung an arm over Lily's shoulder and pulled her close, making her breathe in Chanel No 5. 'Sorry I took so long, I was catching up with a friend, finding out more about the modelling business for twenty-somethings. I was worried you'd be too old, but apparently there are still plenty of opportunities. All we need to do is get a portfolio done. I've already got someone in mind.'

'Oh, that's so kind.' Lily put her glass down. 'You shouldn't have. I mean—' Aubrey frowned and Lily stopped talking. 'Maybe we should discuss it later, I really need to go.'

'Already?'

'I need to get back to Castle Cove tonight. I'm working in the teashop tomorrow.'

'Can't you skip it?' Aubrey whined. 'Make up an excuse, a painful headache?'

'I can't leave Cath alone – it's busy in the mornings and I promised I'd serve in the restaurant tomorrow evening.'

Aubrey's expression darkened and then brightened again. 'I suppose I should be impressed you have such a strong sense of responsibility. That's down to your father's genes.' Her laughter tinkled. 'No matter, we'll be seeing each other again in a couple of weeks. There's a party I wanted to talk to you about.'

Another party? Lily's stomach sank. She'd been wanting to spend some quality time alone with Aubrey. 'Where?'

'Now that's a coincidence – it's at Castle Cove. A good friend of mine is hosting it. Madeline Green. Do you know of her?' Aubrey asked.

'No.' Lily shook her head. Castle Cove was small, but Lily kept to her own trusty circle of friends so she didn't know everyone.

Aubrey looked disappointed. 'She's having a twenty-first for her daughter. There will be more than hundred people attending. I thought it would be another great opportunity to show you off.' Aubrey flashed a smile. 'Let people get to know *my* daughter.'

'Oh, that's lovely.' Lily just about got the words out. If her mother came to Castle Cove, how would she keep their meeting a secret? How would she stop her dad and brothers from finding out?

'And we'll have to sort out a new outfit, so you can really create a splash.'

'Great…' Lily's voice trailed off. Another party and new dress – she'd have to go along with it. But at some point in the future, Lily was going to have to tell Aubrey how she really felt about getting dressed up and being the centre of attention – she just wasn't sure how to do it.

Chapter Fifteen

Late walks were the best kind, Josh decided, as he parked his car on the street and headed along Station Road, intending to take a short stroll. Later he'd detour out of Castle Cove to check out the nearby cliffs at night. In front of him Chester sniffed at the pavement and paused to ogle a lamppost, bringing them both to an abrupt halt. The moon was high and a billion stars seemed to be out, making the rooftops of Castle Cove sparkle. There was a picture here somewhere and if he walked for long enough he'd find it. Josh shivered – he hadn't worn enough. Despite regularly wandering the streets at night taking photographs, he hadn't learned to layer up. His mother was right. He had never listened to her.

'Sit.' Josh tried the command on a whim to see if his new companion would obey. Chester stopped to sniff a large rock on the pavement, ignoring him, and Josh laughed. 'My kind of guy.' He stroked the Labrador's head. 'You know what you want and you're not afraid to go for it – as long as you stay house trained we'll get along fine.'

They approached Castle Cove station just as a train arrived.

'Didn't realise the service ran this late,' Josh said, but the dog didn't answer. 'Nice building too.' He lifted the camera up to his face but Chester pulled on the lead, jerking it down again. 'Stop,' Josh commanded and the Labrador instantly obeyed. Yes, they'd get along fine.

Josh took a couple of photos of the outside of the station, getting a close-up of one of the black wrought-iron posts at the entrance. As he did, he heard the click of heels and looked up just as Lily appeared from the exit in a pair of shoes that made her legs look long and shapely and a dress that should have been illegal, it was so tight. The wrap draped around her shoulders was fit for nothing.

'Are you really walking alone dressed in that?' Josh found himself snapping before his brain caught up with his mouth. Lily stopped dead and narrowed her eyes before dropping her gaze suddenly to Chester. Her expression softened and she bent to pat the dog's head.

'Still alive,' Lily murmured.

'Yep. I've had him for all of three days and I've not sold him to a restaurant yet – *go me*. Where have you been?' Josh's words came out more irritated than he'd intended and he caught the tail end of a flinch.

Lily straightened and Josh had to drag his eyes away from the dress again to face her.

'I've got two brothers already, Mr Havellin-Scott, I'm not auditioning for another.' Lily flushed crimson but held her ground.

'One sibling's quite enough for me. I don't want to plan any *more* weddings. But you're right. I was being nosy.' Josh wasn't going to apologise. He'd learned a long time ago that apologies meant very little – it was actions, not words, that mattered.

Lily watched his face and Josh took the opportunity to scan hers. Her eyes looked tired and she had the air of someone weighed down with something – a guilty conscience perhaps?

'You feeling bad about giving me a hard time about the dog?' Josh guessed, despite sensing it had nothing to do with him. Why he was encouraging Lily to open up he didn't know – he usually lived by the motto *other people's emotions are their own.*

'No.' Lily scowled. 'As you mentioned already, it's only been three days. Let's see how you feel after a couple more.'

'You'll eat those words, Lily King.' Josh smiled, finding her lack of faith in him more challenging than insulting. Plus, Lily didn't strike him as the type of woman who spoke her mind very often so her candidness was actually a compliment. 'You want a lift? Those shoes look expensive.' *Not to mention uncomfortable.*

Lily looked at her feet. 'I was hoping for a cab.' She checked the empty street and car park.

'Mavis not back on the road?'

Lily looked unhappy. 'I'm still waiting for the garage to fix the Beast.' Her eyes scanned the pavement and stopped at his Porsche. 'A lift would be good – it's been a long night.'

They walked to his car with Chester trotting beside them. Josh had already placed some blankets in the small space behind the driver's seat and the dog happily climbed in, leaving Lily the front. She somehow managed to get herself inside despite the tightness of the silver dress. She put on her seatbelt and stared forward, letting out a long, sad breath.

'Want to talk about it?' Josh asked, starting the engine and wondering what had got into him.

'Why, you want some leverage when we choose the wedding shoes?'

Josh let out a quick burst of laughter. 'Hadn't occurred to me, but now you mention it, that's a pretty good idea.'

Lily's shoulders relaxed as she sank back in the seat. 'I'm sorry to disappoint you but I'm far too boring for secrets.'

'You're not boring.' Josh put the car into gear. 'You're repressed.'

'Am not,' Lily squeaked. 'And that's rude.'

Josh tutted. 'The truth isn't rude – there's an awful lot going on under that surface and none of it's boring.'

'You've known me for what – ten minutes – and you understand me better than my family and friends?' Lily didn't sound insulted, more shocked.

Josh grinned. 'Photographer's eye. I see beyond the surface. I'd say you're wild, Lily King, not boring. Just look at that dress.' He kept his eyes on the road rather than following his own instructions. He didn't want to have another accident.

'The dress was my mother's idea.' Lily sounded mildly put out.

'I thought she wasn't on the scene?' They passed Cove Castle and headed along the promenade.

'Ah, well…' Lily trailed off, looking unhappy, and Josh didn't press her.

'Want to go for a drive?' he asked on a whim. For some reason, now Lily was in the car with him he didn't want to let her go. 'Chester and I were planning on hitting the cliffs at the other side of town. There's a great place to park – some incredible views. I often go there to think and I thought I'd take some photos.'

Lily didn't answer for a few moments and when she did Josh was surprised. 'Okay, I'm not tired yet. But I can't get out of the car. These shoes are good for nothing.'

'I wouldn't say nothing but I've got some wellies in the boot. They'll work fine with the dress. If you're lucky I'll take a photo of you.'

'Point that camera at me and I'll give you wild,' Lily growled. Josh grinned and turned right, then left into Charles Street, following the train track out of town. It only took ten minutes to hit the cliffs. As he stopped the car and pulled on the handbrake, Josh realised they hadn't spoken for the whole journey but the silence had been oddly calming.

Josh looked out of the windscreen at the sky and full moon. From here he could see the sea; light shone on the waves, creating a yellow pathway to the horizon. In the distance, he could just about make out a small boat.

Beside him Lily sighed. 'My mother asked to meet me a few weeks ago.' Josh watched her hands wind together and tighten. 'I hadn't seen her for twenty-three years and I've wanted to so much.' Her voice dropped to a whisper.

'You met her tonight?'

Out of the corner of his eye Josh saw Lily shake her head. Her hair swayed, the brown curls catching the moonlight. 'I met her a week ago – tonight I went to Soho and met some of her friends.'

'You don't sound very happy about it,' Josh said bluntly.

Lily's lips tightened. 'It was fine. We don't know each other that well yet, but she's lovely.' Her forehead creased and Josh wondered if the frown was conscious. 'There's a party at Cove Castle in a couple of weeks and she wants me to go with her.'

'And that's a problem because?'

'I haven't told my dad or brothers that I've been meeting her.'

'They wouldn't like it?'

Lily bit her lip. 'I don't know why I'm telling you this. I don't even know if I like you… and that's rude, I'm sorry.'

Josh smiled. 'Don't apologise. I've heard it before.' He wasn't offended. 'Perhaps that's why you're telling me, because you're not sure you like me, and so you're not afraid of what I'll think.'

Lily stroked a finger across her lips, looking thoughtful, and Josh had an overwhelming desire to reach for his camera again. 'Shall we take a walk along the cliff?' he asked instead, not waiting for her answer. Josh opened the car door and hopped out, moving his seat so Chester could join him. Reaching inside the boot, he pulled out his wellies and a fleece big enough to cover the dress, and handed them to Lily. Instead of waiting, Josh marched towards the edge of the cliff, ignoring a red sign he couldn't read in the darkness, and started taking photos of the moon. He'd taken a couple of good shots when he felt Lily behind him. He jumped when she tapped him on the shoulder.

'Will you show me?' Lily pointed to his camera and it took Josh a couple of seconds to reply.

'Okay.' He stepped beside her and switched the camera to VIEW then watched, feeling strangely uncomfortable, as Lily skimmed through his latest shots. There were the ones of the sea, a few close-ups of the post at the train station, pictures of the beach, of Chester, around Castle Cove. Josh stopped watching and gazed out at the sea.

'These are good,' Lily said in the end. 'Do you sell a lot of pictures?'

'Keeps me in dog food and beer. I've been thinking.' Josh changed the subject, unwilling to boast about his work. 'Does your family have to know about your mother? Won't it be a private party?'

'I guess,' Lily admitted. 'I don't like lying...'

'You either tell them or you don't – go or you don't. It's very simple, Lily, just figure out what *you* want.'

A smile played on the corner of Lily's lips and Josh felt a strong wave of desire that was both unexpected and unwelcome, so took a step back, almost tripping over the sign he hadn't read.

'Josh, that says "danger",' Lily squeaked, looking down at the sign. 'We need to go back to the car.' She took off at a trot, still holding his camera, hobbling in his too-big wellies and ridiculous dress, with the fleece clutched around her like a straightjacket.

'Damn right,' Josh muttered, following her. Danger spelled exactly what Lily King was and he'd do well to remember that and steer clear.

☆

When Josh's mobile rang the next morning he ignored it. Instead he tumbled out of bed, almost jumping out of his skin when he opened his bedroom door and tripped over the large black Labrador curled on the hall floor.

'*Woof,*' Chester said.

'Urgh,' Josh responded, heading downstairs and opening the dog food and back door in quick succession. Chester grabbed a mouthful of food before going outside to do his business in the garden. 'Who said men couldn't multitask?' Josh switched on the coffee machine and walked into his living room so he could stand by the windows at the end. The house was large for one person, even with the added four-legged lodger. The living room had an open fireplace and a grey sofa and chairs that had been artfully covered with blankets. Chester had clearly been sleeping on the sofa overnight because one blanket had been ruffled. One end of the room housed floor-to-ceiling patio doors, which opened out onto a deck that Josh hadn't ventured onto yet. Beyond it, a small grassed area led to a gate and the beach. They'd go for a walk this morning, blow off some cobwebs. Josh went back to the kitchen to pour out his coffee just as his mobile rang again. He'd left it charging in his office so quickly grabbed it and answered without checking the screen.

'Josh.' His mother's cool tone could have frozen water.

'Yup.' Josh sipped from his mug, relishing the burn from the hot coffee.

'How are you settling in?'

It was the first time they'd spoken since he'd moved so Josh wasn't surprised by the question. He let his eyes scan the living room as he walked back into it and slumped onto the sofa. Josh had already replaced all the standard rental pictures with his own photos and his eyes rested on one from the beach he'd taken a few years before. There was a piece of driftwood in the foreground and in the background the waves were huge. He'd been out walking with Marta, he remembered – it had been his first visit to see her at Castle Cove.

'How are the wedding plans progressing? Paul mentioned you were helping with the arrangements.'

Josh's mind slid to Lily, to his feelings on the clifftop when he'd wanted to kiss her. He stood and marched to the door to open it for Chester, who came bounding in and headed for his bowl.

'Fine.'

'I've got plenty of experience with events if you find it too much.' His mother's tone gave away the fact that she didn't trust him – but her opinion didn't bother Josh any more.

'Emily's friend has been helping. Between us we're managing to muddle through.' Josh's tone was dry.

His mother let out a long-suffering sigh. 'Have you thought any more about my offer?'

'To send me back to school?' Josh felt the flicker of his temper and tried to bank it by drinking another mouthful of coffee.

'You'd make a great doctor,' she said.

Josh closed his eyes. The conversation had become so familiar he really should engrave it in a piece of wood and send it to his parents. It would save them the bother of recreating the actual words.

'I'd be a terrible doctor. I've got no bedside manner at all.' Josh repeated Marta's words with a curve on his lips.

'You could learn.'

'Mother.' Josh had stopped calling her 'Mum' years earlier. 'Is there anything else, because I've got work to do? You know, photos, art – it's been my living for a few years.'

Josh heard a sniff. 'Pictures are fine, but if you want to make real money you'll need a profession, not a hobby. Just look at Paul, he owns a home in Chelsea.'

'And I'm renting in Castle Cove.' Josh's eyes swept the room downstairs. He could afford this house three times over from the money he'd made from his photographs, but had never felt the desire to stay put for long. Life wasn't about settling down or attachments – it was about living for the thrill, capturing the moment when you could.

'At least try. We'll pay your way and you can even stay here with your father and I.' Josh snorted imagining that. 'Or at Paul's. He seems determined to travel the world for a few years so I expect his house will be free even after this marriage.'

Josh rolled his eyes as Chester bounded into the living room from the kitchen and hopped up onto the sofa beside him – flouting the discussion they'd had the evening before about where he could and couldn't sit. No rules for the dog either. Josh smiled and patted the Lab's head.

'Sorry Mother, I've got to go, there's someone at the door. Speak next week.' Josh rang off before his mother could answer and stood, grabbing his coffee cup so he could refill it, but then changed his mind. 'Walk?' he asked and Chester immediately bounded off the sofa, heading for the back door.

Josh needed to clear his head, to exercise off the conversation with his mother. He'd spent years learning not to care what she thought – he wasn't going to start now.

Chapter Sixteen

When Lily walked into the King's Brewery the first person she saw was her oldest brother Andrew, topping up glasses next to the tasting station.

'Lily.' Andrew spotted her and came over to give her a hug. Her brother was thirty-one, with dark brown hair that had begun to recede over the last couple of years, matching brown eyes and a face full of stubble.

'You been up all night again?' Lily brushed a finger over his chin and gave him a quick hug.

Andrew nodded. 'Doing the brewery's books. Why are you here, is Dad expecting you to work?'

'No, I came for an update on the Beast and I'm not working this morning so I thought I'd come and see everyone.' If she didn't check in regularly she knew one of her family would call in to check on her.

'Dad's in the office.' Andrew pointed towards the back as Josh and Marta walked into the shop, making Lily's heart do an unexpected flip. 'Customer.' Andrew headed for the bar and pressed a small doorbell to summon help before standing back by his sister.

Josh cast an eye over both of them. He wore loose jeans today and a blue shirt, but the camera Lily had gotten so used to seeing slung over his shoulder was nowhere to be seen. 'Is that another brother?' Josh asked.

Lily nodded.

'Got any more?'

'Nope.'

Josh turned to Andrew. 'I drive a Porsche but I don't sell insurance, in case you were wondering.'

'Good to know, but who exactly are you?' Andrew asked, looking suspicious.

'Josh is the brother of Emily's fiancée. He's a photographer,' Lily explained before Andrew questioned him further.

'He's doing a show at my gallery. It opens on the twentieth,' Marta interjected. 'I hope you'll all come, I've got leaflets in the car.'

'A show?' Lily asked Josh, surprised.

'Josh's work is very popular. There are a couple of his photos in the teashop.' As Marta answered, Josh scowled.

'Those are yours?' Lily asked – she'd admired them a couple of times.

'I'm not at all surprised you didn't know that.' Marta blew out a breath resignedly. 'Josh doesn't believe in advertising his work. He seems to think he can gather fans without trying at all.'

'We're here to buy beer, not advertise the show,' Josh complained. 'You work here too?' he asked Lily.

'I did but not any more.'

'You know about beer?'

Andrew slung a possessive arm around his sister's shoulder, making her sigh. 'Raised on it as a toddler. What Lily doesn't know I can certainly fill in.'

'What do you want it for?' Lily shrugged off her brother and headed to the tasting station.

'I thought I'd do a welcome home night in at my house when Paul comes back. Wanted to get some beers in for it.'

'You drink whisky,' Marta said.

'Paul likes craft beer and I'm guessing he's not had a chance to drink it out in Nepal,' Josh explained.

Lily poured a finger into a small glass at the tasting station and handed it to Josh. 'This is our award-winner, Queen's IPA. Where's Chester?'

Josh finished the glass. 'Probably being made into spare ribs as we speak.'

When Lily gasped, Josh laughed. 'You don't think much of me, do you? He's tied up outside with a bowl of water. I assumed you wouldn't want a dog in here.'

'Sorry.' Lily took the glass, filling it up from the next barrel. 'You're right, I'm not giving you a fair chance.' Lily had no idea why. Perhaps Josh reminded her too much of Rogan? Or perhaps it was a defence mechanism because she liked him more than she should – and while she found him attractive, his irresponsible, rebellious attitude to life proved he wasn't the man for her. After her recent experience with Rogan she needed people in her life she could rely on. 'This is King Newt. It's my second favourite – it's got a very hoppy flavour.'

Josh's mouth quirked. 'You drink beer?'

'Do you only think people can drink real ale if they have hairs on their chest?'

Josh rocked back on his heels. 'You're right, it shouldn't surprise me, and I hate people who make assumptions like that. If my grandmother was still around she'd box my ears. I apologise.' He looked serious. 'So, which is your favourite beer, Lily King?' He drank the sample and licked his lips.

'That'll be the next one, Castling.' Lily poured a finger into the glass and handed it to him.

'You going to join me?'

'Can't. I'm working a shift later in the restaurant. If I drink Suze will box my ears.'

Josh sipped. 'Good choice. I'll take a barrel of that and some of the Queens. Do they serve this anywhere locally?"

'At the Anglers in town and Castle Cove Restaurant,' Andrew answered as he walked towards the bar, just as Lily's dad appeared from the back room.

'Sorry folks, I've been on the phone.' Tom hugged Lily as Andrew arranged a couple of barrels into a display on the counter. 'By the way, I'm picking up the Beast later – he's fixed so I'll drop him round to your house.'

'Thanks Dad, I was wondering how he was doing. I can pick him up myself.'

'I'll do it,' her dad insisted.

The bell on the front door rang and Ted wandered in along with Ben Campbell.

'Full house.' Josh took out his wallet and began to flick through it.

Ted marched up to give Lily a hug. 'You okay? Get any more letters?' He whispered more loudly than he'd probably intended because Lily saw Andrew's ears prick up and he came to join them.

'Letters?'

'It's nothing. Someone delivered one to my house that wasn't for me and Ted redirected it.' Lily hated lying but already knew

Andrew felt the same about Aubrey as Scott. If she wanted them to know her mother was back in her life – and she did – she'd have to approach telling them carefully.

From the corner of her eye Lily saw Josh pay for the beer and turn to watch the conversation.

Lily gave Ben an affectionate hug. Like Ted, he was like an uncle to her. 'Have you spoken to Emily recently?'

Ben dipped his head. 'I know she's stuck in Nepal. She said you're helping to organise the wedding?'

'With Paul's brother.' Lily beckoned Josh over. 'Ben, this is Josh Havellin-Scott.'

Ben's expression darkened. 'I've not met your brother and I won't lie, I'm not happy about the wedding. There's a big age difference.'

'Thirteen years.'

'You know Emily's only twenty-three?' Ben said, looking annoyed.

'She's a nurse?' Josh asked.

'Yes.'

'Then she's obviously bright – don't you trust her to make a good decision?'

'I trust her fine, it's your brother I'm not so sure about. Emily's always been so innocent. She's probably only fallen for him because he used to come to Castle Cove on holiday and reminds her of home.'

Lily nibbled her thumb. She ought to say something but all she could feel was the flush crawling up her neck and her heartbeat hammering faster and faster in her chest. She curled her fingers into a fist, conscious of Josh watching her. Maybe expecting something? Lily cleared her throat. 'I think Emily has better reasons than that,

Ben. I'm sure Paul's very nice… I've only known Josh for a short time and he seems…' What? 'Nice' didn't seem adequate. 'Sexy'? No, he wouldn't want to hear that. Lily felt her cheeks heat more as they both looked at her. 'Trustworthy'. Unless you expected him to turn up on time. Drat, she was messing this up. 'I mean…'

Josh chuckled. 'Thanks for the recommendation. I think what Lily's trying to say is I haven't murdered anyone yet and that means Paul's probably okay.'

Ben made a noise that Lily couldn't decipher but it didn't sound positive.

'Perhaps when Emily and Paul get back from Nepal you could come to my house and meet him, unless you've already arranged a date?'

Ben shook his head.

Josh pointed at the barrels he'd just bought. 'There'll be plenty to drink.'

'Perhaps I will,' Ben replied.

'I will too,' Ted added. 'Who knows, there may be even more unexpected visitors we could invite.' He looked sharply at Lily.

'There might be. I'm not sure about all of the people coming to the wedding. Your parents, Josh,' Lily covered as her dad looked hard at Ted.

Josh nodded. 'The chance to see their son getting married isn't something they'd pass up.'

'Parents are important,' Ted said wisely.

'You keep telling her that,' Lily's dad rumbled as he grabbed her for a hug. Lily wanted to ask about Aubrey – really, it was on the tip of her tongue – but when she looked at her dad's face she couldn't.

'What about your mother?' Josh asked. Lily glanced across the room and found Josh staring at her. Her heart flipped in her chest because Josh understood and was trying to add her to the conversation – to give her a way of explaining.

'Lily's mother's not on the scene,' Tom answered, quickly heading to the bar so he could clear up some glasses. He didn't look at them. 'She hasn't been for years. We're her parents, me and her brothers. She's never needed anyone else.'

Josh cocked his head and Lily could almost see what was coming next, could predict the ensuing argument, but before she could stop him Josh spoke. 'Surely every girl needs her mother?'

'Depends on who it is,' her dad said gruffly. 'Lily's mother left when she was a sick baby. She never came back and we never missed her.'

'Is that how you feel, Lily?' Josh's brown eyes bored into her. 'Is it?' he prodded. Lily knew her cheeks were glowing – she opened her mouth but no words came out.

'I'm not sure Lily's given it a lot of thought.' Ted stepped in, patting Lily gently on the back.

'I've wondered about her,' she answered eventually. Her voice sounded strange, like all the emotions that had been swirling through her over the last few weeks were coming to the surface.

'She's not worth your time. Some people are best forgotten,' her dad murmured.

'Amen,' Andrew agreed.

'Besides, if your mother wanted to get in touch she'd have done it by now, don't you think?' Tom said without looking at her. She could see by the straightness of his shoulders that the conversation was bothering him.

Josh narrowed his eyes. This was the perfect opportunity for Lily to say something. The perfect time to talk about the letter, but she couldn't. She opened her mouth but out of the corner of her eye she saw Ted shake his head. 'No. You're right, she would have got in touch by now,' she admitted, crossing her fingers behind her back.

Josh bent to pick up his barrels from the floor. 'We need to go. Bye Lily.' His voice had softened but Lily hoped he wasn't mad because she'd been such a coward. He headed for the door.

Even after it closed Lily could feel Josh's presence reminding her of the opportunity she'd just let go.

Ted patted her hand. 'It's for the best Lily,' he whispered, and this time her brother didn't hear. 'Some people aren't worth the bother.'

'I'm sure you're right,' Lily said quietly, wondering how she'd ever pluck up the courage to tell her family or Ted about Aubrey.

Chapter Seventeen

'I'll take a cassoulet please.' Ted skimmed the menu as he settled himself into a chair, wedging his empty postbag by his feet. He'd come for lunch in the restaurant and Lily planned to join him later if she was allowed to take an early break. 'With a hot chocolate – do you think Suze would let me have chips?'

'Luc's not back, so probably.' Lily glanced towards the kitchen where she knew the team had been working since six a.m. 'You need to pop over to mine for some shepherd's pie.'

Ted winced. 'Any idea when Luc's back?' He handed Lily the menu. 'So you can have your interview?'

'I've no idea. Suze tells me he needs to help at his family's restaurant until his mother's completely better.' Lily longed for the chance to be in the kitchen but she wouldn't get that until the Head Chef returned.

'Talking of mothers, did you decide what to do about yours?' Ted asked in a loud voice. Lily sneaked a look around the room to make sure no one had overheard.

'I… I've seen her a couple of times,' she admitted, desperate to come clean with somebody.

Ted looked shocked. 'You didn't say.'

'I… I've been working up to it.'

Ted looked unhappy. 'What's she like?'

'Beautiful, really nice.' Out of the corner of her eye Lily saw Anya seating Marta at a table for two. 'I need to tell everyone, but I have to work out the best time.'

'I'm not sure there will be a good time, Lily, love.' Ted looked worried. 'Lot of water under the bridge as I told you, all of it bad.'

'You don't think I should tell Dad?' Lily darted a look behind her in case Suze was watching – she was taking far too long.

'If your mother's in your life for good, you can't avoid it – but don't expect him or your brothers to be happy.'

Lily couldn't imagine upsetting her family. 'I… I don't want to hurt anyone.'

Before Ted could comment, Anya appeared beside them. 'Lily, Suze asked if you could decorate the Christmas tree. Simon's carrying it up and Rita's bringing a box of decorations. I can't, I've got to leave early,' she explained. 'And Nate cut his hand on a glass yesterday so he's good for nothing. I'll look after Ted.'

'Can we do it later?' Lily asked. If she decorated the tree she wouldn't be able to continue her conversation with Ted.

'Simon's orders. It has to be now. Apparently, the castle doesn't look Christmassy enough. Don't worry, I'll finish for you here.' Anya tapped her pad.

Lily found Rita by the entrance of the restaurant where the Christmas tree and a couple of boxes of decorations sat alongside a very tall stepladder.

'Thanks for doing this, Lily. There's a plug there.' Rita pointed to a socket in the wall. 'And plenty of lights, baubles and tinsel in the boxes. Simon's keen for the tree to be decorated by the end of lunch. I'll be doing the one at the castle entrance. Call if you need anything. And before I forget, has Suze mentioned she's doing a taster menu for you and Josh tomorrow so you can choose the wedding food?'

'Not to me.'

'It's straight after lunch. I've told Josh and he said he'd try to be on time.'

'Okay.' Lily knelt so she could open the first cardboard box. Inside were about a billion baubles coloured silver, gold, red and green. She searched and found a couple of strings of lights and looked up to the top of the tree. Lily was afraid of heights but hadn't wanted to admit it to Rita in case she thought she was being difficult.

Around her, people chatted as Anya took orders and served food assisted by Nate, whose hand had been lightly bandaged. Lily took the first string of coloured lights from the box and set up the stepladder, wondering how she'd bring herself to climb it.

'Are you going to see if they work before you put those on the tree or have you decided to live dangerously?' Suddenly Josh's voice was in Lily's ear, sending shivers up her spine. He smelled of fresh coffee and cut grass – and both scents seemed a little too wholesome for him.

'You're right. I should check them.' Feeling stupid, Lily plugged in the lights. Nothing happened.

'You might need a new fuse.' Josh studied her.

'Are you meeting Marta?' Anya bustled up to Josh with a pad in her hand. 'Because she's just ordered her main – she didn't want to wait any longer.'

Lily eyed Marta. A book was open beside her glass of wine but Simon had joined her and they were chatting.

Josh picked up the lights. 'I think my seat's taken, at least for now. How about I help with the decorations?'

'I'm sure Lily will be delighted.' Anya smirked before going to greet a couple who'd just wandered into the restaurant.

'Before you ask about Chester, my neighbour Jay O'Donnell told me about a teenager he uses to dog sit. Chester's probably curled up on the sofa he's not allowed to sit on, watching X-rated YouTube videos, right now. He's already been walked,' Josh joked.

'I—okay.' Lily ignored the lump in her throat. 'Aren't you hungry?' she asked, torn between wanting Josh's help and not wanting to delay him.

'I can eat later.' As they talked, Josh fiddled with each of the bulbs on the string of lights. 'Did you talk to your family about your mother?' he asked.

'It wasn't the right time.'

'Will it ever be?'

'Yes. I... I just don't know when, and I don't want to hurt anybody.'

Josh grinned as the lights illuminated. 'Loose bulb.' He handed them back, accidently brushing Lily's hand, giving her goose-bumps. 'I thought you were a cook?' He pointed at Lily's black and white uniform.

'That's more of a wish at the moment.'

'You want me to hand the lights to you?' Josh pointed to the ladder and Lily shook her head vehemently.

'Not keen on heights.'

'And they made you walk up a ladder?' Josh looked annoyed.

'Oh, I didn't tell anyone.'

Josh shook his head and stepped on the ladder, taking the lights. 'Are you doing anything about that wish?'

'I'm going to cook for the Head Chef when he comes home from France. There's a chance of a job if he likes it.'

'And you're worried about it?' Josh guessed, as he wound the cable around the top of the tree before stepping off the ladder so he could trail the lights around the branches. 'Why?'

Lily took a couple of baubles from the box and hung them. 'I'm not adventurous enough. I keep trying to experiment but when I do the food is boring.'

'You can't let go when you cook?' Josh suggested, watching her face.

'I don't understand.'

Josh dug into the box and picked out a blonde, blue-eyed angel with sparkly silver wings. 'She's a lot like you.' He held up the doll. 'Except her hair and eyes are the wrong colour. When you don't look closely she could seem dull and you could miss her. Wait—' Josh said, as Lily's expression and stomach dropped in quick succession.

'Look—' Josh climbed the stepladder again and put the angel on the top, training one of the lights underneath her. 'Let the light shine, let her sparkle show and suddenly she's a whole different person.' He gazed down. 'When are you going to let your light out, wild Lily? It seems to me you use a lot of your energy keeping everything locked inside. Not saying what you think or telling people what you want. Hiding. You're not being honest with yourself or anyone else.'

'What's that got to do with cooking?' Lily squeaked, picking up another bauble, practically throwing it on the tree.

Josh's brown eyes fixed on her. 'Great food requires great instincts. You've got to be inventive and you don't find creativity trying to please everyone. You have to be true to yourself – let the real you out.'

'Making people happy is important to me,' Lily said, so stung by the comment that tears welled up in her eyes. 'At least I'm not rude.'

'Rude is only another word for honest.'

Lily gripped another bauble and looked at Josh, angry suddenly. 'You're trying to justify your behaviour. You do what you want, say what you like regardless.' She pointed to Marta, tucking into a bowl of pasta. Simon had left and she was sitting alone, although her book was open.

'Marta's happy reading and she's known me long enough to know I'll join her at some point. I spent a lot of years trying to please everyone, Lily.' Josh's voice softened. 'Turns out we can't be who we're not. You have to take your own path and be proud of it. There's no point in worrying about what everyone else thinks.'

'But I *do* care,' Lily snapped back. 'My friends and family matter. I'm not going around stomping on everyone's feelings so I can do whatever I want.'

'Is that what you think I do?' Josh asked, taken aback.

'I know where your light is, Josh,' Lily countered, as a hot rush of anger rose in her throat. She didn't know where it came from. Perhaps it had been building for years. But like a dormant volcano suddenly erupting after years of silence, it couldn't be stopped – and God help anyone standing in its way. 'Your light's on full beam,'

Lily snapped. 'Shining in everyone's faces regardless of whether you run them off the road, run them over or blind them.' She came to a sudden and abrupt stop, feeling a gush of guilt. What was wrong with her? She'd never spoken to anyone like that in her life.

Josh stepped down from the stepladder slowly. He didn't look mad, more surprised. Mortified, Lily began to apologise but Josh shook his head, just the tiniest movement, but she saw it.

'Don't apologise for saying what you think, Lily. But remember, I'm not criticising, I'm telling you what I see. Because I lived the life you're living. I've been down that path and I know where it ends.' The corners of his eyes scrunched in tune with his frown and Lily's heart reached out to him. Suddenly, instead of feeling angry, she felt terrible. She held out a hand but Josh murmured his goodbye and headed towards the table where Marta sat.

Chapter Eighteen

The log drifted in the dark waves. Long and broad with a yellowish-brown complexion, it might have been the trunk of a tree once, but even from this distance Josh could see it had been battered and punched, chipped and bruised, until it had evolved from a simple piece of driftwood to a thing of beauty.

Josh tapped his foot as his fingers twitched against the camera. This could be the shot. The one he'd been waiting for. If the damn thing would just make it to the beach he'd be able to position it in the sand, maybe drag over some pieces of seaweed. If he could capture some of the dark light in the sky in the background, maybe the cliffs too, the effect would be moody, almost supernatural. He tapped his foot again and glared down at Chester.

'Fetch.' Josh pointed into the water but the Lab looked at him with watery eyes and he just knew the dog was thinking, *No, you fetch*.

'Dammit.' Josh rocked back on his heels and looked at the sea again. The wood was drifting back and forth just out of reach of the shore. He'd have to go in and pull it out himself before it got dark, or he'd never get the shot and the damn thing would probably be halfway across the North Sea by morning. Shaking his head, he kicked off his shoes and socks, pulled off his jacket, and put them on a nearby rock with his camera. He checked the beach – there was no one around but he didn't intend to stay in the water long anyway. He rolled up his trousers and sleeves and padded towards the waves. Chester whined behind him.

'Well you wouldn't do it,' Josh grumbled, dipping in a toe and yelling as the cold almost made his blood freeze. 'Jeez! And you've got a fur coat.' He waded in a little deeper, feeling his trousers get wet, trying to ignore the minus temperature as the water lapped his legs. He was almost there; once the waves got to his knees he'd be able to reach the log and pull it out. He began to shiver but walked in a little further, grabbing it with one hand.

Chester barked but Josh didn't turn back. Instead he tried to pull the log towards the shore – but the current from the waves was working against him and it was caught on a rock or something, so every time he tried to tug it, it got pushed back. It was too heavy for one.

'Dammit,' he muttered through chattering teeth. 'If you don't help me, dog, you're going to The China Boat.'

'He's more interested in chasing bits of seaweed.' Josh knew the voice from somewhere. He turned without letting go of his prize. Simon Wolf stood on the sand watching him. He wore walking boots, canvas trousers and a stunned expression. 'What *are* you doing?'

'Following my muse,' Josh grunted between gritted teeth. 'This is it. I need a central photograph for my show at Picture Perfect on the twentieth and this is it. I just need to get the damn thing back to shore before I freeze.'

Simon blinked, frowning. 'Does it have to be this log? Couldn't you find one in a wood somewhere?'

Josh remembered his conversation with Lily in the restaurant earlier as he fought the urge to be rude. 'It has to be this one. Are you done chatting because I could really do with a hand?'

Simon began to shake his head and Josh took a chance. 'Marta would appreciate it. The show's in her gallery after all.'

At the mention of Marta's name, Simon's expression softened. 'She is worried about the show and she's mentioned the elusive photograph you've been looking for. Are you sure it has to be *this* one?'

'Yes,' Josh almost shouted, trying to drag the log further into shore again. He couldn't feel his feet any more and his fingers had gone numb. If Simon didn't hurry up he'd have to let go and they'd be back to square one.

Simon swore and began to pull off his shoes and socks. 'I can't believe I'm doing this,' he moaned. 'You're lucky no one else has spotted you or you'd have Jay O'Donnell and the rest of his lifeboat crew turning up any second – and I'm really not sure what they'd make of this. Most normal people would call this reckless and make a run for it.' Simon placed his shoes, socks and raincoat on the rocks alongside Josh's things. Chester sniffed them as he headed towards the waves. He was in the water in seconds. Josh heard a loud curse, some splashing and then Simon was beside him and they were both pulling at the log. Two achieved what one could not and the trunk was on the beach within seconds. Out of breath, they tugged it away from the water onto the sand.

'It's almost too dark,' Josh complained. Ignoring the cold and the way his body was shaking, he grabbed the camera and began to click, picking out the dark sky. The light had changed, but there was still a strange atmospheric glow. He wouldn't have time to create a scene using seaweed – or anything else for that matter.

'No problem, I was happy to help,' Simon said behind him, his tone dry.

'Yes, okay, thanks. I'll let Marta know how helpful you were.' Josh got down onto his knees in the sand and took a few more shots. 'I'll come back in the morning, take more. Think it'll still be here?'

'We'll need to pull it further up the beach to make sure,' Simon said. 'And if you want my help again I might want something in return.'

'I don't do portraits.'

Simon let out a deep belly laugh that surprised Josh. It seemed so out of character for the serious, suited and booted castle owner. 'You've been friends with Marta for how many years?'

'Five.' Josh didn't look up from the camera.

'Then you'll know her better than most?'

'I guess.' He only had a couple more shots in the light and moved to capture the trunk at another angle. Good, this was good. He felt like giving Simon a high five. Maybe he'd have a couple of whiskies this evening to celebrate.

'Does she have a…' Simon paused and Josh looked up. The man's cheeks were actually red. Was he blushing? '… man in her life?' Simon continued, his voice strangled.

'Don't you know? You've been arguing with her for almost eight months.'

'It hasn't come up.'

Josh tutted. 'And I thought I was crap at small talk. There's no-one else, I'm the only one.'

'But you're just friends.' Simon's tone had a challenging quality and for a moment Josh felt like messing with him. But his thoughts flicked briefly to Lily and his mixed emotions when it came to her, and as a nod to male solidarity he decided not to.

'That's right. There's no man – hasn't been for a while.'

Simon jerked his head as Josh stood and slung the camera back over his shoulder. He brushed the sand from his feet and put his socks and walking boots on, ignoring the fact that his toes looked blue and his body was wracked with shivers. 'If you want more information you need to help me move the log. But I'm not going to tell you anything she wouldn't tell you herself.' Josh gave Simon a pointed look.

'I know a few things already and can guess some from what she's said. I'm not asking you to dish the dirt.' Simon bent to pick up the edge of the trunk. Together they pushed and pulled until it sat beyond the rocks above the tideline. He'd come in the morning and take more photos in a different light.

'You're interested in her?' Josh guessed, brushing more sand from his hands and fingers, hoping he hadn't got any on the camera lens. He'd have to shower when he got home. He narrowed his eyes at Chester, who'd been rolling on the beach – the dog might have to join him.

Simon blew a breath between his teeth. 'She's… I haven't met anyone like her before.' He looked puzzled. 'And I really can't tell how she feels about me.'

Josh held up his hands and took a step back. 'Don't ask me. You haven't come up in conversation, if that's what you're asking. Okay, that's a lie,' Josh added, remembering Marta complaining about Simon in the gallery. 'In all honesty, you may have pissed her off.'

A slight smile played at the edges of Simon's lips. The man was good-looking in a chiselled sort of way. If Josh did portraits he'd probably consider photographing him.

'We've had a few disagreements, but I think we've ironed them out. She's very… temperamental,' Simon finished.

'All part of Marta's quirky charm. If she likes you, and if you become friends, you'll be glad of that temper – loyalty comes with it, as does strength.' Josh looked at him intently. 'She's a good person, one of the best. Are you good enough for her, Simon Wolf? Because if she wants you back, you'll need to be.'

'I… I don't know.' Simon stumbled backwards, a worried crease appearing on his forehead. 'I'd like to think so.'

'You've moved here recently like me?' Josh had heard gossip around town.

'I've been in Australia for the last few years. I ran a hotel out there. My grandfather owns Cove Castle and he asked me to run it, gave it to me.'

'Why were you in Australia and not here?' Josh put his hands on his hips, feeling like an interrogator.

'Family fall-out. I like to do things my own way,' Simon confided. 'My grandfather's the same. He's done a good job though – I can't fault him – but the castle still hasn't been making enough. I sent money when I was away to help with repairs but I wanted to expand. My grandfather wasn't keen; he's seeing sense now.'

'Marta likes to do things her own way too,' Josh said, considering him. 'Are you prepared for that? Because this isn't a yes-woman you're dealing with Simon, she knows what she wants and she doesn't suffer fools.'

Simon smiled, his expression almost wolf-like. 'I've got her measure, Josh. I'm not looking for a yes-woman and I don't want to change her. I'm just looking for a way in.'

'Ask her out then. Be direct and be honest. I'll tell you she's been hurt by people who've been less than truthful with her. If you want to know more, you'll need to ask her yourself. Lie to her or cheat and you're out. That's as much as I'll share without being disloyal.'

Simon considered Josh, his grey eyes assessing. 'I appreciate that. I can see she's got a good friend in you.'

'Works both ways.'

'Perhaps one day I might have a friend in you too?'

'Depends on how you treat Marta.' Josh considered Simon. 'And how many more of my would-be compositions you're prepared to help me rescue.'

'That depends on where they are.' Simon glanced at the log again and down at his sandy shoes. 'I think I'll walk back now before you take a fancy to something else in the sea.'

'I'll go with you.' Josh called Chester, who bounded ahead. He fought the urge to quiz Simon about Lily. He needed to shut those thoughts down right now. Lily wasn't the kind of woman you trifled with. Like Marta, she was loyal and true, but unlike Marta she was sweet and vulnerable. Exactly the type of woman Josh usually avoided at all costs. But as he proceeded down the beach in silence with Simon, watching his dog play in the sand as the sun finished setting, he couldn't stop his mind from drifting to the pretty almost-cook with long wavy hair who was so afraid of expressing herself.

Chapter Nineteen

The connection buzzed again and Lily pressed her ear firmly to the mobile. 'Repeat that please Emily, I missed it.'

'Sorry, we're still having trouble with communications. The airport's almost up and running but there's still so much to do here.'

'You'll be back in time for Christmas Eve?' Lily's heart sank – she knew how excited Emily was about the wedding and after all this work she didn't want to cancel.

'Paul promised. We'll definitely make it. I'm hoping to be back before the nineteenth so we will be there in time for Josh's show. What do you think of him?' Lily couldn't tell because the connection was so bad, but she thought she detected a little something mischievous in Emily's tone.

'He's…' Lily considered the question. 'Interesting.'

'I saw a photo. He's quite a looker, a bit of a rebel too if what Paul's telling me is true. Is that right?'

'You could say that.' Lily licked her lips, feeling guilty about her conversation with Josh in the restaurant when she'd all but accused him of being heartless.

'Maybe I chose the wrong brother,' Emily teased. 'What's he really like?'

'Well.' Lily's forehead wrinkled. 'He's late everywhere, says what he thinks. He is nice to look at.' Understatement of the century. 'And he takes really good photographs.'

As a summary it was lame, but Lily couldn't bring herself to list all of Josh's good qualities. How he'd rescued her when she'd come back late from London and had driven her home, how he'd helped her decorate the Christmas tree, how he'd encouraged her to tell her family about Aubrey. Josh hadn't criticized Lily either – he'd wanted her to go her own way, to do what made her happy, and his assessment of her supposed hidden wildness had made her feel interesting and exciting. In return, Lily had judged him and now she felt awful.

'That's good to hear because Josh is doing the pictures for the wedding. Do you like him? Is it okay working with him?'

'Yes.' Lily realised she wasn't lying. It had been fun spending time with someone who didn't care what people thought. 'We've ordered the cake – cakes,' Lily corrected. 'You've got two, but Josh is paying for one.'

'Why?' Emily asked.

'Difference of opinion. Not worth talking about.'

Emily paused. 'You don't have differences of opinion.'

'I do now,' Lily replied, feeling a strange mixture of pride and confusion. 'And we've sorted the flowers. Later today we're tasting the food and wine. Do you have any preferences?'

'You're the cook Lil, whatever you choose I'll be happy with. How about the dress?'

'I haven't tried that yet, but Rita's booking an appointment and she said she'd tell me when today. Also, we've still got to choose the shoes and check the cars.'

'Shoes are your domain. You know what I like. Thank goodness we've got the same size feet. Go all out, I'm thinking Cinderella with a hint of Lady Gaga. Paul says Josh will make a good choice with the car, and Simon should let you drive them, so see if you can take one for a run-around. I've got this vision of me in a white dress and sparkly shoes travelling through Castle Cove with the wind in my hair flapping my veil.'

'You do know it's cold?' Lily's eyes darted to the small fire glowing in her sitting room next to the Christmas tree. She'd had to light it again this morning, even though the heating was on. 'We're a few degrees down from Nepal.'

Emily chuckled. 'I'm looking forward to it, Lily. Tell me about you – how's the quest for the new job?'

'Luc's still away but I'll be cooking for him as soon as I can. I'm just not sure I'm up to it, Em. No matter what recipe I try the result is dull.'

'You work so hard Lily. I can't believe Luc won't give the job to you.'

Lily's silence spoke volumes. 'I saw your dad in the brewery the other day.' She changed the subject.

'How is he? I've only had a brief conversation. He's having a good time with Gayle O'Donnell. I'm so glad they met.' Emily's voice softened. Her mother had died a couple of years earlier and her dad had recently got together with Gayle. They made a brilliant couple and Lily knew the romance had put Emily's mind at rest when she'd left the country. 'Did you talk with Dad about the wedding?'

'He knows we're working on it. Josh offered to host a get-together at his house when you get back so Paul and your dad can meet.'

'Perfect,' Emily chirped, as Lily heard the buzz of voices in the background. 'Sorry, I'm needed. I'll call again as soon as I can. Enjoy the food. I can't wait to see everyone. When you try on the dress get Josh to take a picture and send it to Paul – if the wind blows in the right direction we might even get it.' Emily rang off suddenly, leaving Lily staring at the phone.

Rosemary, cheese, figs, sausages, lamb and chocolate. Delicate fragrances wafted from the restaurant kitchen towards the table where Lily sat, checking her watch. She wasn't even sure why she bothered. Josh was going to be late whether she kept an eye on the time or not.

Nate appeared from the kitchen with a jug of iced water and placed it on the table, frowning at the empty seat opposite Lily.

'Still not arrived?'

Lily shook her head. Nate poured out the water and she pointed to his hand. The bandage was gone, replaced by a long blue plaster.

'All better?'

'Almost,' Nate grinned, his eyes sparkling. 'Don't tell Anya. It's been getting me out of all the mucky jobs.'

Lily sipped her drink and looked around the room. The tree sparkled in the corner of the restaurant and the fairy on top of it winked at her, or maybe it was the lights? All the other tables were laid ready for the evening meal. Lily wasn't working this evening but hoped they'd finish the menu before the rest of the masses arrived — she had a wild date with a book and a bath.

Lily heard the door but didn't turn around. When Josh came into her eyeline she felt her stomach jolt. He'd dressed up in a pair of black trousers and a blue shirt that was unbuttoned at the collar. Lily lifted her eyes to his face and saw the frown on it. She opened her mouth to apologise.

'No,' Josh said. 'No apologies. I will say this: I don't set out to hurt people, Lily, I'm sorry I haven't made that clear. But I do what I want and say what I think because I can't live any other way.'

'I'm sorry,' Lily stumbled over the words but Suze appeared from the kitchen before she could finish her apology.

'I wanted to say hi before Nate brought the food out.' Suze greeted them, shaking hands with Josh. 'I understand Luc discussed menus with Emily on the phone and he had an idea of what he wanted to serve tonight. I've added a few small variations of my own. We'll kick off with a selection of canapes, then soup, a main and dessert. There's a special gin and tonic to serve with the canapes, and wine for the courses. Rita made a list so you can write down your selections. Nate will bring it. Do either of you have a pen?'

'Lily will have one,' Josh answered without looking at her. 'You serve Castling?'

'Of course.'

'Could we both have a half please, before we begin?'

Suze looked confused. 'I've made Christmas Poinsettia punch to go with the canapes.'

'Then bring both.' Josh grinned.

'Luc would have a coronary,' Suze murmured as she headed for the kitchen.

Josh looked around the room and his eyes rested on a couple of his photographs on the wall. Lots of men would have boasted about having them there, but Josh's eyes continued to scan their surroundings until they rested back on Lily.

'You look pretty,' he said.

Lily's cheeks heated as she offered a strangled, 'Thank you.' She'd dressed in her favourite dark green dress and a pair of boots that weren't high because she'd be walking home after the meal. The outfit made her feel sexy, even though there was a lot less skin on display than there'd been when she'd worn the silver body-con.

'I'm guessing that's from your wardrobe rather than your mother's?' Josh let his eyes scan the top of the dress which dipped down, lightly skimming the edges of her cleavage.

Lily felt goose-bumps rise on her skin. 'Yes, it's not as fancy.'

'It's pretty nonetheless. You're lucky – you don't need to rely on what you wear to be beautiful. I'll bet the camera loves you.'

'Ahhh, my mother thinks it will. I've no idea,' Lily stumbled. Compliments or being the centre of attention made her uncomfortable, and she was glad when Nate appeared with two glasses of ale and champagne flutes filled with a red liquid, along with a plate of canapes.

'Suze wants you to sample these with your drinks.' Nate snorted. 'The gin and tonic is good – not as good as the ale, obviously, Lily. Here's the sheet Rita typed up. She said just tick what you like.' Nate handed them both a sheet of paper. 'Try to agree. It'll make life easier.' He directed his words at Josh before disappearing back into the kitchen.

Josh read from the list. 'The canapes include devilled crab on toast, chilli and lime prawn skewers, venison scotch egg, rosemary bread with red onion marmalade and Castle Cove brie – I like the sound of that – and fig and goat's cheese puffs.' Josh picked up his beer and sipped, then picked up one of the canapes and popped it into his mouth.

'Which one was that?' Lily searched in her bag for a pencil.

'No idea, but I liked it. That should get a tick.'

'We need to eat them together so we can agree,' Lily said, exasperated. 'Which one?'

Josh pointed and Lily popped one into her mouth; it melted on her tongue. 'Fig and goat's cheese puff.' She savoured the taste. 'I like it and I think Emily will too.'

'Paul eats anything so we don't need to worry about pleasing him. Have you ticked?' Josh flashed Lily a smile as she marked the page and she had to stop herself from grinning back – those smiles were way too addictive.

Lily sipped some of her beer and looked at the champagne flute. 'Don't you think we should try the cocktail since Suze went to the trouble of making it?'

'You worry way too much about other people, Lily,' Josh said, but he picked up the glass and tipped it in her direction. 'Bottoms up.' He sipped. 'That'll get a tick, but I prefer your ale, so I'll stick with that, at least until the wine arrives.'

Lily tried the cocktail. It was good but she preferred the ale too, but she gave it a tick because Emily loved gin. 'What's next?'

Josh picked up a prawn skewer and waited as Lily did the same, then they both bit into it. 'Too much of something.'

'Salt. I think that's a no.' Lily put a cross on the sheet of paper. 'We're agreeing.'

'Only because we haven't talked wedding shoes.' Josh picked up the bread and brie and gulped it down. 'That's good. If you don't like it I'm going to steal that pencil.'

Lily giggled and ate hers. 'I'm not letting you steal another pencil. Besides, I like it, especially the marmalade. I taste oranges underneath the onion.'

'You do have a flair for food.'

'Lily?'

She almost didn't recognise the voice and when she did, Lily wished she hadn't because she turned and came face to face with her ex-boyfriend Rogan Kelly. 'It is you.' He looked thrown and Lily took her time studying him. Rogan always seemed to have a six-o'clock shadow and today was no exception. He was really tall, over six-foot-three, with light blue eyes that were almost unnatural. He stood frowning at Josh as though he couldn't quite believe Lily was sitting with him.

'Hello,' Lily stumbled.

'And you are?' Rogan raised a black eyebrow at Josh.

'Um, this is Josh Havellin-Scott—' Lily felt herself shrink.

'Lily's new boyfriend,' Josh interrupted, folding his arms so they couldn't shake hands.

'What?' Lily said, shocked.

'Out of interest, do you drive a Porsche or sell insurance?' Josh asked, looking annoyed.

'Both.' Rogan laughed. 'Why?'

'Lucky guess – so you two were together?' Josh gazed at Lily with an amazed expression. Looking at her ex now, staring at them with the arrogant expression she recognised, Lily understood why

Josh was so surprised. Why hadn't she seen how much he'd looked down on her before?

'We dated for a while. Only recently split.' Rogan glanced at Lily. 'Temporarily.'

Lily's jaw dropped. There had been no mention of the split being temporary in their last conversation – it had most definitely been over.

'I think that status might have been updated to permanent.' Josh flashed a fake smile. 'I'm sure Lily would love to catch up but—' Josh looked at their plates. 'We're busy at the moment choosing wedding food.'

Rogan's mouth gaped.

'Emily's wedding menu.' Lily came clean as Josh smirked. 'I'll be in the teashop tomorrow, maybe I'll see you then. Are you back for a while?'

'At least for a couple of months,' Rogan said.

'Did you come to the restaurant for anything in particular?' Josh asked.

Rogan looked around. 'I was going to see if Lily could introduce me to the new owner, Simon Wolf. I thought we could chat about insurance.'

Lily's temper flared but she banked it. Rogan must think she was a total pushover if he thought she'd let him use her again. 'I've no idea where Simon is,' she said. *And if I did, I wouldn't tell you.* The words were on the tip of her tongue but she didn't say them.

'Perhaps you should give his secretary a call like everyone else?' Josh suggested, his expression even less friendly than it had been at the beginning of the conversation, which was saying something.

Rogan's eyes didn't leave Lily's face. 'I'll pop into the teashop tomorrow and we can catch up in private.' His eyes flicked to Josh. '*Ciao*.' Rogan span on his heels and disappeared out of the restaurant.

Josh picked up another canape. 'Scotch egg?'

'Aren't you going to ask about Rogan?'

'Do you want me to?' Josh's brown eyes turned serious. 'I think I got his measure. A user – good-looking I'll grant you – but there's something about him I don't like, despite his awesome taste in cars. He used you somehow?' Josh guessed and Lily felt embarrassed all over again.

'How did you know?'

Josh lifted his hands. 'Photographer's eye, I told you. I see things below the surface. Not that there's much below the surface there.'

Lily pursed her lips. 'Rogan dated me for a while and I helped him encourage my dad to change the King's Brewery insurance policy to his company. Two weeks later, he broke our relationship off.' It still hurt. Maybe not as badly as it had at first, but it was another rejection and dent in her self-confidence she could do without. 'Why did you tell Rogan we were dating?'

'To piss him off. I didn't like the way he was looking at you… I've no idea why. Are you going to eat that?' Josh pointed to the other scotch egg. When Lily mouthed 'no' he ate it. 'I'd give that one a cross. Not fancy enough for a wedding even if it is venison.' Josh finished his beer. 'That leaves the toast with crab. Bottoms up.' He ate it. Now Rogan had gone, Lily began to relax. 'Not sure, I'll leave that decision with you,' Josh said.

Lily picked up the toast and nibbled. 'It needs something spicy to liven it up.'

'Good call.' Josh fixed her with a look again. 'You have a cook's palate, Lily. Luc would be mad not to hire you.'

Nate appeared again to clear their plates before bringing them both a small bowl of soup. 'Leek and potato, with crispy pancetta topping,' he announced. 'The topping can be left off if you're vegetarian. I've got a crisp white for you to try. I'll just go and get it.' Nate disappeared into the kitchen and reappeared almost immediately with a Chardonnay. They watched him open the bottle and pour it.

'I'm glad I'm walking home.' Lily picked up her drink and swirled it before taking a small sip. 'Gorgeous.' She drank a small mouthful of soup. 'What do you think?'

Josh tasted some. 'This agreeing thing is going to become a habit if we're not careful.'

Lily snorted. 'I'm sure we'll be arguing about something before long.' She sipped more soup, marvelling at the delicate tastes and sensations on her tongue. 'Do you get on well with your brother?'

'Paul's hard not to get along with,' Josh answered after a pause. 'He's good-looking, bright, nice to everyone, rich, *oh* and a doctor, which according to my parents is only one step down from God. He's what most would describe as a catch, and since he's a very good man – not to mention brother – he deserves that title.'

Lily cocked her head, wondering if she'd misheard the bitterness in Josh's tone when he'd talked about his parents. 'And you don't?'

Josh laughed. 'I'm not fishing for compliments. I'm more than aware of my shortcomings.'

'Which are?' Lily asked, curious about how Josh saw himself. 'Aside from your dislike of punctuality – and we've said enough about that – and despite what I said yesterday, which I apologise for, you don't seem to be that awful. Chester likes you, and Ted. I'm guessing Marta's a good judge of character and she's your friend.'

Josh finished his soup and put down his spoon before leaning into the table towards her. 'But do you like me, Lily King?'

Lily swallowed, thrown by the question and the way her heart had begun to race.

'Because I remember on our ride in the car the other night you said you weren't sure, and from what you said yesterday I'd say it's doubtful?' Josh watched Lily as she thought about the question. 'You have a very expressive face,' Josh said eventually. 'I can almost see each emotion as it flits across your mind – it's fascinating. I wonder if those thoughts would show up on film?'

'Yes, I do,' Lily answered.

'What?'

'I like you. Despite my better judgement and what every sensible cell in my body is telling me. Is that what you see?'

Josh looked surprised. 'I saw confusion, and vulnerability. I saw that you didn't want to tell me what you felt.'

'I thought I didn't like you at first… especially when you took on Chester so spontaneously, but I think you're actually very kind.' Lily paused. 'And a lot nicer than you pretend to be.'

'I appreciate the vote of confidence, but I'll bet you thought Rogan was a nice guy when you first met.' Josh raised an eyebrow when Lily opened her mouth. 'I'm not that nice. But I will say this: I like you too.' Josh looked conflicted. 'Probably more than I should, *definitely* more than I should, which isn't good for either for us. Because I'm unreliable, and sometimes I'm not kind. I let people down—'

'How?' Lily interrupted.

'I put my work, my photos, before everything, above every expectation anyone's ever had for me. I've never wanted to settle down, I'm not sure I'd know how. I *hurt* people. You said the same yesterday.' Josh looked unconcerned.

Lily put her spoon down, absorbing the words, trying to see the truth in them, definitely seeing the lies. 'Yesterday I was mad and I lashed out, which isn't like me.' She pulled a face to show she was sorry. 'I've had time to think on it. As I said, you have a friend in Marta, and as far as I can see – despite my own misgivings – you're proving to be a good owner to Chester. So maybe we've both got you wrong?'

Josh shrugged as Nate came to collect their bowls and glasses, ready to bring the second course. 'An anomaly,' Josh said, and when Lily stared at him he added, 'Two anomalies. Don't go expecting more.'

Lily smiled, warmed by Josh's words, by the fact that he'd admitted to liking her despite his better judgement. Because even she – without the photographer's gift of seeing below the surface – could see beyond the words and could tell Josh's opinion of himself was flawed, and he was a far better man than he believed. It just might take some time to prove it to him, but for some inexplicable reason, she wanted to.

Chapter Twenty

The Castle Teashop buzzed. It was early afternoon and they'd been busy all day. Probably because the light rain that had started this morning had quickly turned to sleet and at least two coach loads of visitors had headed for the teashop instead of exploring the castle grounds.

'We ought to add a revolving door,' Cath grumbled, stopping to chat to Lily on her way to table three near the window. 'I've no idea what the kitchen looks like, but if Alice comes in, for goodness sake don't let her in there before we've given it the once-over. The woman will have a coronary.'

'White Christmas' began to play on the record player, making Lily smile.

Cath whizzed past her again, heading for the counter. 'Rogan came in before we opened this morning, looking for you. I told him you'd moved to Australia but he said he saw you yesterday afternoon having dinner with a strange man. Which strange man was that?' Cath asked cheekily, as she began to cut up slices of carrot cake. 'Make me a couple of cappuccinos, will you?'

'I was tasting Emily's wedding menu with Josh,' Lily blurted, grabbing a couple of mugs before turning her back to make coffee so Cath couldn't read her expression.

'How was it?' Cath asked.

'The food was great.'

'I mean how was Josh? Did he walk you home afterwards?'

'No, Ted popped in to deliver Christmas cards just as we were leaving and he offered to walk me home. Josh had left Chester on his own and wanted to get back.' Lily wasn't sure if she'd felt relieved or disappointed. After their conversation when they'd both admitted they liked each other despite their better judgement – when Josh had effectively warned her off — Lily wasn't sure what she wanted.

The bell tinkled at the front of the teashop again just as Lily put the two coffees on the tray beside the slices of cake. At exactly the same moment, Rogan strode in, as if by talking about him they'd somehow conjured him up. His choppy brown hair looked windswept but he didn't take the time to fix it even though he passed a mirror. Instead his light blue eyes immediately fixed on Lily.

'There's no room.' Cath charged past him on her way to serve a customer. 'Perhaps you could come back later – say in ten years?'

Rogan ignored her and walked to the counter. 'Are you due a break?' he asked, looking around the room and spotting a table near the back by the toilets. 'I'll sit over there. Just a black coffee and bung on a slice of that chocolate cake.' Rogan had his back to Lily and had almost reached the empty seat he'd spotted before she'd even thought about saying no.

The bell above the door rang again and Lily could have howled because unless she was mistaken — or had begun to hallucinate due to chocolate cake fumes— Aubrey Dean, a.k.a. her mother, was making her way through the teashop, wearing a pair of huge dark glasses and a white fur coat. Why was this happening to her?

'Darling,' Aubrey said, walking around the counter to kiss Lily on both cheeks. 'You look terrible.' She glanced over her shoulder at Albert who followed behind, looking dejected, carrying a large portfolio over his right shoulder. 'It took me ages to find you. We've been all over the place. I knew you worked near the castle but someone in the restaurant told me exactly where. I know you're busy so I thought I'd pop in and say hi instead of calling.' Aubrey dismissed Lily's look of dismay. 'I was in the area. The friend whose party we're going to lives about ten miles from here and I've been invited to a dinner at her house this evening. I've found the perfect photographer for you. He does the most incredible work and specialises in older models.' Aubrey looked critically at Lily's skin. 'With a good facial, haircut and some decent clothes, he'll be able to put a fabulous series of shots together. I've been so excited. I didn't want to wait to tell you.'

'Oh wow...' Unsure of what to say, Lily looked around the teashop to see if anyone would recognise Aubrey. 'Why don't you sit over there?' She pointed to a table near the back of the teashop underneath one of Josh's photos. It was dark and out of the way. 'I'll make you drinks and maybe slice some cake? It's my break in ten minutes so we can chat then.'

'I'll have a herbal tea please, and definitely no cake. Albert will have the same,' Aubrey added before the poor man could answer for himself.

Lily walked behind the counter, checking the clientele. Most were tourists so there was little chance of them recognising her mother. If she took her break soon, she could probably persuade Aubrey to leave and there would be no chance of her dad or brothers turning up. Andrew, her dad and Scott would all be at the brewery.

The bell tinkled above the door again and Lily was almost afraid to look up. When she did, she wasn't sure whether to laugh or cry as Josh walked in and headed for the counter.

'I'm going to the beach with Chester. There's a piece of driftwood I need to photograph for my show so I thought I'd grab some cake. What's he doing here?' Josh spotted Rogan.

'I've no idea,' Lily said, as Cath reappeared at the counter.

'I bumped into Ted this morning. We had quite a gossip and he told me Rogan's back in Castle Cove for a few months – probably doesn't want to be alone so he's sniffing around Lily. What did he order?' Cath asked.

Lily told her.

'I'll serve him, you sort out that couple over there.' Cath pointed to Aubrey and Albert as she went to give Rogan his cake.

'What's wrong?' Josh asked as Lily nibbled her lip.

'That's my mother,' she whispered, as the bell above the teashop rang again and her father and Ted wandered in, making her stomach hit the floor. 'Oh no, my dad's here!' Lily jerked her eyes back to Aubrey who was talking intensely to Albert. 'Unbelievable! He never comes in the daytime. What am I going to do?'

'Make their drinks and sit your dad as far away from your mother as possible. I'll hide her.'

'How?' Lily asked, her nerves jangling as she imagined coming clean. They were all going to find out and everyone would hate her.

'Stop worrying. It'll be fine.' Josh's voice softened. 'Go and distract your dad before he comes over.'

Lily didn't wait. She headed for the front and sent her dad and Ted to a small table by the front of the teashop. When they sat, the counter would obscure the view of Aubrey and as long as they didn't go to the loo, and her mother didn't leave, they'd never know she was there.

'Just hot chocolate and cake please, love.' Lily's dad patted her hand. 'How's the Beast?'

'Doing great.' She darted her eyes beyond the counter where she could see Josh pulling up a chair to sit with Aubrey and Albert. What would he talk about? 'I didn't expect to see you. Who's in the brewery?' Lily's voice wobbled as she tried to cover her emotions.

'It's quiet today. Scott and Andrew have it covered. Ted mentioned Rogan was back in town.' Her dad's eyes darted to her ex. 'I thought I'd come and see how you were doing.'

'Great.' Lily hid the lie behind a big smile. 'I'm over him, Dad. You don't have to worry about me – no broken hearts here.' She patted her chest.

'Good to know, but there's no harm in us spending a little time in the teashop, making sure Rogan knows you're not alone.' Her dad narrowed his eyes at Rogan and Lily stopped her sigh. Maybe it was a good thing. If her dad was so focussed on *her* ex, he might not notice his own.

'I've got customers to serve, Dad, I'll pop into the brewery later for a catch-up. Shall I get your order to go?'

Tom shook his head as he glared at Rogan again. 'No, we'll stay.'

Lily ground her teeth but smiled. 'Okay, give me a sec and I'll get your order, or Cath will.' She whizzed back to the counter to make drinks and cut the cake as Cath arrived to serve them.

'Rogan asked when your break was.' Cath looked annoyed. 'I told him you were too busy to have one. Who's that woman Josh is talking to? She looks familiar.'

'Long story.' Lily grimaced. 'Complicated too. You'll be doing me a massive favour if you make sure my dad doesn't see her. If you think having Rogan here will cause a few ripples, she's likely to start a tsunami.'

Cath grinned. 'Now I'm intrigued. Lily King has secrets – about time too. I'll distract your dad and Ted, so long as you promise to fill me in later.' Lily nodded. 'Josh is doing a fine job of keeping the mystery lady happy, which just leaves the scumbag ex for you. Perhaps you could poison his coffee, or take a leaf out of Alice's book. When she first arrived here she chucked an ice cream over one of our more annoying customers.'

Lily laughed. 'Tempting, but since I'm after a permanent job in the restaurant I guess I'll have to do it the nice way. I'll go and talk to him. I can't avoid it forever.'

'Don't be too nice.' Cath pointed a stern finger in Lily's direction. 'Dig deep and find your inner bitch – we all have one. It's just yours is buried deeper than most, but sometimes you need her, and today is that day.'

Lily curled her hands into fists as she headed to Rogan, ready to do battle. He'd already eaten his cake and had picked up one of the newspapers from the rack on the wall and started to fill in the crossword. He looked up when she approached.

'Cath said you didn't have time for a break.' Rogan flashed a smile that would have melted her insides a few short weeks ago.

'I don't really.' Lily pulled up the chair opposite and dug deep. 'There's someone else I need to talk to so we need to keep this short.' She crossed her legs and let her foot tap on the floor, signalling her impatience.

Rogan looked surprised. 'You seem different. I'm not sure what's changed but it suits you.'

'That might be the first compliment you've ever paid me,' Lily said, surprised by the vehemence of the statement and by her ability to make it. 'But I'll thank you for it anyway. You wanted to see me?' Rogan opened his mouth to speak. 'If you're going to ask me for an introduction to Simon Wolf I'm afraid I can't help. I'm after a new job in the castle myself and I'm not planning on doing anything to jeopardize that. As Josh said last night, I'd advise you to speak to Rita Thomas. She's Simon's PA and if he's looking to change his insurance company, she'll know.'

'You are different.' Rogan's eyes glittered. 'Almost feisty.'

Feisty – she liked the sound of that. Lily's eyes flicked across to Josh, deep in conversation with Aubrey. She had him to thank for it. Funny how learning to be honest with one man made it so much easier to be the same with another.

'Thank you.' She rose from her seat. 'Now we've got that cleared up I've got places I need to be. Good luck with your business. I'll see you around.'

'Soon I hope.' Rogan stood and folded the newspaper. 'I'll give you a call – perhaps we can catch up over a drink?'

'I don't think so.' Lily turned her back. It took effort to be rude and she could feel the shake in her legs as she walked away – but she was proud of herself, and the way she'd handled Rogan. Lily glanced across at her dad, now deep in conversation with Ted, and watched her ex walk out of the teashop. One down. Now it was time to deal with her mother.

Josh must have felt Lily approach because he glanced up. He obviously sensed the unsteadiness she was hiding behind her smile, because he stood and offered her his chair.

'Glad you could join us.' Josh pulled up a seat for himself and Lily sat, checking again that her dad was hidden behind the counter on the other side of the teashop. 'Aubrey's been telling me about the photographer she's lined up for you. I had no idea you were interested in going into modelling.' He tipped his head.

'Ah, well.' Lily's skin tingled with the lie. 'I'm not exactly fully decided on that.'

'Nonsense,' Aubrey exclaimed. 'With a face and figure like that you could have the world at your feet.'

'I'm really happy here.' Lily glanced across the teashop towards her dad again instead of at her mother. 'And I'd like be a chef someday.'

'One day you'll be able to afford your own cook. Leave it with me, darling.' Aubrey patted her arm. 'I'll set up a shoot with the photographer and my agent will take you on if I ask. You could have a whole different life, dear.' She looked around the teashop. 'A world away from this.'

'I like it here.' Lily's voice was small, and she could feel the confidence she'd gathered dealing with Rogan disappear. Beside her, Josh exhaled noisily, but she ignored him. She'd waited years to meet her mother – now wasn't the time to upset her.

'You don't know anything else,' Aubrey argued, frowning at Josh as if she could detect the brewing disagreement. 'Albert, show the girl the portfolio. This is a model whose mother I'm friends with. My agent represents her.'

Albert picked up their empty drink cups and put them on the teashop counter along with the small vase of flowers Lily had filled this morning. Now the table was empty he had room to open the book. A tiny blonde girl lay in a bed of flowers wearing a small pair of hot pants and a t-shirt. Albert flicked the page over. In the next shot the girl wore a bikini, and in the next a body-con dress similar to the one Aubrey had given her.

Lily couldn't imagine ever looking like that, or wanting to. It wasn't exactly attire for a chef. 'This girl looks amazing, but I'm not sure that's my style. I don't normally wear clothes like that,' she stammered.

'We'll choose an appropriate wardrobe, obviously – your silver dress for one,' Aubrey added.

'Josh takes photos.' Lily changed the subject. 'He's really good. That's one of his.' She pointed to the photograph of the beach hanging nearby.

Aubrey glanced up. 'It is very good, but photographing models is a different art form.'

'I don't photograph people. It's a very different skill. This photographer is good – if this is what *you* want, then you probably won't find better.' Josh stared at Lily and she willed herself to be honest but the words wouldn't come.

'I'll set something up.' Aubrey snapped the portfolio shut. 'Now that's settled, I really need to leave. *Oh,* I got you this.' She dug into her bag and pulled out a small box and handed it over. 'Make-up from one of my clients. I thought you might like to practice. It must have been difficult for you to experiment living in a houseful of men. Try some darker colours around your eyes.' Aubrey looked at Lily's face critically. 'A pinker lipstick. I'll book someone to do your hair and make-up at the shoot, but you need to think about your everyday image. Remember, one day everyone will be looking at you.' Aubrey rose and Lily did the same, darting a panicked look towards her dad and Ted. If her mother left now she'd walk straight past both of them.

At the counter Cath mouthed something.

'I've got to go,' Lily said, as Aubrey walked around the table and gave her an air kiss.

'Soon this life will be behind you.'

'You need to get back to work, Lily,' Josh cut in, obviously trying to help by pointing at Cath, who was now madly signalling.

'I need to powder my nose before we leave.' Aubrey headed towards the loos in the opposite direction to the entrance. Lily raced to the counter. That was close. She breathed a huge sigh of relief.

'They're leaving – Dad can't see them. What can I do?'

'I'm on the case, just give it a minute.' Cath grinned. 'Lily, this is a whole new side to you.'

'I haven't got a minute. She'll be out of the toilet and walking this way any second.' Lily panicked.

The bell above the door rang and Anya rushed towards Lily's dad and Ted, gesturing with a beer tap. After a few seconds of commotion, they put some money on the table and waved at Lily before following Anya out of the teashop.

'What happened?' Lily's pulse began to slow. She honestly couldn't believe she'd managed to keep her parents apart.

'I asked Anya to say someone wanted a glass of King Newt but she couldn't figure out how to open the barrel – she's a great actress. I only hope there isn't a barrel open in the cellar already somewhere.'

'Thanks Cath,' Lily whispered as her mother and Albert waved goodbye and then left the teashop. 'I owe you.'

'You can fill me in on the whole story when we're washing up.'

Josh came to the counter. 'I said I'd pay for their drinks,' he explained. 'I didn't think you'd want them hanging around.'

'I owe you too.'

Josh's expression turned serious as Lily rang the order up. 'Do you want to be a model, Lily?'

'It's complicated,' she murmured.

'It's not.' Josh rested a hand over hers as the till opened. 'It's very simple, and it's about time you realised that.'

Chapter Twenty-One

Happily Ever After was situated on Castle Cove's main high street. As Lily made her way along the pavement, she admired the Christmas lights twinkling above the shops even though it was only four in the afternoon. Cath had let her leave the teashop early today and she'd had time to quickly bath and change before walking along the promenade. Lily hadn't rushed, aware Josh would almost certainly be late, so it was a complete surprise to find him standing outside the shop as she approached.

'Have you seen sense and bought a watch?' Lily teased.

'I'm just excited about seeing you get all hot and bothered about wedding shoes. Paul's vetoed anything pink, but I've a hankering for rainbows and sparkles.' Josh grinned. He wore a thick leather jacket but Lily could see he'd dressed up again – this time in black trousers, what looked like a navy shirt and proper shoes. Even the five-o'clock shadow he regularly wore had been shaved off.

Lily giggled. 'Whatever Paul wears, you'll get some to match, so I wouldn't go too wild. They've already chosen the suits and dress. Emily said you're taller than Paul, so we'll have to work from measurements for his clothes, but you can try yours on. Rita arranged for your suit to be brought here along with some shoe choices. I need to check the dress is the right length and size. Also, Emily wants pictures.'

'One for the portfolio?' Josh asked quietly.

'There isn't going to be a portfolio. I'm *not* going to be a model. I just haven't found the right time to tell Aubrey yet.'

'Make sure it isn't in ten years after you've starred on the cover of *Vogue*. Your mother strikes me as a very determined woman, and I ought to know. I have a mother like that myself.'

'So what's the story with your mother?' Lily arched an eyebrow. 'Doesn't look like she got her way.'

Josh laughed, unoffended, and she grinned. It was great having someone you could be honest with, someone you didn't have to worry about offending.

'I took after my grandmother – she never did anything she was told either. I owe her a lot. She paid for me to go to college and to set up as a photographer, encouraged me to follow my own path.'

'Where is she?' Lily asked, imagining an octogenarian skydiving somewhere.

'She died a few years ago.'

'I'm sorry.'

'Don't be. My grandmother lived the life she wanted – it was full, wild and just a little bit naughty. She taught me a lot.'

'A free spirit?' Lily guessed.

'Not entirely. She did what suited her – got married, had kids, ran her own business for a while, which I think she even enjoyed. She didn't suffer fools and wanted nothing to do with living for convention, or what some might call doing the right thing.' Josh looked annoyed. 'My mother never understood her; they didn't understand each other. Funny how one set of genes can create their polar opposite – in cooking terms, my grandmother was a knock-your-socks-off curry, while my mother does her best to imitate boiled cabbage. She tried to have my grandmother committed to a nursing home when she hit the age of seventy-five, which was the final turning point in their relationship – ours too – and the start of my grandmother's demise. So now it's just me keeping the delinquent gene alive.'

'You're not a delinquent,' Lily said, as Josh opened the door of the shop and let her walk in.

After that, Lily got caught up in the magic of weddings.

Happily Ever After was all about sparkle and lace with a little bit of magic thrown in. A white Christmas tree decorated with pink and silver lights, topped off with what looked like a bride, sat in the corner of the square room. A mannequin stood to the right of the door dressed in a gorgeous flowing white dress with a long veil. In the opposite corner an inanimate groom clothed in a full morning suit and black shoes stared happily at his bride. A chandelier dominated the ceiling and on the left wall a huge silver mirror reflected a rail of dresses. Towards the end of the shop Lily could see changing rooms, and next to that a squashy white sofa and glass coffee table already laid out with chocolates and a bucket of chilling champagne.

As they looked around Lily heard the tap of heels, then a tall blonde woman appeared from behind the changing rooms.

'You're here.' She beamed, taking Lily's hand. 'I'm Julie Evans and this is my shop. You're here to help with the fit for Emily Campbell's wedding dress?' The woman must have shopped for jewellery at the same place as Rita Thomas because the long chain on her necklace ended with a bobbly pink heart made from rubber.

'And the bridesmaid dress and suits,' Lily added. 'I'm sure I recognise you from somewhere.'

Julie smiled. 'I come to the teashop sometimes.' She squeezed Josh's hand. 'Emily chose the designs via Skype. She says you're almost the same height and size?' Lily nodded. 'If you try the dress on first we can check it fits. I'll make the adjustments based on you and the measurements Emily emailed. Your suit is out back,' Julie said to Josh. 'I've got your sizes and you need to choose the shoes. I've got a collection to show you.' Julie clapped her hands. 'Shall we start?'

'Please,' Lily said, excited.

Julie led them towards the changing room. Inside, a wedding dress hung ready on the rail. The white satin sparkled under the overhead lights and Lily could see it had a dramatic off-the-shoulder neckline, a diamanté belt and a long train that would trail behind Emily as she walked. Lily slid the silky material between her fingers.

'It's beautiful.'

'It's one of my favourite dresses of the season. Do you want champagne?' Julie asked. 'This is a celebration, even if Emily isn't here to enjoy it.'

'I'm not sure.' Lily chewed her lip.

'I'd say one won't do any harm,' Josh said. 'Besides, it means we're less likely to argue when we choose those shoes.'

'Getting me drunk isn't going to make me agree with you.' Lily laughed.

Josh popped the cork and filled the two glasses on the table. He gave one to Lily and watched her sip.

'It's good,' Lily admitted, feeling the bubbles hit her head and her shoulders start to loosen.

'Ready to try the dress on?' Julie asked, as a phone began to ring. 'I need to answer that but if you want to get undressed and make a start on putting the dress on, I'll be back to help button you up in a jiffy.'

Julie pulled the screen across to give Lily privacy. Lily peeled off her coat and jumper and hung them on a hook. She smelled lavender on her skin from her bath earlier and hoped it wouldn't transfer to the silk. She'd worn make-up because Emily wanted a picture but had taken care to resist the darker colours Aubrey had given her. Her hair was in a messy bun because she didn't want it to get caught in zips or buttons while she dressed. Thank goodness she only owned white underwear – anything colourful might have shown through the sheer material.

Lily took the dress carefully off the hanger and managed to undo and step into it, covering herself, but she wouldn't be able to do up the mass of silk buttons that worked their way up from below her waist to the middle of her back. Treading carefully, Lily poked her head out of the changing room. Josh hadn't been asked to change yet so he'd spread himself across the sofa, opening his arms wide along the back, stretching his shirt across his chest. He was lean and muscled and Lily could just make out the edge of his collarbone peeking from the small v at the top of his shirt, where a few buttons were left undone. What did he look like under that shirt – would he be tanned?

Josh must have caught her watching because he cleared his throat. 'That dress looks a little big,' he observed, just as one of the shoulders drooped, exposing the top of Lily's bra.

'It's not done up.' Lily clasped the top of the dress so it couldn't drop any lower, her eyes darting around the room. 'Julie said she'd help.'

'I think she's still on the phone. I can do it?' Josh stood as Lily looked at him critically. 'I've washed and everything.' He held out his hands. His nails were clipped and clean so there were no excuses.

'Okay, um—'

'Here.' Josh didn't give Lily a chance to argue; in seconds he was standing in the changing room beside her and the space that had felt so ample seconds earlier seemed to shrink.

'Um,' Lily said again, staring at Josh's chest, at the tiny buttons that held his shirt together. A minute ago, she'd been wondering what he looked like under that shirt. If she were brave enough she'd reach over and undo it to find out. 'There are buttons at the back.' Her voice sounded strange to her ears. 'I'm not sure I can turn. There's so much dress.' She looked down. 'You'll need to be careful where you tread.'

'No problem.' Josh slipped off his shoes and dropped them on the carpet outside the changing room. 'I'll be careful.'

Lily felt Josh behind her, she heard material being moved, probably the train so he didn't tread on it, then warm breath tickled her shoulder as Josh got closer and began to do up the buttons.

'There are millions of them,' he murmured. Lily felt her skin prickle as Josh's fingers worked, brushing the bottom of her spine. She cleared her throat as the dress tightened, trying to think of something to say, but as his fingers brushed her spine again she found herself swallowing. It had been a long time since her blood had stirred like this – not that she could remember when it last had – and she didn't know what to do. 'I'm not sure this is the right underwear for this style.' Josh's fingers stroked Lily's bra strap at the top of her shoulder. 'The dress is off the shoulder, so you're going to be able to see this.'

'Um—' Lily mumbled again. What did he want her to do, take her bra off?

'You should probably take it off so we can get a full picture of the fit,' Josh read Lily's mind. The words came out so matter-of-factly that he couldn't possibly have any idea of the effect he was having on her – and she obviously wasn't having the same effect on him because he was forming complete sentences.

'Well—' Lily knew her cheeks were crimson.

'I'll undo it for you if you like?' Josh's voice deepened and she felt his fingers stop at her bra strap, hovering over it, obviously waiting for her answer.

'Okay,' she squeaked and felt his fingers move as he unclipped her bra and waited. She felt warm breath on the back of her neck and tried not to squirm.

'Do you want to take it all the way off?' Josh asked after a few more moments. 'I've not done it myself but if you tug the straps through the arms of the dress, you could probably just pull it off.'

'I know how,' Lily suddenly snapped, knowing the flush on her cheeks would have travelled all the way down her back by now. Her skin prickled, and her legs felt like jelly, and all because she was standing so close to this man, completely exposed, while Josh's voice hadn't even wobbled.

Embarrassed, Lily did as Josh suggested and pulled one of the straps out of one sleeve of the wedding dress before tugging the whole bra out of the other. She held her underwear in her hands, bunching it up, unsure of what to do with it.

Behind her Josh sighed and then continued to do up the buttons without saying anything until Lily felt the top of the dress tighten.

His fingers lightly brushed her skin as he moved the straps so they were off her shoulders, positioned in line with her collarbone. He paused for a moment before moving around the changing room to stand in front of her.

'It's um…' Josh trailed off and Lily looked up into his face. His brown eyes had darkened and instead of looking self-assured and unaffected like she'd been expecting, he looked unsure, perhaps a little overwhelmed. 'You look beautiful.' His eyes dropped to the bottom of the dress and scanned upwards, stopping at the diamanté belt for a beat before continuing. He paused at Lily's collarbone before moving up again and stopping at her mouth.

'It's the dress,' Lily found herself saying as awareness prickled across her body. Even her lips were tingling —not surprising given Josh's eyes were still fixed on them. Then he took a small step forwards, his eyes tracking upwards until they met hers and held.

'It's not the dress.' Josh looked serious, then his brown eyes danced with humour. 'I know this sounds predictable, but may I kiss the bride?'

Lily opened her mouth but words wouldn't come, so she nodded, unable to stop herself.

Josh wasn't what you'd call conventional, so Lily didn't expect the kiss to be sweet. She'd been thinking he'd dive in, rush and take what he wanted, perhaps with little thought for what she needed or liked.

But she was wrong. He didn't rush. His lips were gentle. The man didn't own a watch, didn't follow or care about time, which perhaps explained why he seemed to focus on sensation rather than next steps. The first brush of his lips felt like feathers, just a tiny movement, then Josh moved his hand up to stroke the edge of her face and Lily found herself leaning into him, felt the hunger inside of her climb as his lips played on the surface, seemingly in no great hurry to move on.

It wasn't Josh who took the kiss deeper and it wasn't Josh who took control. Lily surprised herself by dropping the bra she'd been holding onto the floor and grabbing the collars of his shirt, pulling him towards her, so the kiss that had started so slowly took on a life of its own.

Now she could feel the heat burning between them, and the promise of it became a fire deep in her bones, making her impatient. As the moment deepened, Josh edged even closer, letting his hands fall from the side of Lily's face to her arms, which were still clutched around the collar of his shirt. For a brief second, she thought about letting go and undoing one of the buttons on the shirt she'd been obsessing about. It was only the quiet cough behind them that brought her to her senses.

Josh must have felt the retreat because he instantly dropped his hands from Lily's arms and they simultaneously looked out of the changing room to where Julie stood with her arms folded, a bemused expression on her face. Lily sprang back, away from Josh.

'Well, if the dress gets that reaction for Emily, I'd say it works.' Julie walked around Lily before kneeling down to take a closer look, then she checked the waist and shoulders. 'The length and size are almost perfect.' She tugged at the dress, checking the fit. 'Wouldn't you agree, Josh?' Julie's expression didn't change but Lily could sense the humour in her tone.

'It fits fine.' Josh said eventually. He moved away and headed for the white sofa, dropping back onto it, his face strangely blank.

'I wouldn't get too comfortable, it'll be your turn next,' Julie said, adding a couple of pins to the shoulders of the dress. 'I think you'll need to try some shoes before you change, Lily. We know you'll need six-inch heels because the dress will work with that exact height. There are a few pairs out back. Just give me a minute or two to dig them out.' Julie smiled at Josh. 'I'm sure you two will find a way to amuse yourselves until I get back.'

The room fell silent as soon as Julie left and Lily clenched her hands into fists, fighting the sudden wave of embarrassment as she took in Josh's pale cheeks and confused expression. She'd launched herself at him – perhaps he'd only meant to give her a small peck on the lips and she'd notched it up from a tame PG to an almost X rating?

'I'm sorry.'

'Why?'

'For—' Lily's eyes widened, willing Josh to guess. When he didn't, she added, 'For hurling myself at you.'

Josh smiled as some of the earlier colour returned to his cheeks and he seemed to relax. 'You've got nothing to apologise for. I think the hurling was mutual – I can't say I was expecting to get so caught up, but…' He considered her. 'I knew you were wild, I really should have expected it,' he teased.

'I'm sorry,' Lily said again, trying hard to read his expression.

'And that's another thing you shouldn't apologise for. Wildness is most definitely a good thing, some might say devastatingly so.'

Before Lily could ask Josh what he meant Julie returned with three shoeboxes in one hand, holding a suit bag in the other.

'Here.' Julie handed Josh the suit. 'If you go in there' – she pointed to the changing room beside Lily's – 'and try this on, we can see if it fits. You,' Julie said to Lily, pointing at the three boxes. 'Check out these shoes.'

Lily lifted the lid off the first box and pulled out a pair of simple white stilettos. The second contained a pair of open, strappy shoes which she quickly discarded. 'They'll be too cold for December,' she explained to Julie, opening the final box. The third pair of shoes were white too, only they were sparkly with silver piping and a shimmery strap across the top, plus there were peep holes at the ends. 'I love them,' Lily said, stroking the heels as Josh appeared from the changing room dressed in a dark blue morning suit that seemed to make his eyes even darker. The white shirt he wore set off his skin, making him look tanned and rugged. The image set off a cacophony of butterflies in Lily's stomach.

'This looks good too,' Julie said, checking the sizing on Josh, pulling at his waistband and the shoulders of his suit without asking if she could. It didn't seem to bother him. Instead he stood quietly, letting Julie tug at his clothes, looking more than a little amused. 'I'll say that's a pass. You'll need to choose shoes as well in a minute,' Julie said. 'But Lily needs to make her decision first.'

'Oh, I choose these.' Lily held up the third pair of shoes. 'I'm just not sure how I'll put them on.'

'I'll do it.' Josh walked across the room to Lily. He took the strappy white shoes from her hands and examined them.

'I can't really argue about these – they're very pretty.' He looked down. 'I'm guessing the only way we'll do this is if I kneel.' He grinned.

'It'll be the first time I've had a man at my feet.'

Josh didn't say anything. He knelt and moved the dress to uncover Lily's bare feet, then helped her into the shoes, taking time to do them up. His fingers were gentle and he kept his head bent so he could concentrate. Lily drew in a breath as his fingers stroked the skin on the top of her feet, making nerve endings tingle. When they were done, he looked up with the faintest hint of mischief in his eyes. 'I'd say they're perfect. I like the sparkles and straps, it makes them conventional and pretty but with just the right amount of *wild*.'

Josh stood as Julie came to bustle around Lily, checking the fit of the shoes and the length of the dress. All the while Josh and Lily kept their eyes fixed on each other and she could feel emotion burning inside her again. Heat seemed to reach outwards, leaving a strange sensation on her skin. It was only when Julie stood again that she looked away.

'I'd agree, they're perfect,' Julie agreed. 'We're done with the wedding dress — Emily is going to look absolutely gorgeous. Do you want me to help you out of it, Lily?'

'I'm more than happy to do it,' Josh answered quickly. 'But we promised my brother and Emily a photo.' He went into his changing room and returned with his phone, holding it up to look through it. 'You look beautiful, Lily, and I was right, the camera loves you.'

Lily felt embarrassed. Should she pose? She didn't know how, so she stood staring at Josh. After a moment, he dropped the mobile from his face. 'I'll send the picture in a minute. If Emily looks half as good as you in that dress, my brother's going to be mute for most of the wedding.'

'I'll go and find the men's shoes and get your bridesmaid dress.' Julie bent to pick up the other two boxes. 'If you're happy for Josh to help you get undressed, Lily?'

Lily jerked her head, watching Julie leave. When Josh bent at her feet again she wasn't sure what to say so didn't speak as he slowly removed her shoes before returning them to the box on the coffee table.

'Do you want to go into the changing room?' he asked. 'You don't have to look so worried, I'll just undo the buttons and leave you to it. No hurling, I promise.'

'You may have kissed me first, but it wasn't you who was responsible for the hurling. Maybe I'm just worried about myself.'

'Are you saying I'm irresistible?' Josh teased.

'I'm blaming the champagne,' Lily muttered. 'Or perhaps it's the dress.' She looked down at the demure floaty skirt and diamanté belt.

'You could. Or you could admit there's a certain amount of chemistry between us. Perhaps even decide to act on it.'

'I did,' Lily squeaked, her eyes darting to the changing room. 'I did act on it, and if Julie hadn't come along, who knows what might have happened...' Who knows how long it would have been before she'd started to unbutton Josh's shirt, before he'd begun to help her out of the dress? Her body flushed at the memory. 'And that's not me.' She frowned. 'I don't do things like that.'

The corner of Josh's mouth twitched as he considered her. 'Except you did. I wasn't expecting you to, I wasn't expecting that…' He stopped, looking surprised. 'But now you have, it's difficult to undo those feelings…'

'We're very different.' Lily nibbled her thumbnail, fighting the need to throw herself into Josh's arms, despite her better judgement.

He studied her. 'We are. But I think somewhere deep inside, in a place neither of us probably wants to admit to, we're similar too.'

'Here they are.' Julie's voice sang as she appeared again from the back room, startling both of them and effectively ending the conversation before it had reached any kind of conclusion. She put three boxes on the table and nodded at Josh as if to say *it's your turn*.

He opened the first and pulled out a pair of black brogues.

'They're nice.' Lily stood beside him – the dress trailed on the carpet behind her. She really needed to get changed, but inexplicably didn't want to leave Josh.

'Mmm.' He opened the next box, revealing a pair of black slip-on shoes. 'I think I'd prefer to wear your shoes. I don't think even Chester would deem these chewable and that dog likes to *chew*.'

'Check out the third.' Julie stood beside them both. Josh did as he was asked and pulled out a pair of patent black leather lace-ups with red suede across the top and down to the heels.

'That's more like it.' He smiled, pulling them out.

'They're eye-catching, and they'll go with the suit,' Julie agreed.

'And the flowers – plus they're the right side of interesting.' Josh put them on to check the fit, his eyes darting to Lily as he straightened. 'What do you think Lily – are you going to agree, or are they too unconventional?' His eyes held hers with just the slightest hint of challenge. 'Do you need another glass of champagne before you decide?'

'No.' She looked at the shoes thoughtfully. 'I'd say they'll work. They're not conventional and they're definitely not what I was expecting, but if you think Paul will like them they'll work for me. You're right, they are interesting with a hint of unusual. They'll go with the suit and they go with you,' she said, feeling strangely light and more than a little confused. 'Julie, I'm not going to be able to undo these buttons by myself. Will you help me out of this dress, please, so I can try on the bridesmaid dress? I don't want to get anything on it.'

As Julie freed her from the dress, Lily fought a strange mixture of emotions, because it wasn't Julie she wanted in the changing room with her – it was Josh. She knew that getting involved with a man like him would be a total disaster for her. Why was she so tempted to be swept away by him?

Chapter Twenty-Two

'How are you getting along with the show?' Marta asked Josh, bending to pick up a stick from the beach and throwing it for Chester.

'The show's fine,' Josh said, as the dog looked at Marta and then at the stick before sniffing a piece of dried seaweed.

'It's almost uncanny how alike you are,' Marta snorted, shaking her head. 'Think he's any good at photography?'

Josh fought a smile as he walked beside her, taking in a deep breath of sea air. 'Chester will do anything for food – give him a biscuit and a camera and you might find out.' The Labrador began to chew the seaweed. 'Of course, he might just eat them both.'

'I'll risk it if you don't show me the rest of your photos soon.'

Josh chuckled. 'If we walk a little further I'll show you my newest model. I've caught quite a few shots and I'll definitely use some, but I haven't taken the *one* yet.'

'Don't tell me that, Josh,' Marta protested. 'We've got less than two weeks and I'm beginning to panic. I'm used to your unorthodox ways. I've given you more time to put this show together even though every other photographer I've worked with had theirs finalised and planned months ahead. But I can't wait forever, even for you.'

'It's not like you to stress.' Josh stopped walking and turned to face his friend. 'What else is going on?'

Marta glowered. She'd tied her hair up to keep it out of her eyes but the wind whipped it around her face. She looked tired and her skin was dull. 'The electricity's been playing up at the gallery. I've got someone coming to fix it but it's been a stressful afternoon. Simon keeps popping in to check on me and I'm…' Marta ran a hand through her hair, pulling it out of her eyes. 'It's annoying.'

'You don't like him?' Josh turned to walk along the beach again. He knew from experience that Marta shared best while walking.

'He's irritating and totally fixated on profit and money,' Marta moaned. 'He argues about everything and I've no idea what he's thinking half the time.'

'You do like him.' It wasn't a question.

Marta sighed. 'I've no idea why.'

'You like irritating men?' Josh joked, but Marta didn't answer. 'If it's any help, he likes you too. I probably shouldn't say, but I don't think he'll mind. He told me the other day on the beach.'

'You were talking about me?' Marta shrieked.

'Not how it sounds.' The log came into view and Josh pointed to it. 'That's the picture, or it will be – I know it's in there somewhere. The log was in the sea and Simon helped me pull it out. In return he wanted to know if you were single and how he should go about asking you on a date.'

'And you *told* him?' Marta's eyes widened.

'I told him to ask you, to be honest and that you'd been hurt,' Josh replied, undaunted by the murderous look in his friend's eyes. 'Nothing you wouldn't tell him yourself.'

'What was he doing asking you for dating advice? It's not like you're doing such a great job with your own love life,' Marta snapped.

'What does that mean?'

'You've mentioned Lily King at least four times in the last hour.'

'I've talked about the dog too, doesn't mean I'm planning on dating him.' Josh's mind switched to the changing room of Happily Ever After when Lily had taken their kiss from a tentative peck to a full-on blow-your-socks-off smooch before backing off. She'd let Julie into the changing room to help her try on the bridesmaid dress and had made up an excuse about having to visit Ted when they'd finished, so they couldn't walk together or pick up the conversation from earlier. It was a good thing, Josh knew that – they were totally wrong for each other. He kicked a pebble across the beach, feeling frustrated.

They approached the log and Josh watched Marta as she marched around it, checking each angle with a crease marring her forehead. 'Simon hasn't asked me out,' she confided eventually. 'And he was checking the fuse box most of the morning so there were plenty of opportunities.'

'I guess he's working his way up to it,' Josh said, out of his depth. 'Or he could have changed his mind. If you want, I can beat him up?'

Marta's face brightened. 'Tempting, but I really don't need your help. There are plenty of other ways to torture Simon Wolf. I've got a dress to wear at your opening that will do just the job and a man I can ask to accompany me if necessary.'

'Ouch.' Josh studied the log. Perhaps if he lay down in the sand and photographed it on the same level he'd get the effect he wanted? 'I'm not sure Simon is ready for you.'

'Few are,' Marta agreed sadly. 'And if he can't even work himself up to asking me for a date, he isn't the man I think he is – and he's definitely not the right one for me.'

'Give him a chance.' Josh folded his arms and studied the log from another angle. 'Sometimes it takes time to get what we want.'

'Are we talking about Simon, that log or Lily?' Marta's tone was dry but Josh knew she was teasing him.

'All of them. But I'm not interested in Lily,' Josh said firmly. 'I like beautiful, uncomplicated women who know that what they want doesn't include me. My work comes first and that girl has strings and vulnerability written all over her.' Not to mention a powerful pull on him. 'We're planning my brother's wedding together, nothing more.'

'You keep telling yourself that, Josh. Perhaps you might even believe it. But I see the way your face lights up when you talk about her. I see something in you I've never seen before. My question is, are you brave enough to go after her, or are you just another Simon Wolf?'

'It's not me who isn't brave enough,' Josh murmured, picking up his camera to take a shot. 'Not interested,' he said aloud, because he was done talking about Lily King. If she wasn't bold enough to take their chemistry further, if she was too afraid of where it might lead, then she wasn't the woman for him. He didn't chase after people who didn't want him and he wasn't about to start.

☆

Josh didn't hear the doorbell at first. He was too caught up in going through his photos from the day before and checking the canvases that had been couriered to him this morning ready for the show. The sitting room was a mass of canvases large and small, black and white, pictures in colour. Dogs, rust, logs, waves, Cove Castle, one of Lily looking mad in the restaurant kitchen, even a few of the cliff he'd taken a few days before. It was only when Chester barked and nudged his knee that Josh realised someone was at the door.

'Good boy.' Josh gave the dog a treat and nudged him aside. He could see a blonde bun through the frosted glass and for a brief unguarded moment thought it was his grandmother.

'Josh.' His mother's brow knitted as soon as he opened the door, and she wrinkled her nose at Chester, who padded past him to greet her. 'What is that?'

'A dog. My dog.' Josh stood aside so his mother could enter. She stopped at the doorway to give him a perfunctory air kiss and continued through the hallway into the living room. Chester followed, padding behind, possibly hoping for food or friendship, neither of which he'd find. Josh closed the door and followed. Olivia Havellin-Scott scanned her eyes around her son's living room and wrinkled her nose. Josh's mother was tall and skinny. She wore an expensive black suit with a skirt just below her knee and a long orange scarf wrapped around her neck. Her handbag hung from the crook of her arm and she narrowed her eyes at Chester.

'Where did that dog come from?'

'He got dumped and I offered him a home.' Chester whined so Josh opened one of the big glass doors at the end of the room and let him out. A blast of cold air shot inside so he closed it again quickly. 'He's a good dog,' Josh said, making conversation. He already knew why his mother was here and braced himself. 'Want a drink?'

'Earl Grey.'

'Sorry, no tea, I wasn't expecting you.' He heard the deep sigh and decided to ignore it. 'I have coffee.'

'I like it black.'

'I know.' Josh disappeared to the kitchen to fill up the cafetière. When he returned his mother was looking out of the window. Was she deliberately ignoring all of his photos piled around the room, or did she truly not see them?

'I came to talk about your future.'

'I know what you came for,' Josh said, feeling resigned. 'And we've had this conversation a hundred times already. I really don't see the point of repeating it. Where's my father?'

His mother's face dropped, making her look tired and unhappy. 'At work. He got called into surgery.'

Josh picked up one of the canvases from the sofa and placed it on the floor. His mother didn't comment on that, or on the picture beside it, so Josh didn't say anything. He'd been down that road too many times before.

His mother sat and looked around the room. 'So, you're renting?'

'Yep.' Josh sat opposite, spreading himself out in the chair, trying to release the tension in his chest. 'It's a good house. Suits me for now.'

'And the dog?'

'Same.' Josh smiled. 'I'm not renting him though, he's permanent.'

'How will that fit in with your nomadic lifestyle?' His mother twisted her mouth as if the subject were unpleasant.

'He's portable so he fits fine. And he looks good on a canvas so he'll earn his keep.'

His mother looked uncomfortable. 'Your grandmother liked dogs. Had a few of her own while I was growing up.'

'I know,' Josh said, aggravated by the sad expression on his mother's face, because as far as he could tell, she'd never felt anything for his grandmother except bitterness. 'And you hated them.'

His mother looked thoughtful. 'Hate is a strong word. I don't have an affinity with animals.'

Or much else, if his childhood was anything to go by. 'You're here to talk about me being a doctor?' Josh cut to the chase – he wasn't in the mood for reminiscing. Too much water had passed under the bridge, and there were too many resentments to ignore them.

His mother looked surprised. 'Yes. It occurred to me that the reason you don't want to be a doctor is because you might be worried about money.' She reached into her handbag.

'No,' Josh barked. Chester scratched on the glass doors at the end of the room. 'I appreciate the gesture but I really don't need your money,' he said as gently as he could, opening the doors and following his dog into the kitchen where he poured coffee before bringing his mother one. She had a long drive home and he wasn't going to let her do it thirsty. 'I'm a photographer.' He didn't point at the evidence surrounding them. 'I love what I do and I'm good at it. I'm not built to be a doctor.'

'You're clever enough.'

'Perhaps, but I love taking photos.'

'This is your grandmother's doing.' His mother's lips thinned, making her look old and mean.

'If by that you mean she listened to what I loved and gave me the room and support to do it, I suppose you're right. And I'll thank her for it every day of my life.'

'If you just tried to see it our way.' Josh tried to interrupt but the expression on his mother's face stopped him. 'It's not easy living without. When your grandmother decided to become an artist, we ended up having to sell our house. I was only fifteen.'

'And then she gave up her painting to open a laundry business. Bought two houses in the same amount of years, as I recall?'

'Doesn't make up for it,' his mother sneered. 'Nothing will ever make up for the embarrassment of losing my home.'

'I don't have children to let down or embarrass,' Josh said gently. 'Unless you count Chester, who'd be content living anywhere. I'm not about to lose my house or anything in it. I'm doing pretty well.' He waited for his mother to ask about it. Waiting for her to finally show an interest in his passion. Instead she shook her head.

'You're embarrassing me and your father. We raised you for better things than this.' She glanced around the room.

'Then I'm sorry I don't measure up,' he said, not meaning a word.

'I don't understand you, Josh. You've got everything: looks, brains, family support. You could be anything you wanted.'

'I'm exactly what I want to be.' Josh heard his tone, and felt his heart harden, closing the tiny gap he'd just left open. 'I'm a photographer and I love it. I'm great at it too.'

'Your little hobby. You're so like your grandmother,' she said bitterly. 'Following your creative whims, ignoring everyone else's needs.' She stood, putting her untouched drink on the coffee table.

'I've just remembered, I need to be somewhere. Perhaps we could pick this up another time?'

'Not on my account.' Josh followed as she marched through the sitting room and hall, stopping at the front door, not even bothering to give him her usual perfunctory kiss. After he'd closed the door, Josh stood for a couple of seconds shaking off the feelings of disappointment. Then he tracked back to the sitting room, closely followed by Chester, and picked up the canvases and frames, putting them back on the sofa and around the room, ignoring the hollowness in his chest. That was why he didn't let people close – the reason relationships of any kind were a bad idea. He didn't live up to expectations, he *hurt* people without meaning to – and he'd do well to remember it. Which was yet another reason why he was determined to keep his distance from Lily.

Chapter Twenty-Three

'I'm nervous.' Lily's hands wobbled as she arranged the prawns and Marie Rose sauce on the plates in the teashop kitchen, adding pieces of lemon and some rocket for colour. She ground a little black pepper onto the top for effect. Beside her Cath sliced freshly baked soda bread and put it into baskets.

'Don't be.' Cath picked up four of the plates and the bread, bumping the kitchen door open with her bum before turning back to Lily. 'Tonight is going to be magnificent. If you want to hone your cooking skills before Luc returns, what better way could there be than creating a fabulous meal for your friends and family? And they're all here, Lily. Ted, Olive, Ben, Anya, your dad, Andrew and Scott – ready to cheer you on and eat up. I just wish I'd had the idea of cooking a meal for your friends and family instead of Suze. It's the perfect chance to try out your cooking skills.'

Lily's stomach contracted as she squeezed lemon juice onto the remaining starters. Had she added too much? She couldn't tell.

'I'd say you need a little more.' Cath read her mind, nodding at the plates, and Lily squeezed the lemon again, feeling her heart sink. She'd been nervous all afternoon about adding too little of this and too much of that to the point that Cath had ended up making suggestions about seasoning, encouraging Lily to add her secret ingredients – a single chilli and half a bottle of Malbec – to the main course. The result had been flavoursome but Lily couldn't help feeling like it wasn't her work, and that the cooking *force* Suze had talked about had totally bypassed her. She had no idea how to rely on instinct while cooking and couldn't seem to let go of the fear of getting things wrong and disappointing people. Worse, the excitement she used to feel while creating dishes seemed to have evaporated.

'How many are here?' Lily asked, trying to distract herself.

Cath looked into the teashop and counted. 'It'll be fifteen in all. Shaun's sitting with Jay and Alice is serving wine. Ted and Olive have a table with Ben and Gayle. It's Anya's night off and she's sitting with your dad, Andrew and Scott – there's a place there for you too. *Oh*, and Marta and Josh just walked in. I didn't know you'd invited him?'

'I didn't.' Lily's stomach churned.

'Marta must have brought him. I thought she was coming with Simon.'

'Simon's coming?' Lily felt sick. It was enough that most of Cove Castle had turned up to try out her latest trial menu, without the big boss coming along too. At least Suze was working and couldn't check the meals. While the sous chef had been trying to help her access her inner cook, Lily was nervous that Suze wouldn't be impressed with the food tonight. Lily closed her eyes and opened them again as the door to the kitchen swung shut and Cath went to serve the starters.

What was Josh doing here? She hadn't seen him since their kiss in the changing room at Happily Ever After when she'd suddenly got cold feet. Somehow just knowing he was in the teashop, about to try her food, had her body tingling in anticipation. She went to the Aga to stir the beef bourguignon. Inside the oven, five dishes of gratin dauphinoise bubbled, and next to them freshly cut green beans, already seasoned, were waiting to boil for exactly four minutes, or maybe it was five?

The kitchen door bounced open and Josh walked in. He wore jeans, a dark blue long-sleeved t-shirt and a five-o'clock shadow that should have been illegal. Lily's pulse perked up and she turned back to the starters, adding more black pepper so she had something to do with her hands.

'You look frazzled.' Josh studied her. 'Meal not working out?'

'It's fine,' Lily grumbled, wishing he'd leave. Josh being here made her feel unsettled and exposed. It was like he could see inside her head, see all of her thoughts and feelings, and if he could read her now, he'd know she was terrified of getting the food wrong tonight.

'You sure?' Josh cocked his head as though trying to read her.

'Yes, really,' she lied, glancing at Josh from under her lashes. He looked hot and she was tempted to wrap herself around him like she had in Happily Ever After so she could treat herself to another one of those mind-numbing kisses.

Before she could do it, Cath burst into the kitchen. 'Sorry, I got held up, Olive asked what was in the sauce. What are you doing here?' she asked Josh.

'Extra pair of hands.'

Cath grinned and picked up four more starters before disappearing out of the kitchen.

'You don't look like you're having much fun.' Josh stood beside Lily and stared into the huge pot. 'Smells good.'

'It doesn't feel right. The food.' She wasn't sure how to explain it. 'And I'm not sure why.' Josh didn't try to comfort her, or to tell her everything would be okay. 'I like that you never give me the reaction I expect,' Lily admitted, feeling a little better. 'Anyone else would tell me it looks great and that I'm being stupid.'

'I'm not going to tell you how to feel,' Josh said. 'If this feels wrong to you then it probably is. Not because the food isn't good, it smells great,' he added, 'but food's a kind of art Lily, it's an expression of your heart and soul. If yours aren't in this, I guess you're not going to feel right about it.'

Lily opened her mouth and closed it again because Josh had got it exactly right. Cath burst back into the kitchen and grinned at them.

'Remember, only your opinion counts, it doesn't matter what anyone else thinks,' Josh advised before picking up a couple of plates and a bread basket and disappearing out of the kitchen.

'You going to tell me what that was all about?' Cath asked, her green eyes dancing.

'Just wedding stuff,' Lily lied.

Cath giggled as if she knew exactly what Josh had been doing there. She picked up four plates. 'You want to bring the rest? You're not staying in the kitchen Lily – I told you. You need to sit and eat, hear the wonderful things people are going to say about your food. Besides, it's all organised. I thought you'd rather sit with Josh and Marta so I pushed some tables together so you can sit with your dad and brothers too.' With that she disappeared out of the kitchen.

Lily checked the pots on the hob again before heading into the teashop. Her chest felt tight, she was so nervous. What if they hated the food? She wouldn't be able to look anyone in the eye.

Cath had rearranged the tables so Lily would be facing Josh, Marta and her dad. Scott sat on one side of her and Anya on the other while Andrew had moved to sit with Olive and Ted. Lily put the final plates on the table and pulled up her chair, putting a napkin on her knees. The room hushed as Cath shouted, 'Dig in!' Suddenly knives and forks were lifted and there was a clatter as they hit the plates, a collective hum as her friends and family sampled the food.

Lily had a bite of a prawn and nodded. It was okay, not amazing, and it probably wasn't the taste sensation Luc would be looking for, but the food was passable.

Beside her, Scott muttered, 'It's fantastic, Lily.' Her dad agreed, scooping more into his mouth. Marta ate a prawn and hummed her approval.

'I'm sure Luc would be impressed. Simon too if he were here,' Marta added after a few more mouthfuls.

'Where is he?' Josh asked, earning a glare from his friend.

'Planning world domination, or poring over his company books, I really couldn't say.'

'So you rescinded his invitation here tonight?' Josh smiled wickedly.

Marta's lips thinned. 'After he'd played with my fuse box for over two hours without speaking three sentences to me, I suggested he might have better things to do tonight.'

'I almost feel sorry for him.' Josh took a swift bite of the starter.

'What do you think?' Lily asked, impatient now. A chorus of 'wonderful' and 'brilliant' echoed around the room, but these were her friends and family, and while she valued their opinion, she didn't trust it – but Josh would be honest.

'It's good, but it's not you, wild Lily,' Josh said softly. 'I'm sensing something is missing—'

'It's great, Lily,' Scott interrupted, his cheeks flushed with annoyance. 'I've never tasted better. I'm sure Luc is going to give you the job.'

'I love that you want to make me feel better, Scott, but it's not great.' Scott looked surprised at Lily's outburst. 'The food's just okay and the whole point of this was I need honest feedback. I want to be a better cook.'

Scott's expression softened. 'We were raised on dad's cooking, so I'd probably be happy if you fed me a raw steak so long as you put ketchup on it.'

'What's missing?' Lily looked at Josh.

'You said it didn't feel like your food when we were in the kitchen. Maybe you're trying so hard to please everyone, you've forgotten what *you* like. What do you like?' Josh's brown eyes fixed on Lily's face with such intensity that she had an urge to drop her fork and throw herself at him. The desire was so unexpected that a flush crawled up her cheeks.

'I've no idea. I did as I was told, what I thought everyone wanted.' *Same as always.* Lily nibbled her bottom lip. 'Let's see what you think of the second course.' She pushed her chair back and picked up her half-finished starter and gathered a couple more plates. Most were empty, which made her feel better, but the fact that she wasn't excited about the next course told her more.

Cath and Alice met Lily in the kitchen. They'd cleared the starters between them and bustled around the room tidying while Lily boiled water ready for the beans.

'Thanks for today,' she said.

'I'm sorry it's not working out.' Cath looked worried. 'I wasn't trying to take over the cooking, I wanted to help.'

'Don't be silly.' Lily gave her friend a swift hug. 'The dishes are incredible and I honestly couldn't have done it without you. I just wonder if I need to find my cooking instinct another way.'

'How?' Alice asked, efficiently packing plates into the dishwasher.

'Honestly, I've no idea.' Lily put the large pot of beans on to boil.

'Maybe you need to do something you've never done before. Cook blindfolded, make up your own recipes?' Alice suggested. 'When I came to Castle Cove, I tried lots of things I'd never done, had adventures. It helped me figure out what I really needed. Now everything's changed for me. I'm living with the man of my dreams, we're talking about going travelling together someday. Maybe it'll be the same for you?'

'You think I need to try something different?' Lily asked.

Alice spread her arms wide. 'It's what I did.'

'Like what?'

'Maybe you need some passion in your life, Lily?' Cath beamed. 'That'll get those creative cooking juices flowing.'

'Josh is very handsome,' Alice added, tapping a hand on her heart.

'And about a million times nicer than Rogan,' Cath agreed. 'He seems to like you too, which proves he has excellent taste.'

'And he is handsome,' Alice repeated, making Cath laugh.

'Josh has nothing to do with whether I can cook or not,' Lily mumbled, embarrassed. She stirred the casserole. The beans looked ready so she pulled the hot plates out of the oven and put them on the table.

'We don't mean he'll suddenly help with your cooking – it's just, I don't know.' Cath's green eyes turned serious. 'I never feel like you let go. Maybe spending time with him will help you learn how?'

'I am spending time with Josh,' Lily admitted, serving each plate with a hot slice of gratin dauphinoise.

'With or without your clothes on?' Cath teased, adding a ladle of casserole to each meal. Alice giggled as she served green beans.

'It's not like that,' Lily lied as her mind conjured an image of Josh in the changing room of Happily Ever After, of all those buttons she'd been itching to undo.

The kitchen door opened and Ted walked in and checked the food. 'That looks great.' His cheeks reddened. 'I was worried you'd be serving shepherd's pie.'

'That's off the menu, Ted.' Cath handed him a couple of plates. 'Can you help us take these out, please?'

Ted took the plates and Alice, Cath and Lily followed him, balancing dishes and serving everyone in record time.

Lily watched as everyone began to eat. Within seconds the chorus of compliments began but she brushed them off. Instead she watched Josh sample the beef and nod. His eyes caught hers and he put down his fork. 'Not eating?'

'Not sure I'm hungry.'

'It's good,' Josh said. 'But I think you're more of a knock-your-socks-off curry kind of girl.'

'Do you like curry, Lily?' Scott looked confused.

'More than I like boiled cabbage.' Lily's voice turned husky. 'How's the show?' She changed the subject before her brother asked what she was talking about.

'Yes, how is the show, Josh?' Marta pinned him with a look that made Lily regret the question.

'It's fine.' He smirked, looking unconcerned. 'Not finished, but I've got another week, right?'

'Not if you want a leaflet, or a price list; not if you actually want to sell your work.' The words hissed from between Marta's teeth.

'I'll finish in plenty of time before the opening. I just haven't found the *one* yet. I've been taking pictures of the log and I've got some good shots, but nothing's right.' Josh looked unconcerned. 'It'll come, always does.'

Marta grunted, sipping her wine. 'So long as it arrives before the twentieth.'

'How are the wedding plans progressing?' Lily's dad changed the subject.

'Almost there,' Lily replied. 'We have to choose the car – we've got an appointment with Rita in three days. After that we just need the bride and groom and they're supposed to get here on the nineteenth.'

'In time for your show?' Marta asked Josh.

'At least we know two people will turn up.'

'I'll be there,' Lily promised. 'I'd like to see what you've been photographing in Castle Cove.'

'Logs apparently,' Marta said.

'Don't forget the rust,' Josh added. 'Everything's going to be fine.'

☆

'I want to help,' Cath said, bustling around the kitchen as Lily filled the sink with hot water and added a squirt of washing-up liquid.

'And I appreciate it, but I'm honestly fine. You spent all afternoon in between serving in the teashop to help with the cooking. You and Alice mainly served and cleared up – let me finish off,' Lily pleaded.

Cath began to protest.

'Honestly, I need some time alone – tonight was good, but it didn't wow and I need to figure out why.'

Before Cath could respond, Alice burst into the kitchen with more glasses.

'You need to leave too,' Lily grumbled. 'I know Shaun and Jay are waiting for you both in the teashop and I'd honestly like to be by myself.'

'How will you get home? We're not going to leave you here alone and Jay will refuse – you know what he's like.' Alice's expression turned dopey.

'The Beast is parked at the station so I don't have to walk,' Lily said, already knowing they wouldn't leave her.

Cath looked concerned. 'It's late and dark and there are tons of glasses to wash up.'

'I'll help.' Josh's voice came from the doorway of the kitchen. Lily turned – her hands were dunked inside the sink of bubbly water and she felt her heart leap into her throat.

'You left?' she murmured, feeling stupid.

'I took Marta home, walked Chester and saw the lights were still on so I dropped him off and came back.' He glanced at the washing-up bowl.

'It's great you're here, Josh,' Cath said with a sly smile. Grabbing Alice's bag from the floor, she tipped her head towards the teashop. 'We were just leaving. You'll make sure Lily gets home, won't you?' She didn't wait for an answer; instead she pushed Alice through the doorway. Lily heard giggles and chairs being moved, then the sound of the bell above the door at the front before the room fell silent.

'You didn't need to come back, I'm fine on my own.' Lily picked up a wine glass and washed it, placing it on the draining board.

'Maybe I like washing up.' Josh grabbed a tea towel and dried the glass.

Lily snorted. 'Rebels don't wash up. Rebels leave their plates and cups for someone else to sort out, or they smash them into fireplaces.'

Josh laughed. 'Not if they have a mother like mine.' He dried another glass and put it on the table in the centre of the kitchen. 'Although if I'm busy, I have been known to resort to paper cups and plates to save time.'

'Figures.' Lily giggled, imagining that. The room fell silent as she continued to wash up and she could feel Josh watching her. She didn't look up; instead she tried to fight the sensations inching up her body, the tingles spreading across her skin. It felt like she was being touched, slowly and gently being brought to life. She fought the feelings, fought the desire to act on them. Instead she picked up a pan and began to scrub.

'I think it's clean – unless you're planning etching your name in it,' Josh observed. His eyes darkened as he watched her, making Lily's heart thump. This wouldn't do. She wasn't going to let herself fall for this man. He was the opposite of what she needed.

'So what's going on with Marta and Simon?' Lily asked, working hard to clear the chemistry building between them. Josh nodded, perhaps acknowledging what she was doing.

'That's anybody's guess. They like each other but Simon seems reluctant to make the first move and I know Marta won't – she's a little relationship shy. If Simon wants her, he'll have to fight for her and I'm not sure he's got it in him.'

'I don't know.' Lily put the pan on the draining board. 'Some things take time to build up to.' She swallowed, wondering why she'd just said that. Her cheeks heated as she stared into the bowl of bubbly water.

'What things?' Josh said, gently moving closer. He smelled of the outdoors, like he'd brought in a blast of fresh air from his walk.

'Gosh, I don't know.' Lily's washed up another glass. 'Not everyone's like you. We can't all throw caution to the wind and do whatever we want, be with whoever we want.' The words rushed out. She wasn't even sure where they came from or why she'd said them; surely this was the conversational equivalent of poking a bear? One she'd been determined to leave alone.

'Why not?' Josh asked, moving closer still. Lily felt his presence across her shoulders, like a pleasant breath of warmth. She knew she was in danger of giving into her feelings – her need to turn around – but fought it. Josh, with all his rebel ways, wasn't the man for her.

'Because not everything we want is good for us,' she said sharply. 'Some things aren't meant to be.'

'How do you know?' Josh asked softly. 'Who told you what's okay to have and what you need to avoid?"

'No one,' she answered, feeling cross. 'Me. I know what's good for me. I know what I need.'

'Is that the same you who won't let herself go in the kitchen? The same you telling herself she's not good enough?'

Lily washed up the last glass, keeping her hands in the water, unsure of what to do with them. If she turned, she knew she wouldn't be able to stop herself from falling into Josh's arms, into that seductive voice with all those promises wrapped inside it. 'I don't know,' she admitted, eventually feeling her shoulders go limp, tired suddenly of fighting her feelings.

The admission had Josh taking a step backwards and inexplicably Lily felt the loss of his warmth and the closeness of his body. He reached for the last glass she'd washed up and dried it, putting it on the centre table with the others.

'You must be tired,' he murmured.

Lily turned to face him but didn't find the disappointment or irritation she'd been expecting. Instead she found understanding, mixed with an unexpected dose of affection, maybe even a hint of restrained lust.

'Shall I walk you home?' Josh asked, bumping the kitchen door open.

'You don't have to…' Lily trailed off. She was doing it again – not asking for what she wanted. 'I'd like to walk. I drove here but the Beast will be fine in the car park.'

Josh waited for Lily to dry her hands and pick up her handbag and walk through the kitchen door before switching off the lights. She stood while he locked up the teashop and checked it was secure. The moon was out and the street looked quiet. Even the castle only had a few lights on upstairs. Simon was most probably sitting in his office calculating something. Even the restaurant would be closed by now. Lily pulled her jacket tight, feeling a chill in the air and wishing she'd brought her big coat. Josh pulled off his own jacket and wrapped it around her shoulders.

'That's very gentlemanly of you,' she teased, keen to erase the tension between them.

'You're right,' he said, reaching for the jacket again. 'I really ought to take it back before you get the wrong idea – a man is nothing without his reputation.'

Lily laughed, batting his hand away, and pulled the coat on as they walked down the promenade towards the high street. The moon was high and light sparkled on the sea. The effect was romantic and she walked a little faster, ignoring the hammering in her chest, and the stirring on her skin.

They walked a few streets more with very little conversation and a whole heap of chemistry and then they were standing outside the door to Lily's flat and she was handing Josh his jacket, ignoring the instant hit of cold and overwhelming desire to ask him inside.

She dug in her bag and pulled out her keys, and he took them from her so he could unlock and open the door. Before she headed through it he tipped her chin and looked into her eyes. Lily thought Josh was going to kiss her, felt the tingles on her lips and moistened them ready for it. She didn't move a muscle, afraid that once she started, she wouldn't be able to stop.

But instead of kissing her, Josh stepped back. 'Sleep well.' He looked thoughtful. 'And think about what you need, Lily, not about what everyone else thinks. You know where I am when you're ready to embrace who you are – or if you need a friend, I'll still be there even if you're not.'

With that he turned and walked into the darkness, leaving Lily staring after him, wondering once again what it was she wanted and needed and if she'd ever truly find out.

Chapter Twenty-Four

Lily carefully eased herself out of the Beast and pulled the skirt of her red ball-gown up to her knees so the expensive silk didn't scrape on the gravel. She'd parked in the car park across from Cove Castle so she wouldn't have to walk too far in the mile-high shoes her mother had sent a few days before – along with the dress and a sparkly ruby handbag.

The outfit was stunning but over the top. Lily hadn't wanted to wear it, especially when she'd noticed that the bodice dipped between her breasts, exposing creamy white skin she usually kept hidden. But she hadn't been able to bring herself to refuse it, especially when her mother had called to tell her about the designer and how lucky she was to borrow it. Lily shut the Beast and locked it, then pulled a jet-black eye mask from her handbag and put it on. It wasn't like anyone would recognise her if they saw her now, but just the act of hiding her face made her feel more confident.

Cove Castle was lit with red, white and green Christmas lights that ran along the sweeping staircase and up to the front door where a huge glittering lantern lit the way inside. The effect was magical. As Lily slowly approached and headed up the staircase she took a moment to appreciate the view. She'd lived in Castle Cove her whole life but had never been invited to a private party or been given the chance to work at one so had no idea what to expect.

When she arrived at the grand entrance, a man she didn't recognise took her coat. Lily knew Aubrey's friend had hired private caterers to provide the food and serve at the party which meant hopefully she was unlikely to bump into anyone she knew, but her blood still pumped unnecessarily fast, making her a little dizzy. Even Suze had been given the night off and the main restaurant had been closed, although the kitchens were being used by the caterers who'd be serving canapes and champagne all night.

The hallway of Cove Castle always gave Lily's heart a jolt and today was no exception. The vaulted ceilings had been decorated with lights and foliage and the huge marble fireplace facing the main door had a large fire roaring inside it. Above it, on the mantelpiece, candles burned amid sprigs of winter holly. To the right Lily could hear laughter and music coming from the library. The servant who'd taken her coat directed her towards the noise just as a waiter appeared with a tray filled with glasses of champagne, water and real ale. She swiped a glass of King Newt as Aubrey appeared.

Her mother was in a sweeping black dress that tucked in at the waist and then puffed out in an arch of material which glided downwards and across the floor. The bodice was slim and low cut, exposing smooth creamy skin that could have belonged to a twenty-year-old. Aubrey had obviously spent hours getting ready. Her make-up looked perfect and her hair had been woven with sparkles and piled high on her head. Long earrings sporting about a million diamonds dripped from her ears and she wore a jewelled face mask that covered her eyes but left her sharp cheekbones bare.

Aubrey gave Lily a quick air kiss and swiped the glass of ale from her hand, quickly replacing it with champagne. 'Sparkling wine is more feminine, darling. Come on.' Aubrey pointed her own glass towards the library. 'I'd like you to meet some of my friends.' As they walked Aubrey filled Lily in.

'Madeline Jones is holding this party for her daughter Eve. Eve turned eighteen a couple of weeks ago. I guess you could call this her coming out party.' She snorted. 'She's young and pretty, but not a patch on you so don't worry about that.'

'Okay.' Lily stopped to admire the red lights around the library doorway. As they entered the large room she took in a sharp breath. All the usual furniture – including chairs, a sofa and long desk – had been removed and a small orchestra played in front of the large window to the left.

Lily loved the library. Two walls were filled with bookcases that started on the ground and travelled upwards, covering every inch of the wall surface, stopping only as they hit the high vaulted ceiling. Simon's grandfather had collected books his whole life. There were sections dedicated to non-fiction, leather-bound classics, newer contemporary works, as well as six shelves packed with romance – a nod, apparently, to Simon's grandmother who'd been a voracious reader. Simon hadn't spent much time in the library but he had brought a few guidebooks from Australia. Those languished in the corner along with a collection of *Lonely Planets* and *Rough Guides*. All the staff at Cove Castle were allowed to borrow up to three books at a time if they wanted to and Rita was responsible for signing them in and out.

Someone had hung tiny white fairy lights from the ceiling and they followed the path of the bookshelves. It must have taken hours to set up, but the effect was worth it because every shelf shone, lighting up colourful book spines and making the room look magical.

Throughout the room huge balloons with 'Happy Birthday' and '18 today' emblazoned across them floated in the air. Lily could see a young woman, dressed in a glittery white ball-gown with a matching mask, standing next to the orchestra shaking hands with a never-ending queue of guests. Aubrey tugged Lily through the crowd, stopping every now and again to introduce her to another masked person who looked at her blankly. Finally, they joined the queue of people and waited until they got to shake hands with the birthday girl.

'Eve, this is my daughter.'

Eve barely acknowledged them as she moved on to the next guest. Aubrey nudged Lily along the line to an older woman with shiny black hair who was obviously Eve's mother.

'Madeline.' Aubrey pushed Lily forwards. 'I want you to meet *my* daughter.'

Madeline gave Lily a perfunctory once-over before nodding at Aubrey. 'I understand you've only just found each other?'

Madeline took Lily's hand and squeezed it before dropping it again. 'What do you do?' Madeline scanned the room, checking on the other guests.

'I work here—' Lily began, but Aubrey interrupted.

'Lily's going to be a model. I've set up a shoot, she's going to be huge; my agent has agreed to take her on.' Her mother spoke quickly, her eyes shining with excitement.

'Oh really?' Madeline's red lips thinned as she took a proper look at Lily. 'Have you done any modelling?'

'No,' she admitted. 'I've been working as—'

'Lily's very excited about getting into the business.'

'That will be nice for you, Aubrey, finally having someone to follow in your footsteps.'

'Madeline worked all over the world – we often worked together,' Aubrey explained. 'Her daughter is a model.'

Madeline's eyes flicked briefly to the young girl still greeting guests.

'Eve is very successful. We're flying to Paris tomorrow for a shoot,' Madeline explained as a passing waiter offered Eve a glass of champagne. 'No.' She waved him away before sipping from her own glass of water. 'How did you find each other? It must be odd for you Lily, finally seeing your mother again after all these years – how long has it been?'

Aubrey looked like she wanted to interrupt.

'I'm not sure,' Lily lied, unwilling to embarrass her mother. 'It's a dream come true though.' She sipped her drink. The champagne tasted expensive and the bubbles danced on her tongue. She hadn't eaten much today and could already feel the alcohol going to her head. 'Aubrey wrote to me a few weeks ago. It was a lovely surprise.'

'Lucky timing,' Madeline murmured.

'I'd been meaning to get in touch for years,' Aubrey said. 'But you know how hard it is to find the time to do anything these days. My career takes up so much of mine and young children can be demanding. I didn't want to get in touch until I knew I could be a proper mother.' Aubrey smiled indulgently. 'And now we've found each other and we're catching up. Once Lily starts modelling she'll move to London and we'll be able to spend even more time getting to know each other.'

Lily nibbled her lip.

'You're moving to London?' Madeline looked surprised.

'Ah, I'm not certain,' Lily stammered.

'We haven't worked all the details out yet,' Aubrey interrupted. 'It'll be difficult living all the way down here once the work starts pouring in, but we don't need to think about that quite yet.' She laughed, tossing her hair, looking every bit in her element. Another woman approached and Aubrey introduced them without giving Lily an opportunity to respond.

Lily sipped her champagne while the women chatted and looked around the room at the couples catching up. Few seemed to be eating, which was a shame because the food looked good. Even fewer people were smiling which was strange considering this was a birthday party. Even Eve looked bored, but at least the constant queue of people waiting to shake her hand had tailed off. A photographer stopped to take a picture of Eve and Lily shrank into the corner. She didn't want to appear on the front of *The Castle Cove Gazette* next week; it would be difficult explaining that to her dad and brothers.

Finishing her glass, Lily grabbed another from a passing waiter. One more drink wouldn't do any harm and she'd planned on walking home or getting a cab anyway. Unlike the night when Josh had rescued her, she had a spare pair of flat shoes ready in her handbag.

A waiter came to offer Lily a canape but as she went to take it she noticed the frown on Aubrey's face and snatched her hand back.

'I'm not hungry.' She ignored the grumble in her stomach as she watched the waiter disappear with the full tray.

Aubrey leaned across to whisper in her ear. 'Someone over there is eyeing us up.'

Lily's eyes slid to a man dressed in a sharp suit with almost-black hair and an angular jaw. 'He's a trader in the city apparently, I'll introduce you.'

'Don't worry, I'm here to catch up with you.' Lily drank more champagne and swayed on her heels, wishing she could eat something.

Aubrey made an irritated sound. 'Your admirer's been cornered by someone, we'll try to catch him later. I hear he's got a very good job.'

But was he nice? Lily wondered. Would he help her wash up, walk her home or give her his coat like Josh?

'You did a good job on your eyes.' Aubrey studied Lily, pulling the mask away so she could take a better look. 'Darker definitely suits you and you've done well making your lips look plumper, that can be difficult. When we do the photos for the portfolio I'll hire someone to do make-up and they can give you some tips.'

'I'm not much of a make-up girl,' Lily admitted.

'We'll soon change that.'

She had to come clean. 'Aubrey… Mum—' Lily began as the orchestra began to play 'Happy Birthday' and a huge cake was brought out for Eve. The girl didn't even smile as the staff serving canapes surrounded her and broke into song.

'Eve's a funny thing,' Aubrey observed as the singing died down and the guests went back to their conversations. 'Madeline's had such a hard time with her. She didn't want to be a model – can you believe it?'

Lily nibbled her lip.

'Madeline soon wore her down though and it sounds like she's doing well,' Aubrey confided. 'I think you'll do better, even if you are older – you're taller and you have my bone structure.'

Lily watched Eve for a few moments. The girl didn't look happy. In fact considering this was her party she looked downright miserable.

The orchestra started playing again and the man Aubrey had pointed out earlier came to join them.

'I saw you across the room. My name is Hugh Walker,' he murmured. He was handsome, probably in his forties; you could see flecks of grey in his hair which had been slicked back. Aubrey giggled as he took her hand and then leaned in to give Lily a kiss on her cheek. 'I don't think I've seen either of you at one of Madeline's parties and I'm used to knowing everyone,' he said.

'I've missed the last couple and my daughter Lily has only come into my life again recently,' Aubrey purred.

'Goodness, you don't look old enough to be a mother,' Hugh gasped.

'It's nice to meet you.' Lily smiled, even though her face ached and her feet hurt. She glanced around the room. It would probably be hours before she could leave. She couldn't go early or she might upset Aubrey.

Hugh picked up a couple of glasses of champagne from a waiter and passed one to them both. Lily had a small sip – the bubbles were refreshing so she drank more, quickly finishing the glass. Her mother continued to chat with Hugh, breaking into laughter every few minutes.

Feeling like a gooseberry, Lily let her eyes glide around the room, checking out the other guests. Everyone was beautiful and there were some incredible clothes. Her eyes drifted across the walls, to a photograph next to one of the bookshelves. It was one of the castle and Lily already knew it had been taken by Josh. Just having his picture here made her feel inexplicably better and she let her mind drift to the man who kept confusing her.

What would Josh be doing if he were here now? He definitely wouldn't be standing alone, drinking champagne. He'd probably be photographing the bookshelves or irritating the guests by speaking his mind.

A few weeks ago, Lily would have found the idea of Josh annoying – he was so at odds with the way she lived her life – but now she wasn't sure if she just plain admired him.

A waiter walked past with a tray of canapes and for a moment Lily thought about taking one. Instead, she let him walk away. Josh would have eaten his fill by now. He'd be drinking ale too, if he hadn't got bored already and left. Feeling irritated with herself, Lily grabbed another glass of champagne from a passing waiter and gulped it down before excusing herself. She didn't have to ask the way – she already knew where the bathroom was.

She locked herself inside one of the toilet cubicles and leaned her head against the doorway, realising too late she felt dizzy. She should have stuck with the ale, it never went to her head. She checked her watch – how long would it be until she could leave? Maybe she could pretend she had a headache? But what if Aubrey didn't believe her?

Lily stood, straightening the top of her dress. She was about to step outside the cubicle when she heard the door to the bathroom open and close.

'I can't believe she'd go to the lengths of digging out a daughter just to outdo me,' a familiar voice complained as Lily heard handbags opening and a tap running.

'Madeline, you know what Aubrey's like, she always has to be top dog. Do you remember when she eloped with her second husband on the same weekend you announced your engagement?'

'She ruined my party,' Madeline complained.

'And look how long that marriage lasted,' another woman added.

Madeline huffed. 'Bringing some random stranger to my daughter's birthday party so she could show off is out of order.'

As their words sunk in, Lily stilled.

'The girl is pretty.' The woman paused. 'Do you think Aubrey hired her?'

Madeline laughed. 'Where from, Daughters Are Us? I've no idea. Perhaps she is Aubrey's daughter – the point is, why haven't we heard about her? I worked with the woman for over fifteen years and this is the first time she's mentioned having a child.'

'It is funny timing – the first I heard about the daughter was six weeks ago, around the time Eve's party invitations went out.'

'Aubrey said the girl's father wouldn't let them have a relationship but I'm not sure if that's true.'

Lily nibbled her fingernail. Would her dad have done that? Lied, kept her from her mother for all those years? Were her brothers in on it too? She felt sick.

'If I know Aubrey, having a child in her life wouldn't have been convenient. To be honest, I think the only reason she's materialised the girl now is so she can boast about her. Give it six months – especially if the modelling career doesn't take off – and this mystery daughter will disappear again, I guarantee it. Probably Aubrey will have lost interest. Did you see her poring over Hugh? Think she's lining her next husband up?'

'Wouldn't put it past her.' Someone else joined in, her tone bitchy. 'Do you think she's paying her agent to take the daughter on?'

'Probably, but the girl would have to show real promise, like Eve, to make any money at it.'

'The girl's pretty but she's quiet,' someone observed.

'She probably does exactly as she's told, which is just the way Aubrey likes it,' Madeline said nastily as Lily heard a handbag snapping shut. She waited as heels tapped and a door closed, leaving the bathroom empty.

Tears pricked Lily's eyes. Why had Aubrey got in touch? Was it really just so she had someone to show off? She sat on the toilet seat, ignoring the way her head spun and her stomach churned. It was hard to think when her head was filled with champagne. She opened her handbag and pulled out a handkerchief and dabbed her eyes, then picked out her mobile which she'd switched off earlier and fiddled with the switch.

She put it away again. There was no one to call – no one knew about tonight except for Josh and she couldn't go and see him. Turning up on his doorstep at this time of night, in a dress that left so little to the imagination, was tantamount to saying she wanted to sleep with him – and she wasn't the type of girl who did things like that. Was she?

Chapter Twenty-Five

Josh fussed with the photograph on his laptop as he took another sip of whisky. The close-up of the wood looked good. You could almost feel the texture and colours, to the point that even *he* felt tempted to reach out and run a finger across it.

But it still wasn't the *one*.

Frustrated, Josh stood and walked out of his office, into the sitting room where he could see out of the floor-to-ceiling windows. It was bitter outside and the wind blew, stirring up the sea so waves battered the beach, throwing buckets of rain along with it – he knew it first hand, he'd been out an hour before, stomping across the sand walking Chester. The dog groaned in his sleep and stretched, making the most of the roaring fire Josh had recently lit. Josh already knew if he left the room, the Labrador would hop up from the rug he was currently on and lay claim to the sofa.

'I'm watching you, dog,' Josh murmured, a smile tipping his lips as he took another swig of whisky.

Chester might have heard because his ears pricked suddenly and he shot up, heading for the front door, inexplicably barking as his tail wagged.

'What?' Josh asked, walking past him. He could see a silhouette through the glass and took a deep breath, praying it wasn't his mother on another ill-conceived mission of persuasion – he truly didn't have the patience.

He wasn't expecting to find a windblown and miserable Lily King – wearing a silky red dress that exposed a whole host of cleavage – shivering on his doorstep. 'You lost?' he asked, standing out of the way so she could walk inside. He closed the door, intrigued, as Lily bent to pat Chester and kicked off her shoes in the hallway, before walking unsteadily towards the sitting room.

'Perhaps,' Lily murmured, slumping in front of the fire and pulling her knees to her chest. 'Do you have wine?'

Josh studied her before answering – she didn't look right, not like Lily at all. 'No. I have whisky and Castling.'

Lily sighed. 'Whisky please. Make it a large.'

Lily lay back on the rug, stretching out where Chester had been only moments before. Her wet hair and smudged make-up did little to erase the hint of wanton sexiness from the pose and Josh took a step back, shocked by his reaction, which hovered somewhere between protective and all-out lust. Even from here, Josh could tell Lily had been drinking, which made acting on those feelings a no-no.

'Rough night?' Josh walked into the kitchen where he picked up a towel and filled a large glass with ice and water before adding a not-too-generous dose of his favourite single malt. 'Want to talk about it?' He shook his head at his own words – why did he keep encouraging Lily to open up? He handed Lily the towel so she could dry her hair and took a seat in the black leather chair to the left of the fire. Here he could see Lily and talk, but she was far enough away to keep some distance between them.

Lily grabbed the drink from his hand and swallowed the whisky down in one. 'More,' she asked, holding out the glass, ignoring the towel.

Josh made her another one, adding more water this time, and Lily gulped it down again. This time when she held out the empty glass Josh placed it on the coffee table.

Lily glared at it. 'You said you thought I was wild, Josh. Well here's my wild side. Or don't you like me like this?'

'I like you just fine, Lily,' Josh said gently. 'But wild and drunk are very different things.'

'Nonsense,' Lily slurred, standing on wobbly legs. 'Do you have any music? I want to dance.'

'No,' Josh said, trying to pull his eyes away from her.

'There was music tonight and no one danced,' Lily said, looking into the fire. 'Perhaps if we had, things would have turned out differently.'

'Why?' Josh asked, feeling confused and a little conflicted as Lily ignored the question and reached a hand to the top of her zip.

'I'm soaking wet and I'd really like to take off this dress,' she said huskily, pulling the top of her zip undone and wriggling her bottom suggestively. 'It's very uncomfortable.'

Was the sexy striptease an act of deliberate seduction or did she really not appreciate the power of her words, Josh wondered. He wasn't going to wait to find out – he didn't have *that* much willpower. 'I'll get you my dressing gown.' Josh averted his eyes and headed up the stairs to find the unworn dressing gown that his mother had bought him one Christmas buried in the back of his wardrobe. As he grabbed it, Josh tried not to think about Lily undressing in his living room.

When he returned, Lily's zip was half undone and she'd turned on some music and was swaying to it in front of the fire. Lily looked like a magical nymph and Josh fought the urge to pick up his camera. He handed her the dressing gown and looked away as she undid the zip on her dress and it dropped to the floor.

'Want to tell me what happened?' Josh asked, once Lily had wrapped the warm dressing gown around her. He searched the room for his glass, wondering if he could get away with drinking another shot, without Lily noticing, to erase the tension in his shoulders. 'Tonight was the party, right?' He knew it was. He'd been thinking about Lily earlier when he'd been walking on the beach, wondering if Aubrey was behaving or trying to manipulate Lily into doing something else she didn't want to.

'Tonight was super,' Lily murmured, lying on the sofa and putting her forearm over her eyes. The movement made the dressing gown shift, exposing that creamy white skin Josh shouldn't be looking at. He gazed into the fire instead. 'My mother introduced me to lots of her friends, only it turns out none of them knew I existed a month ago,' she admitted.

'Ah.' Damn, where was his whisky? 'Perhaps she wasn't ready to share you? Maybe she was worried about what your father would think?' He tried to think of another excuse but couldn't.

Lily snorted. 'Or maybe the reason she didn't get in touch was because of my dad – someone mentioned that too. Right after they said they thought I'd been hired for the night, that I probably wasn't even Aubrey's daughter.' Her voice broke. 'She wants me to be a model, just like her friend's daughter. I figured it out on the walk here. It's never been about me, I've never been good enough. I can't believe I ever thought I was…'

'It's not you who isn't good enough,' Josh said, fighting the emotion building inside him. He could see the hurt and disappointment crawling across Lily's face, sinking into her skin and soul, and he wanted so badly to erase it. But he didn't know how.

'I could really do with another drink,' Lily whispered, moving her arm away from her face.

Josh watched a tear slide down her cheek. Dammit. Angry on her behalf now, he picked up her glass and went into the kitchen to pour a small glass of whisky for Lily and a larger one for himself. Then he headed back into the sitting room.

Lily was sitting now and she'd adjusted the dressing gown so it covered her properly. The towel sat around her shoulders like a shawl and she stroked Chester, murmuring into his ear.

Josh handed her the glass. This time she took a small sip and put it down.

'I'm sorry. I'd planned on coming here and seducing you, to show us both I could be wild – but I've messed it up.'

Lily looked so sad and lost that Josh had to fight the overpowering urge to tug her to him – the only thing that stopped him was knowing where that would lead. 'Wild, not wild – you need to be yourself, Lily. You need to find out who you are,' he said instead.

'What if I don't know?' she asked, her voice small.

Josh cleared his throat. 'Do what you want, what makes you happy. That's the only place to start.'

'Is that what you do?'

Josh laughed, swiping a hand through his hair, feeling off-balance. 'Not always. If I always did what I wanted we'd both be naked on that rug right now, probably giving Chester an X-rated show.'

Lily squinted at him, but Josh could see the flush climb her cheeks as she caught the meaning in his words, could see the smile lifting her cheeks. 'You want to do that?'

'Since the day we met, wild Lily.'

'And you really think I'm wild?'

He laughed. 'To your very core. You just need to find the real Lily and let her out. Stop trying to be who you think everyone else wants you to be.'

She tucked a wayward strand of hair behind her ear, frowning. 'I left the party tonight. I didn't even tell Aubrey where I was going. I left my phone switched off and the only place I wanted to be was here. I've been avoiding you, not doing what I know we both wanted, and now I'm not sure why.'

Josh sighed long and deep, wanting to kick himself. He might be a rebel at heart, but he wasn't going to take advantage. 'Tell me the same in the morning and we'll have a whole different conversation. Right now, you need to go to bed.'

Lily grinned.

'Alone,' Josh said firmly, wanting to kick himself all over again. 'There's a spare room. No one's ever slept in it but I'm guessing it's comfortable and it's made up. I'll get you some headache pills and a glass of water. Sleep this off and we'll talk in the morning.'

Lily looked dejected. 'This isn't how I thought tonight would go.'

Josh laughed. 'Believe me, I'm on the same page, but whatever happens, whatever you decide, you need to do it sober.'

'Nonsense,' Lily repeated herself from earlier, but this time with a smile. 'I like you Josh Havellin-Scott. You're a better man than you think you are, far better than you make out. Perhaps I wish you weren't – but I'm not going to argue with you.' She winced. 'My head's started to hurt and you might be right, I am a little tired.'

'First door on the right,' Josh said, his jaw tight, wishing she wasn't right because if that were the case Lily wouldn't be heading up his staircase right now, flashing her legs as she walked, and he wouldn't be going to the kitchen to fill up a glass and fish out the packet of paracetamol she'd no doubt need.

But in the morning, if Lily still wanted him when she was sober, he wasn't going to say no again.

Chapter Twenty-Six

Lily's head had split in two, and a marching band was giving a free concert in what was left of her brain. That was her first thought on waking – her second was *where the hell am I?* The room wasn't familiar. Neither was the dark blue duvet cover on the bed. She eased herself into a sitting position, wincing at her dry mouth, and spotted the glass of water and paracetamol on the bedside cabinet.

Knocking back both, Lily pulled the duvet up to her chest, noticing for the first time that she was wearing a soft green dressing gown.

Josh's.

She remembered now: the party the night before, stumbling from the castle along the promenade to Josh's house on the beach. She'd wanted to seduce him, to let herself go and she'd tried. Lily winced. Had she actually started to undress in front of him – had she danced?

'*Nooooo*,' she groaned, picking up a blue cushion from the bed and pushing her face into it, feeling the burn climb up her cheeks. She should leave. Looking up, Lily saw the red dress she'd worn the night before slumped across a straight-backed chair in the corner. Would she have to do the walk of shame this morning, made even more shameful by Josh's refusal to take her to bed? Had she read everything wrong and did he really not fancy her?

Lily slid out of bed and made use of the en-suite bathroom and the shower and hair products inside. Ten minutes later she dried off and checked the small wardrobe in the bedroom and slipped on a long shirt, which must have been one of Josh's. Maybe he'd have some trousers she could borrow too? If she used a safety pin and rolled them up she'd probably be able to make it back to her house without embarrassing herself. But she'd need to find Josh first.

Lily crept downstairs into the living room, taking care not to make any noise.

'Good morning,' Josh murmured, making her jump. He was sitting in the black chair by the fire she remembered from last night, with Chester curled at his feet. 'How's the head?'

'Um, okay,' Lily answered, rubbing her hands across her forehead. 'I'm so sorry about last night.'

'Which bit?' Josh's lips curled. 'For drinking all my single malt, dancing or for the almost striptease?'

'Oh gosh,' Lily groaned. 'I'm so sorry.' She tiptoed further into the living room, aware now that her legs were exposed and Josh was sitting in a pair of sweatpants and a long-sleeved t-shirt that had seen better days. He had a five o'clock shadow again and he looked sexy and amused and her stomach tumbled.

'You don't need to apologise,' Josh said gently. 'In all honesty, I enjoyed your company, watching you let out your wild side.'

'You didn't enjoy it that much. You made me go to bed. Alone.' Lily knew she sounded annoyed but couldn't stop the sudden hot wave of temper or need to blurt her feelings out.

Josh studied her. 'What kind of man would I be if I'd taken you to bed when I knew you'd been drinking so much?'

'I don't know,' Lily admitted, feeling tired and disappointed that he hadn't leapt up as soon as she'd come downstairs to finish what she'd started last night. 'Do you have any tea?'

If Josh was surprised by the change in subject he didn't show it. 'There's coffee.'

Lily's stomach grumbled and she remembered she hadn't eaten the night before. 'Yes please.' Her stomach complained again, this time louder.

'Sounds like you're hungry – there's probably something fit for human consumption in the kitchen, unless you want dog food? Chester has plenty.'

'I'll stick with human – I can make us something?'

Josh waved a hand in the direction of the kitchen before heading for it. He poured her coffee and pointed to the fridge. 'If you can make something interesting with what I've got in there you're a better cook than me.'

'Mmmm.' Lily opened the door and surveyed the offerings before searching through a couple of cupboards. 'You seem to be missing some of the basic food groups, but I can do us an omelette. I used to make them for my dad and brothers sometimes when I was younger. We called them Lily's surprise.' She smiled – she'd forgotten. 'Once I made one and added chocolate.' She shuddered. 'It was horrible but everyone ate it and I think they even thanked me too.'

'It's a little early for chocolate but other than that, I'm easy.' Josh took a seat on one of the metal barstools next to the long oak counter in the centre of his kitchen. It was a nice room, probably caught the light on summer mornings. The view outside the window was less interesting than at the back, but Lily could see Josh's Porsche parked in the gravel driveway and beyond that the quiet street outside where snow had begun to fall. She opened one of the glossy white cabinets, searching for pans. In the third she found what she was looking for and pulled out a large frying pan and glass bowl.

'You want any help?' Josh asked lazily, gulping more coffee before getting up to fill his mug again. 'I don't really mean that by the way – I'm just being polite.'

Lily snorted, relaxing, and Josh took a seat again, watching her with an odd expression on his face. 'Do you mind if I take photos?'

'Of me?' Lily squeaked as she placed eggs, tortilla chips, cheese, beans, tomatoes, chillies and a half-empty bottle of lime juice on the counter. 'I thought you didn't take pictures of people?'

'I didn't do dogs a couple of weeks ago. There's an expression you get on your face when you're looking at food – I'm wondering if I can capture it.' When Lily looked startled Josh added, 'All in the name of research. You look good in my shirt, by the way, I almost prefer it to the red dress.'

Lily put a hand to her neck as he hopped up and disappeared before returning with his camera. 'I didn't say yes,' she said, shaking off her embarrassment and cracking eggs into the bowl.

'You didn't say no either. Think of it as helping me with my professional growth. I really don't do people.' Josh held the camera up to his face and took a couple of shots. Lily tried to ignore the ball of tension building in her chest. It wasn't uncomfortable, more confusing.

'As long as what happens in the kitchen stays in the kitchen,' she countered, finding a knife and chopping board and arranging the ingredients into a row. She studied them, feeling a wave of excitement.

Josh didn't respond, but he continued to take photos as she got started, crushing tortilla chips and chopping whatever vegetables she could find in the fridge. She took a swig of coffee, finishing it, and held out her mug. 'Please?' Lily grinned as Josh scowled.

'I said wild Lily, not demanding,' he grumbled, putting his camera on the counter before filling the mug and refilling the coffee machine. 'I'm not used to sharing my coffee or whisky.'

'And I'm not used to cooking in a man's kitchen or modelling for photographs – so I guess we're both trying something new.' Lily fired up the hob. It looked clean, which inexplicably made Lily like Josh even more – he might be a rebel in many ways, but the man was no slob.

Lily added the vegetable selection into the pan, enjoying the hiss as it began to cook. A salt and pepper grinder sat to the right of the cooker and she quickly seasoned the eggs and added them too.

'You look relaxed,' Josh observed, taking another quick shot.

'Making an omelette isn't rocket science.' Lily pulled out some plates and placed a couple of cut tomatoes and crushed tortilla chips onto them. 'Herbs would be good if you have some?'

'I've got pictures of a basil plant somewhere. Look.' Josh brought the camera over to show her a couple of the photos he'd just taken. Her damp hair tumbled around her shoulders in wild waves, her cheeks were pink and Josh's shirt was half undone, exposing the top curve of her breast. She held a spatula in one hand and looked flushed and excited, perhaps even a little bit wild.

'Wow. I had no idea I could look like that. I could do with some make-up.' Lily studied the picture critically, barely recognising herself.

'You look good.' Josh stared at the camera. 'Better than that log I've been working on.'

'It's a mercy you don't make a living from giving compliments. I'm glad you like it. Maybe you'll use me in your show?' Lily laughed, imagining that. Her half undressed, on show for everyone to see. 'Shame you don't do people,' she laughed.

Josh didn't say anything. He stared at the photo, probably wondering whether he could delete it without upsetting her.

'Can I have a copy?' She'd have to hide it from her dad and brothers and if Aubrey saw it she'd have a coronary – there was no gloss here, no posing or high fashion.

Josh seemed to wake up. He put the camera down and sat at the counter again, studying her. 'Depends on how good breakfast is.'

Lily didn't respond, instead she cut the omelette in half and served it. She searched a couple of drawers before finding cutlery and pushed a plate towards him. For some reason, her heart was in her throat. She wanted him to like what she'd cooked.

Josh picked up a knife and fork and sliced a piece of the omelette, chewing slowly with his eyes closed. 'Perfect,' he concluded. 'Try it.'

Lily ate a little. The tastes blended well – there was the crunch of tortilla chips, the bite of chilli, it worked with the other vegetables and cheese. If she'd had some herbs the combination would have been perfect. 'It's' – she sampled some – 'good. I guess I'll be getting that picture after all.'

'Think Luc would be impressed with an omelette?'

'Maybe.' Lily considered. 'Or perhaps a different variation.'

'Did cooking here feel different?'

'I guess.' Lily thought about it. 'I just threw in what I thought would work. I wasn't thinking about what was right. It wasn't like there were a lot of options, so less to worry about.' Was that the cooking *force* Suze had talked about? Lily took another bite of omelette. 'And I wanted to please you but I knew you'd probably like whatever I cooked, especially when your only other choice was dog food.'

'It's pretty good dog food,' Josh teased. 'But this is better.'

Lily watched him finish eating, watched his long fingers slice his breakfast. He'd put his beloved camera on the counter after taking a couple of shots of her eating. 'Why did you photograph me?' she asked suddenly. 'You don't do people but you've taken pictures of me, why?'

Josh put down his cutlery. 'I like capturing your expressions. Most people aren't as honest in front of the camera.'

'I wasn't trying to be honest,' Lily admitted.

'You're not trying to please me either, you're being yourself.'

Lily frowned.

'What's wrong?' Josh asked.

'I just remembered Aubrey. I left last night without saying goodbye. I probably need to check my phone in case she got worried.'

'Check now. I'll clear up.' Josh cleared their plates before refilling their coffees as Lily found her mobile and switched it on. Instead of the hundred messages she'd been expecting there was one lone text from Aubrey which looked like it had been sent when she'd been in the bathroom at the castle.

Lily, sorry to cut and run. Couldn't find you – left with Hugh.
Speak tomorrow x

'Wow.' Lily put her phone in her bag as her heart dropped to her feet.

'Everything okay?'

She nodded mechanically. 'Aubrey had already left. I didn't need to worry about her looking for me. I guess I was right, I really was there so she could show me off. After that I was redundant – she doesn't care about me.' She tried to fight the wave of disappointment. 'All those years of thinking about her, of wishing she'd get in touch so we could have a relationship, I never even thought about what her motives might be.' She blinked away tears.

'People are intrinsically selfish,' Josh said gently. 'They want people to be what they need them to be.'

'You're not. You keep encouraging me to be myself.'

Josh stared at her. 'Doesn't mean I'm not selfish, or that I don't have my own motives for doing that?'

'Why are you selfish?' Lily asked. 'And what motives?'

'Photos are my life. They come before everything – expectations, love, loyalty, friendship. I'd call that selfish,' Josh said. 'And I'm encouraging you to be yourself because I prefer the real Lily King.'

'So do I,' Lily said carefully. 'Although I'm not sure I know exactly who *she* is yet. I like that I can be myself with you. But I've got to ask—' Lily felt her cheeks heat.

'What?'

'If you like me so much why haven't you… I mean, why haven't we… been to bed?' Lily felt her body cringe with embarrassment, but held Josh's eyes, watching them darken as his expression changed from confused to predatory.

'I've been waiting for you to be sure. And sober,' he added with a smile. 'Sober helps.'

Lily held Josh's gaze, feeling the ball of warmth in her chest expand. 'I'm sure and I'm sober.' She squeezed her hands into tight fists, fighting her desire to run. Fighting the coward inside who wanted to pretend they weren't having this conversation, the girl still so afraid she wasn't good enough. Josh got up and walked around the kitchen counter and Lily could feel the warmth move into her stomach, morphing into a wave of hot lust.

Josh stood for a few moments, looking down. He didn't touch her, instead he took his time searching her face, looking into her eyes. But she didn't want to wait so reached her hand up, intending to pull his head down for a kiss.

'No,' Josh said gently, taking Lily's hand. He stepped closer so her chest brushed against him. 'We're going to take this slowly. You need to be sure.'

'I am sure. I was sure last night, and I'm still sure this morning. I don't need time to decide what I want – I'm ready for this, ready for you.'

Josh looked into her eyes again as a smile tugged the corner of his mouth. 'You're brave too, Lily – I saw a hint of that before and now it's clearer. You're nervous?'

'How do you know?' she asked, irritated that she'd shown it.

'Your hand's shaking.' Josh lifted his to the curve of her jaw and leaned down. This time he moved quickly, perhaps as impatient as she was for this to happen – for all the promises that had been growing between them over the last few weeks to finally become real. There was no slow build today, no easing them into the chemistry. Josh must have listened when Lily had said she was sure because his lips met hers all of a sudden and she was pulled into a heat that rocked her right down to her core.

Lily reached her hands up to tug Josh's head down as the kiss deepened. He wrapped his arms around her waist, so their chests touched, then she ran her hands into his hair just as Chester came to nuzzle up against them.

'We've got an audience.' Josh looked down at his dog. 'I'll need to put the TV on so he'll leave us alone.' He took her hand and led her into the sitting room before switching on the TV. They both watched Chester hop up onto the sofa with a groan before lying down. 'I'm not sure he can see it, but he likes the noise,' Josh said as Chester began to snore.

'You're good with him.' Lily smiled. 'My reservations were unjustified.'

Josh guided her towards the stairs. 'The dog's just grown on me, despite his refusal to follow any of my instructions. I guess he reminds me of me. You sure about this?' he asked as they arrived outside of his bedroom.

'Very.' She pushed the door open and yanked him inside.

Josh's room was large but the bed seemed to fill most of it – it was made, which Lily wouldn't have expected, and the sheets and duvet were white. There were no decorative scatter cushions like in the spare room but everything looked clean and fresh. Her eyes were drawn to the walls which were filled with a number of framed photos. She walked closer; there was one of Cove Castle, another of a sunset, and a field with a lone tree. 'They're good,' she said, still holding his hand.

'They're cheaper than wallpaper.' Josh closed the dark blinds at the windows. Without the light from outside, the room dimmed to a romantic glow and Lily felt suddenly shy. Josh guided her back from the window towards the bed and sat, so she stood between his knees, looking down.

'I'll understand if you're not ready for this,' he said, gently searching her eyes.

'I'm fine, I'm just, it's just…' she trailed off.

'You need whisky and music – perhaps your red dress?' Josh guessed, his expression amused as he watched her wrestle with her emotions.

Lily gulped. 'I just want you to know, I'm probably not as experienced as you…'

'Well hell. You might think of me as a rebel but I *am* discerning.' He looked a little put out.

'No, I don't mean that. It's just, I'm not. And I don't always, um…' Lily's cheeks were probably glowing even in this light. 'I don't always, actually, I don't ever… not everyone does.' She grimaced. 'And I really don't mind. For some reason, I just wanted to tell you that up front so you aren't disappointed.'

'I'm not sure I understand.'

'I don't, you know…' Her face flamed. She wasn't going to spell it out.

'Are you saying you don't orgasm?' Josh looked aghast. 'Dammit Lily. Who the hell have you been dating? Actually, don't tell me, I know about the Porsche driver, and I don't particularly want details on any others.' He reached up to the buttons on her shirt, undoing them one by one, muttering something under his breath about hidden wildness and men being selfish in the bedroom.

'Oh, I'm not wearing a bra,' Lily whispered as the top of the shirt fell open making every one of her nerve endings stand to attention.

Josh stood suddenly so he could finish unfastening the buttons. 'You say that like it's a problem.' He eased the cotton from her shoulders and let it drop to the floor until she was left standing in just her white knickers. They weren't particularly sexy, but they were the laciest pair she owned. Josh looked down and shook his head, making Lily suck in a breath because for a moment she thought he didn't approve. 'Too many clothes,' he murmured instead, before dropping to his knees so he could tug the tiny garment off, leaving her naked and a little embarrassed.

'What about you?' Lily asked, regaining her composure as Josh stood again and looked down, making her whole body tingle. 'Or is this a one-woman show?'

'You don't see me complaining.' Josh grinned as he pulled his t-shirt over his head, exposing a tanned chest and muscles Lily had only imagined underneath. She tried to drag her eyes back up to his face instead of down to where the hard ridges of muscle dipped underneath his clothing.

'You work out?' Her voice came out strangled.

'I have been known to lift a camera, and the walking helps.' Josh stepped backwards so he could look at her.

Lily did the same, letting her eyes follow the path of his torso. 'I may not be that experienced but I know the trousers need to go.' She surprised them both by pushing him backwards so he fell onto the bed, then helping him take off his jogging bottoms. When he was naked, she jumped onto the mattress with him, ignoring any embarrassment, ignoring everything but the look on his face.

Lily didn't want to wait for Josh to make the first move. Since she'd been the one holding back, she knew she ought to be the one to go for it, but before she could he reached out and hugged her to him.

Lily had been kissed before, but this was the first time her whole body seemed to melt on contact. Josh guided her gently back onto the bed so he could explore her mouth and all the while his hands trailed across her collarbone and cheeks, setting off a cacophony of shivers.

'Cold?' He pulled back as his eyes dipped downwards.

'It is December.' Lily nibbled her bottom lip.

'Then I'll have to warm you.' Josh lifted the duvet over both of them before disappearing underneath it. Lily's eyes widened as he kissed his way down her cheeks and collarbone, moving lower still until her eyes drooped and closed, giving in to the sensations, blocking everything else out. Josh's lips worked their way to her breasts, stopping for a while as his hands stroked their way across her hips and stomach, dipping lower still. Lily felt herself melt into the bed, felt her body on fire. When Josh moved down further still she almost levitated. 'Woah,' she groaned. 'That's – oh gosh.' Her hands gripped the sheets.

She was climbing, that's all she could think, climbing to the top of something, up and up. 'Oh,' Lily hummed, wanting to stop the feelings building, they were so powerful, almost too much for her to handle. 'You need to stop.' She put her hands in Josh's hair, feeling off-balance.

He eased himself up so he could look at her. 'You scared? Because some would say this is all about you letting go – are you still afraid to do that with me?'

'I don't know,' she whispered. 'I don't want you to stop. It's just, the feelings scared me for a moment. I'm okay now.'

'Good to know.' Josh smiled and gave her a swift kiss before easing his way downwards again.

This time Lily didn't ask Josh to stop, this time she closed her eyes and let herself fall into the sensations, to experience everything without worrying about anything else. Within moments she fell, tipped over the edge, diving headlong into warmth. Her skin felt tingly and sensitive, and she loosened her grip from the sheet as Josh moved back up her body to kiss her again.

'I think that can't just became a can.' He grinned, looking satisfied.

'Ha.' Lily kissed Josh firmly on the lips. 'I'm not sure whether to feel annoyed because I wouldn't let myself go before, or angry because no one's ever tried to make me.'

'I'd go with angry. It's not like you took much persuading.'

Lily laughed as he dropped himself down to the side of her. 'I'd like to say let's do that again but I think I'm being greedy.'

'Oh, we're not finished,' Josh promised, his eyes sparkling. 'If you think that was it wild, Lily King, just wait until I make you scream.' He pulled her closer and leaned in for another hot kiss.

Chapter Twenty-Seven

'I arrived this morning to this.' Marta scowled at the gallery as Josh paced the room. It was early evening and so dark he couldn't see the framed muddy puddle on the wall. He flipped the light switch on and off a couple of times, knowing Marta would have tried that already.

'You've checked the fuse box?' Josh asked, earning himself an eye roll.

'I called an electrician too. He came earlier. He's got no idea what's wrong so he's going to send a specialist engineer, but he told me it could take a while to figure out the problem and he's not even sure when someone will come and look.' Marta stamped her foot. 'Your show opens in five days. I've got used to the fact that you haven't got a centrepiece but I want my customers to be able to see the photos you *have* taken.'

'I've got the centrepiece.' Josh recalled the picture he'd taken of Lily this morning before they'd gone to bed. He hadn't decided he'd use it until that moment – although subconsciously he'd probably known it all along. It worked, unlike the log which had given him a few good pieces but nothing with the emotion he'd been looking for.

More importantly, it was *exactly* what Lily needed to finally accept and declare who she was. He knew she'd be reluctant but once she saw the photo she'd understand.

'I'm not sure if knowing you've finished your show makes me feel better or worse,' Marta admitted. 'If there are no lights no one will see anything. Think I should reschedule?' she asked as Simon walked through the gallery door and stopped dead.

'Reschedule what?' Simon looked around the room. 'Why's it so cold and dark in here?'

'The electricity's completely gone,' Marta grumbled.

'Have you checked the fuse box?' Simon repeated Josh's question from earlier.

'Do you both think I'm completely stupid?' Marta's voice went soprano. She paced the gallery and ran a hand through her hair. 'I've checked the fuses and most of the bulbs – everything's dead. I don't know what to do about the show.' She glared at the light switch as if merely being angry with it would make it work.

'You've got five days. Surely someone will be able to fix it?' Simon said. 'I can take a look again if that would help?'

Marta didn't look at him. 'I think you know my fuse box better than you know me Simon, you've spent so much time with it. And I appreciate you trying, but someone's already checked today and I'm guessing I've got a bigger problem than a dodgy fuse.' She stepped behind her desk and sank into the chair beside it. '*The Castle Cove Gazette* is supposed to be coming. Josh's show was going to be huge. If I cancel they might never come back – or take me seriously.'

'So have it at the castle,' Simon suggested.

'Sorry?'

'The library was cleared out for a party yesterday and we haven't put the furniture back yet – it would be a great venue for an art show.' Simon looked thoughtful. 'I've been thinking of spreading our wings. It would be a place to start. The kitchen could cater, we could set up a bar. I know it's a private event but maybe some of the guests from the restaurant could join you?'

Marta looked annoyed. 'What cut would you expect to take from my sales for saving the day?'

Even in the dim light, Josh saw Simon pale and he stared at Marta for a moment before replying. 'I'm offering to help, not exploit you.'

'And I appreciate it,' she said, her sharp tone suggesting otherwise. 'But I've been doing this on my own for a long time, I'm perfectly capable of sorting out a solution for myself.'

'Then I'll leave you to it.' Simon barely hid the dark flash of temper underneath his smooth smile. He turned on his heels and headed for the door, stopping before he went through it. 'Good luck, Ms West.'

As the door slammed behind him, Josh turned to Marta. 'I'm not known for my charm, but even to me that was harsh. Seems to me the man was only trying to help.'

'I can never tell what's going through his mind. When he came to Castle Cove it was all about money, then I thought he liked me but he's never got further than popping in for a chat. Now he's offering to rescue me?' Marta narrowed her eyes at the door, looking suspicious. 'It doesn't add up.'

'It adds up fine,' Josh said, suddenly feeling sorry for Marta as well as Simon. 'It's just you're adding up wrong. Just because you had one man in your life cheat and another lie, doesn't mean every person you meet will do the same.'

'How do you know?' Marta looked pained.

'I suppose you don't,' Josh said, feeling bad for his friend. 'But pushing people away because we're afraid they might hurt us seems a sad way to live.'

'That's not what I'm doing.'

'Isn't it?' Josh asked, watching Marta process the question. 'You've admitted to me that he confuses you but you like him anyway?'

She looked uncertain but didn't respond.

'Then perhaps your anger has more to do with him not asking you out than your belief that he's trying to take advantage.'

'You think I need to apologise?'

'Depends if you feel bad.' Josh glanced around the dim gallery. 'And whether you're planning on putting on my show.'

'You're right.' Marta dug in her handbag. 'I'll call Simon now.' She pulled her slim mobile out and stared at it. 'And perhaps I won't take anyone to your show after all. Trying to make Simon jealous was beneath me. But I'm still planning on torturing him. There's that dress I told you about… so if he's not interested I can at least show him what he's missing.'

Josh didn't respond. Simon Wolf didn't strike him as the type of man who'd want to be played. The opening of his show was going to be a very interesting night… a very interesting night indeed.

Chapter Twenty-Eight

Josh glanced at the classic black Mercedes again and checked his mobile. Lily should have been here ten minutes ago and it wasn't like her to be late. Had she had a run-in with Aubrey or had one of her brothers heard about their morning in bed yesterday and decided to lock her in the brewery for getting involved with another Porsche driver?

Jeez – exactly when did he become such a worrier?

'I'm sure Lily will be along soon,' Rita soothed, making Josh feel even more ridiculous. She wore another eccentric necklace today filled with what looked like green parrot feathers. Josh had an urge to take a photo until Chester rolled in a muddy puddle on a patch of grass beside them, making him curse under his breath.

'Looks like someone's going to need a bath or your furniture is going to get ruined,' Rita observed, making Josh feel like a useless pet owner as well as an idiot. What was happening to him? He went with the flow, heading in whatever direction the wind blew – he didn't worry about mucky dogs or absent women. A month in Castle Cove and one morning in bed with Lily shouldn't have changed that.

'Sorry I'm late.' Josh heard Lily trot up beside him and stopped himself from looking round even though he wanted to. He caught a waft of something delicious and sugary as Lily leaned in to give him a swift hug and kiss on the cheek. 'Someone dropped a cappuccino all over the floor of the teashop and I helped clean it up. Are those the cars?' Josh turned to face Lily and his heart jolted as her face brightened and her brown eyes shone. Her skin looked clear and fresh, probably from the walk around the castle to meet them, and the sunshine hit the curls at the ends of her hair, making Josh want to reach for his camera again. He swallowed, feeling out of sorts.

'Simon drove them around this morning.' Rita moved out of the way so they could take in the gleaming cars. The vintage Rolls Royce was part-cream and part-black with high sides and shiny black and cream wheels. Josh looked inside at the red leather interior. There was even a drinks cabinet in the back ready to hold the post-wedding champagne. In short, it was a beautiful car, traditional and perfect for a wedding. Josh could just imagine the white ribbon attached to the front, the suited and booted chauffer and beautiful bride drawing up to the castle.

Rita flipped open her notepad. 'You want a chauffeur to pick Emily up from Ben Campbell's and to drive her here. Then Paul wants the car overnight so he can drive to the honeymoon suite, is that right?'

'Correct.'

'That's fine. We'll need a deposit and his driving licence but Simon discussed it with me earlier and it should be okay.'

'How fast does the Rolls go?' Josh asked Rita, who consulted the notepad again.

'Over eighty-seven miles per hour, but Simon likes to keep it under fifty. It's an old car, belonged to his great-grandfather, and he wants to keep it pristine.'

'Sure,' Josh grunted, knowing Lily would be pinning her hopes on this car and wondering why all of a sudden her wishes mattered so much to him.

'I can imagine Emily in the back in her dress,' Lily said, her face beaming.

Yep, and Josh could imagine Paul's face if this rolled up outside Cove Castle on his wedding day instead of a sports car.

Beside the Rolls Royce stood a Mercedes. The car was long, matt black and sleek and could have been driven off a Bond movie set. The top had been put down, even though it was probably only eight degrees outside, and the leather seats shone in the sunlight. The car looked fast and – unlike any wedding car he'd ever seen – Josh knew Paul would love it.

'How fast does the Mercedes go?' Lily asked, surprising Josh. Why did she care?

'Over a hundred,' Rita responded. 'But Simon likes the drivers to keep to under sixty-five. This car belongs to him and he doesn't like it going too fast. Something to do with depreciation and lifetime of the tyres.'

Josh rolled his eyes. That sounded like Simon. But what was the point in having a car like this if you didn't take a risk and put your foot down?

'Are we allowed a test drive?' Josh asked. If they were going to go with the Rolls, he'd like to at least take a road trip in the Mercedes. If the show went well – if Marta made up with Simon and he had a show at all – he might make enough money to put down a deposit. He loved his Porsche but every time he went near it now he was reminded of Lily's ex, and that had definitely taken the shine off.

'Of course.' Rita nodded. 'Simon mentioned you might want to. He doesn't usually say yes but apparently for you the rules are different.' She looked stern, as if she didn't quite approve. 'If you take the road along the promenade you could head out of town and take it along the coast. The views are beautiful up there and at this time of day there won't be much traffic. If you could keep to the speed limit specified I'd appreciate it. I'll need to see your licences.'

'I don't have mine with me.' Lily looked at Josh.

'Sure.' Josh pulled his wallet from his jeans pocket and rifled through before handing it over. Rita studied it before putting it in her pocket.

'I'll let Simon know you're taking the cars out for a quick run to get a feel for them. Remember, I know where you live.' Rita gave them a scary look.

Lily opened the door of the Rolls and checked the back. 'Plenty of room for a dog, although—' She considered Chester. 'He might need a bath.'

'You can leave him with me,' Rita offered hastily, screwing up her nose. 'I'll take him to the teashop and get him a bowl of water – looks like he might benefit from a rub down with a towel. If I let that dog get in either of those cars Simon will have my guts for garters. I assume that's okay?' she asked.

'You can have Chester, so long as I get him back. Just give him one of these and he'll follow you anywhere.' Josh dug in his coat pocket and pulled out a handful of dog biscuits, catching Lily's warm look. 'He doesn't understand the word obey, but he responds to bribery.'

'Thanks.' Rita laughed as she handed Josh the keys to both cars and took the biscuits. 'Will you be long?'

'I'm sure half an hour in each will do it,' Lily answered, surprising Josh by opening up the passenger door of the Mercedes and climbing inside. She was wearing jeans and a pink sweater today, which made her look wholesome and appealing, and Josh had a sudden flashback to the way she'd looked in his bed.

'Are you sure it's worth driving this?' he grumbled, dropping into the driver's seat and firing the engine. 'I thought you'd have your heart set on the Rolls?'

'Isn't the point of the test drive to make a decision?' Lily checked the controls on the dashboard and stroked a hand across the leather interior without looking at him.

They took off down the drive and headed out of the castle, turning right onto the promenade. The sun was out and it was cold today but people were still on the beach walking their dogs and a couple of kids played in the sand. As they headed out of town towards the cliffs, Josh put the heater on so they didn't freeze and almost simultaneously Lily shivered.

'Do you want me to put the roof up?' he asked, expecting her to say yes.

'I'll be fine.' Lily smiled at him. 'In answer to your first question, the reason we're driving this car is because I saw your face when you looked at it – you got that expression you get when you pick up a camera so I wanted you to see what it was like.'

'It's not very traditional,' he said, feeling off-balance at Lily's cool assessment. He wasn't so sure he liked the camera being turned on him. They hit the road that ran along the edge of the Castle Cove

Cliffs and Josh looked over at the sea where sunlight sparkled on the waves. There were dozens of dark clouds near the horizon but here the sky looked clear.

'Nope. But if we're choosing a car to take Emily to the castle on her wedding day, and then for Paul to drive to their honeymoon suite in the evening, I'm wondering why we can't go with two cars – one for before and one after?'

'What about the budget?' Josh asked, driving the car to a beauty spot on the edge of the cliff and parking.

'I'm thinking to hell with the budget.' Lily grinned when Josh mock gasped. 'Actually, I'm hoping Simon will do us a deal if we ask nicely. Besides, you only get married once – at least I'm hoping Emily and Paul will.'

'I certainly hope so,' Josh said drily. 'I'm not sure I'm up to planning another wedding.'

'I think it's been fun.' Lily looked crushed, making Josh wonder why he'd said that.

'Have you heard from Aubrey?' He changed the subject.

'She's left a message and texted about the photo shoot she's organised. I'm still trying to figure out what to say.'

'I don't want to be a model, I want to be a chef?' Josh suggested. 'One word in front of the other – in that order. It's really not that difficult.'

'I know you're right.' Lily said. 'And I will tell her, I'm just working my way up to it.'

Josh laughed. He couldn't help himself. 'Lily, there's a world of difference between delaying something and never ever doing it. You're going to have to tell Aubrey eventually.'

'I know. You're right of course, I'm being ridiculous. I'll do it today. Probably.'

'What are you worried about?'

'It's clear Aubrey only got in touch so she had a daughter to show off, that it wasn't about me. I'm scared if I say I don't want to be a model Aubrey won't want to see me again,' she admitted.

'If she doesn't, she's a fool and not worthy of you,' Josh said quietly.

'I know, but it doesn't make it easier. When I tell Aubrey, I have to be prepared for her to walk away, to say goodbye to the mother I've wanted for so long. Perhaps I'll even have to admit I'm not good enough for her.' She squinted at the horizon. 'Do you think it's going to rain? Should we go back?' Lily changed the subject, clearly uncomfortable.

Josh ran his hands over the steering wheel. 'I'd like to take the car a little further down the coast. Get a feel for it. If Paul's going to drive this to his honeymoon, we need to know it's safe.'

'Are you worried the wheels are going to fall off?' Lily teased.

'I need to make sure the brakes work in case Paul and Emily run into any Micra drivers in the dark.' Josh grinned, firing the engine and backing the car up into the road before putting his foot down. The air was cold, but he loved the wind in his hair. He hit sixty and notched it up – cars like this were built for speed. Out of the corner of his eye he saw Lily's eyes on the speedometer so tapped the brake. He didn't want to get her into trouble with Simon.

'Fast—' she said, but the wind caught the rest of the sentence.

'I know, I'll slow down.'

'Don't,' she shouted. 'I said faster. Cars like this aren't meant to go sixty-five. There's a longer stretch of road coming, and an airfield to the left that only gets used on the weekends.'

'Seriously?' Josh spotted the sign for the airfield and took a left. The road was wide and open and the mesh gates which he'd expected to be bolted and closed lay open. 'Is this usually accessible?' he asked, driving through the gateway onto the open tarmac. The stretch of road was so huge he couldn't see the end of it. He could see a small control tower to the right along with a couple of strips of open space most likely used for taxiing.

'It's normally left open during the day in the week. It's an open secret. The owner lets learner drivers come here to practise. Andrew used to bring me and I know Simon comes when he wants to let his cars loose, but you didn't hear that from me.'

Josh nodded, wondering what to make of Simon Wolf — perhaps there was more to the man than met the eye, something even he couldn't see?

He drew the car to a stop and they both looked at the stretch of grey tarmac surrounded by trees, topped by open sky dotted with dark clouds. Josh felt a bubble of excitement in his stomach as he gunned the engine and gripped the steering wheel.

'Go!' Lily shouted suddenly, wriggling in the seat beside him. Her eyes were bright and she giggled as Josh put his foot down and the car shot forwards, hitting sixty in a few seconds. Wow, he felt his heartrate spike as the speed shot up, blowing freezing wind into the car.

'Faster,' Lily roared as the dial continued to climb, hitting ninety. If Simon could see them now he'd probably have a coronary. Then again, if what Lily had said was true, Simon headed to this place every now and again to let off his own steam.

'Emily will love this car,' Lily screamed. Josh could hardly hear because the wind was so noisy. 'She wanted a place to show off her sparkly shoes, a car she could set herself free in. Go faster!' She laughed and Josh's face stretched into a grin.

'Is that Lily King in the passenger seat – keeper of rules, worshipper of the safe road, woman voted most likely never to offend anyone?' Josh put his foot down and hit a hundred.

Lily threw her hands in the air as they hurtled down the tarmac. 'Not any more, this is wild Lily King – breaker of rules, user of her own road, woman most likely to follow her heart.'

'What happened?' Josh asked, surprised.

'You,' Lily replied, making Josh's heart lift and fly even though he knew it was a mistake. Letting people in, giving them space in his affections was dangerous, but with Lily he couldn't seem to help himself.

Josh saw the end of the tarmac approaching so swung right, bringing the car to an abrupt halt in front of the control tower, unsure whether to act on the intense need racing through his blood to reach for the woman beside him – the one who seemed to fill so many holes in his soul, so many needs he hadn't even known he had.

They sat for a few moments, absorbing the cold biting their faces, acknowledging the feelings fizzing between them.

Josh didn't know who reached for who first – perhaps it was him, he honestly couldn't remember. But suddenly Lily seemed to be straddling his lap and he was tapping the button so the seat slid backwards and down to give her space, reaching forwards to fumble with the controls on the dashboard to figure out how the bloody hell to put the roof up while Lily ripped at his shirt, undoing four buttons before sliding her hands inside and settling freezing fingers on burning hot skin.

Josh looked into Lily's face, into her bright eyes, pink cheeks and smiling lips. This was Lily King in all her glory, doing what came naturally, doing what she wanted and all of a sudden he felt something inside him open up – a part he'd kept closed off for far too long, perhaps since his grandmother died – and then Lily slid through the gap, just as he reached up to draw her mouth down to his, knowing even then that she'd stolen his heart.

Chapter Twenty-Nine

Too many clothes. There were too many clothes. That's all Lily could think as Josh deepened their kiss, pulling her closer. She had her hands in his shirt, trapped against his skin, but she hadn't managed to undo all of the buttons yet. She wanted to be close to him, wanted skin touching skin. She felt Josh's hands fumble with the buttons of her jeans and pulled her hips back to give him access. Thank goodness he'd figured out how to close the roof of the car, but the windows were still open, leaking in icy air, covering every part of her body with goose-bumps.

'Too many clothes.' Josh read her mind, easing back from the kiss so he could thump the buttons on the door, sending all of the windows sliding upwards in a synchronised nod to sanity and warmth. He tugged the bottom of Lily's jumper and drew it up over her head, quickly undoing her bra, leaving her naked from the waist upwards. Despite the fact that the air was still freezing she felt hot.

'I hope these windows steam up soon,' Lily joked, not bothering to look out of the car. They were unlikely to have any visitors and even if they did, right now she couldn't care less. All she cared about was getting closer to Josh, having his hands on her, his mouth kissing and licking her skin, sliding across her collarbone towards her breasts, making her gasp and her nipples peak.

'You want to stop?' Josh asked just before his mouth clenched over a nipple, making Lily almost scream as she squeezed her thighs against the outsides of his legs. Ignoring how uncomfortable she was, ignoring the driver door and gear console both digging into her calves.

'Are you mad?' Lily muttered, dipping her hands below where Josh's mouth was working on driving her crazy so she could pull at his belt, attempting unsuccessfully to undo it.

Rain began to splatter on the windscreen and she thanked God for it. At least the bad weather would keep all the sane people away from the airfield. She tugged at Josh's belt again as his mouth began to slide across her skin to the other nipple, leaving a trail of fire.

'Wait,' Josh laughed, lifting his head and pulling away so he could undo the belt himself and chuck it on the passenger seat. Then he undid the jeans button and began to work on the zip until Lily stopped him.

'Let me do it.' She smiled, sliding it down and pushing her hands inside his jeans, pushing his boxer shorts aside, setting him free and setting her hands on him. She slid them up and down on the soft skin, making Josh groan until he stopped her.

'It's your turn,' Josh said quickly, undoing Lily's jeans zip before tugging the material downwards until they stuck at the top of her legs. Josh pushed his hands into the back of Lily's jeans, underneath her pants, warming the delicate skin, and squeezed, making her insides burn with need.

Lily wanted more, but she was straddling Josh, and that was as far as the clothes could go.

'Not sure this car has enough room to manoeuvre.' Josh glanced at the gear stick and up to Lily's face, looking frustrated.

Lily laughed and eased herself up, bumping her head on the roof of the car. A few weeks ago if someone had suggested she'd be half naked, trying to get undressed in Simon Wolf's car, she'd have told them they were crazy – but now… would Simon be mad?

'Stop thinking, Lily.' Josh read her mind.

'It's Simon's car.'

'Strictly speaking I think it belongs to the castle. Besides, you're sitting on me.' He looked at the window, at the rain thundering down it. 'Unless you want to go outside, or would you rather stop?' He dipped his head and slid his tongue across Lily's nipple, driving her insane – which was probably exactly what he intended.

'Can't stop,' Lily said because that was the truth of it. Sod Simon, sod decorum, sod doing what was right. Desperate now, Lily half stood, bumping her bottom against the steering wheel, and managed to create enough space to kick off her shoe and manoeuvre one side of her jeans over her bottom, thigh and foot before sliding the other to her knee and then flipping the garment to the side. Almost fully naked, aside from her pants, socks and one half-leg of jeans, Lily sat back on Josh's lap and slowly slid forwards.

'Oh,' Josh groaned, capturing her mouth in a deep kiss and pushing his hands inside her pants again, squeezing her bottom, making her squirm. 'Still too many clothes,' he murmured, moving his hands forwards and pushing her knickers aside before directing her upwards and down again so he slowly filled her.

'Woah,' Lily bit her lip as Josh began to move, lifting his hips, holding hard onto hers as he guided her up and down. Up and down. 'Gosh, woah, wow,' she added because sentences were a thing of the past – and making sense, having the ability to create any kind of conversation, seemed like a lifetime ago. Instead her heart lifted as Josh continued to move, as his tongue explored her mouth as they rode up and down, up and down. Lily felt herself building, felt her heart open like a flower, as she acknowledged her feelings for Josh, and accepted what they were doing to her.

Because of Josh, she wasn't the woman she'd tried to be; because of him, she'd become a woman who expressed herself, one who was brave and happy. Perhaps one who would finally face Aubrey and tell her what she wanted, laying claim to her future as a chef. She might even be honest with her dad and brothers. And it was all because of Josh – the rebel inside and underneath her, the man who'd got under her skin before edging further inside still, filling her heart.

Lily felt herself building upwards, felt a warmth hit from her toes to her core. Sensation rocked her as she rode faster and faster, matching Josh's pace. Then she tipped suddenly, crashing over the edge of whatever bubble of need she'd been holding onto, and was joined quickly by Josh as they panted their way to completion. Then Josh claimed her mouth, kissing her hard, before easing back to look into her face.

'That was wild, Lily King,' he murmured after a few seconds of shell-shocked silence.

'Just the way I like it.' Lily grinned, thinking for the first time in her life that she might actually mean what she said, and hoping things would always be this way.

Chapter Thirty

'Table eight in the corner needs clearing.' Cath whizzed past Lily on her way to the teashop kitchen holding a tray full of plates before stopping to stare at her. 'You're looking very pleased with yourself this morning.'

'I… um…' Lily knew her cheeks were probably luminous because Cath chuckled and nodded.

'Been having fun with Josh I'm guessing,' Cath clucked before disappearing through the kitchen door. Lily thought back to the day before and the ride in the Mercedes, which had been both incredible and surprising. Josh kept showing her sides of herself she hadn't known existed and it was becoming addictive.

'Lily.' A familiar voice had her stumbling backwards, leaving the cups she'd started to clear on the table. She turned around.

'Emily?' Her friend was standing next to the Christmas tree looking tanned and excited, her blonde hair shining underneath the harsh lights of the teashop.

'Are you a mirage?' Lily launched herself across the teashop to give her Emily a huge hug. 'You look amazing.' Emily's skin glowed and she looked happy and healthy. 'I thought you were back on the nineteenth?'

'We got an earlier flight – arrived this morning.' Emily looked around the teashop. 'We got a cab because we didn't want to bother you. It was all very last minute so I decided to surprise you. It looks great in here, so Christmassy, I can't believe how much I missed Castle Cove.'

'We missed you too,' Lily said, squeezing her friend again. 'And I can't wait to tell you all about the wedding plans. We chose the car yesterday.' Lily felt her skin tingle which probably meant a blush was crawling up her cheeks as she remembered what had happened with Josh last night.

'What's it like?'

'Amazing.' Lily's blush deepened. 'Sit over there and I'll see if I can take a quick break.'

Lily returned a few minutes later with a couple of hot chocolates, a slice of Death by Chocolate and two forks. 'Cath said I can take ten minutes. I thought you'd be hungry.'

Emily picked up a fork and took a swift bite of cake. 'Wow, I missed this… and I really shouldn't be eating any, I won't be able to fit into my dress.'

'You'll be fine.' Lily picked up a fork and dug in. 'You can definitely eat half a slice of cake. You're glowing. Paul clearly agrees with you.'

Emily grinned. 'He's gorgeous, I can't wait for you to meet him. But tell me more about the wedding plans first. I saw the photo Josh sent – did you like the dress?'

'It's gorgeous Em, you'll look stunning. The length was spot on and I just love that sparkly belt.' Not to mention Josh's reaction to it.

'I can't wait to see it up close. I'm heading over to Happily Ever After later today to try everything on and see the shoes you chose.'

'They're sparkly and impractical, as ordered.'

'I knew I could rely on you.' Emily chuckled. 'And what about the cake— cakes. I want to know the full story behind why there are two of them.' She looked around the teashop which was getting busier again. 'Perhaps we'll have to save that for later though — which reminds me why I came. We're staying with Josh and Paul's invited some people over tonight for a celebration so I wanted to invite you myself. Dad's coming and I'll need reinforcements when he meets Paul. I know he's still not happy about the wedding – and I think Paul's mum is going to pop in too and she sounds terrifying. Please say you can come?'

Lily grimaced. 'I'm meant to be helping in the restaurant but I'll see if someone can cover for me. I'll talk to Suze.' She couldn't let Emily down and somehow after what had happened with Josh yesterday she felt braver about asking. 'I'll do my best to come for a bit, even if I'm late. What time does it start?'

'Seven.' Emily's eyes shone. 'You've got to come, I need you to meet Paul. He's so dreamy you won't be able to help but fall in love with him. Although Josh said you'd been seeing a lot of each other.' Emily waggled her eyebrows. 'He's hot too.'

Lily blushed.

'Something's going on between you?' Emily gushed, reading Lily's face. 'Maybe we can have a double wedding?' She giggled.

'Ah, we're not serious.' Lily stumbled over the words. 'I mean, I'm not sure I know what we are.' It wasn't like they'd talked about it. For all Lily knew Josh behaved like this all the time. Although a very big part of her hoped he didn't because, unless she was mistaken, she was in danger of falling head over heels in love with him.

Chapter Thirty-One

Josh filled another glass with Castling and looked around his kitchen. Emily and Paul were staying with him until the wedding and Emily had bought a ton of Christmas stuff this afternoon and proceeded to fill his house with it. There were fairy lights dancing across the kitchen window and above the cooker and a large Father Christmas candleholder in the centre of his breakfast bar. Emily had even connected her phone to the speaker system so non-stop festive hits had assaulted his eardrums for the last hour. Lily would love it. Josh grimaced, surprised that he was thinking about her again as Paul wandered into the kitchen and caught his expression.

'I missed that grumpy face in Nepal. What's wrong, are you worried about the show?'

'Why would I be worried?' Josh asked, handing his brother the drink. 'It's almost ready to go.'

'Because it's the day after tomorrow and most normal people would be nervous,' Paul said drily, sipping his Castling. Josh watched his brother – he looked good, there was still the same dark brown hair, the same serious expression, but Paul had a lightness to his face that was new.

'Are you worried about the wedding then, because that'll be happening in less than a week?' Josh picked up his whisky and sipped, relishing the feel of it sliding over his tongue. In truth he was nervous about the show, but more because of the content and what it meant than any concerns that it wouldn't be successful.

'I'm looking forward to it,' Paul admitted, looking especially dopey. 'Emily's wonderful. As long as you haven't mucked up the arrangements we're good to go.' He grimaced suddenly. 'Aside from getting her dad's blessing...'

'I'll keep filling up Ben's glass.' Josh tipped a beer in his brother's direction. 'And you've always been the charming one so I'm guessing you'll get her dad's blessing even before I get him drunk. Mind you, that is some age difference.'

'When you know, you know,' Paul murmured quietly. 'Regardless of all the silly things people worry about.'

Josh heaved a sigh, feeling a strange mix of curiosity and fear. 'What does *you know* mean?'

Paul tipped his head and gazed at his brother. 'I can't believe after twenty-seven years you don't know how it feels to be in love?'

'Perhaps I'm checking, *you know*?' Josh shot back. 'Or maybe I need material for the best man's speech?'

'Steer clear of ex-girlfriends and stories about hangovers please. If that's a serious question.' Josh nodded and Paul continued, 'Being in love feels like you're dancing on air. You can't stop thinking about the person... what they want is more important than any need of your own. I imagine being in love is very much like how you feel about your camera.'

Josh's mind drifted to Lily, to the memory of her in the Mercedes, to the framed canvas sitting in his office. Did he love her or was it something else? His mind was so full of her, he couldn't think straight.

When the doorbell rang Josh looked at Paul. 'That could be the almost father-in-law – do you want to go? I expect you'll get points for greeting him.'

Before Paul could move, they heard the door open and Emily and Marta's voices. Seconds later Marta marched into the kitchen holding a bottle of champagne.

'Paul,' Marta gave Paul a swift hug. They'd met a couple of times over the years and had always got on. 'Congratulations, Emily is wonderful.'

Marta pulled back and Josh noticed her dress for the first time. It was figure-hugging and bright red which set off her auburn hair.

'Any special reason for the knock-out outfit?' Josh teased, putting the champagne in the fridge. 'Want some fizz now or fancy a whisky?'

'White wine please, and the dress is a practice run for the show. I believe Simon is coming tonight?'

'Yep.' Josh handed Marta her drink. She smiled wickedly, pointing at the Christmas decorations over the window. 'That's either Lily or Emily. I know you wouldn't bother.'

'Lily?' Paul asked. 'Emily's friend?'

Marta nodded. 'Josh and Lily have been planning the wedding together.'

'Lily's the one who ordered the Fruit Cake?' Paul shuddered.

'She helped choose the shoes, food, flowers and car too – gave up a lot of her time to do it,' Josh snapped.

'Which I'm grateful for of course,' Paul said, looking at this brother with a bemused expression.

'So these pictures I've been waiting to see,' Marta said, changing the subject. 'Can we look at them before my hair turns grey?'

'Sure.' Josh felt the inexplicable burst of temper evaporate as he marched through the kitchen into the hall, leading Paul and Marta to his office. On the way, they passed the sitting room where Emily sat by the fireplace chatting with Ted and Olive while Chester sniffed their shoes.

Josh closed the door, ignoring his damp palms as he glanced at the pile of framed photographs and canvases propped against his bookshelf. There were thirty pictures in all and some had only arrived this morning. 'I haven't decided which to use as the main focus of the show,' Josh lied, picking up the first canvas. It was by far the largest and he propped it on the small sofa in the corner of the office.

In it, Lily stood whipping eggs in a silver bowl, wearing his shirt. Her hair was partially damp and sunlight – Josh couldn't even remember there being any that morning – slid from the window across the side of her face, giving her an almost ethereal quality. On the kitchen counter, an array of eclectic ingredients added colour to the composition.

'It's called *Wild*.' Josh cleared his throat.

'That's Lily.' Marta's voice sounded strange. 'But not like any Lily I've ever known. Why is she wearing your shirt?'

'Long story,' Josh said, feeling unexpectedly protective. 'And not what you probably think.' Not when he'd *taken* the photograph anyway.

'How did you get Lily to pose for you?' Marta looked closely at the picture. 'I thought you didn't do people?'

'It happened. I took it and somehow it worked.' Josh couldn't explain it. Nor could he explain why this was the picture he wanted to use as the focal point of his show. If pressed, he'd probably say it was because the world needed to see Lily for the incredible woman she was. Only that sounded way too sentimental for a man like him. 'I'm not going to start taking portraits – this is a one-off,' he added, so no one got the wrong idea.

'I like it,' Marta admitted eventually. 'I've no idea why. It might be the colours and textures, it could be the subject. It's different but I like it and I'm sure my customers will too. It's emotional, a departure for you, but a good one and a new angle for the show.'

Josh picked up the next canvas from the pile and placed it beside the one of Lily. 'This is the best one I took of the log. It's called *Battered* – the other option for the main showpiece.' The picture was dramatic. Somehow after days of trying Josh had managed to capture the wood at exactly the right angle. The clouds behind it had been dark and Chester had stood miles in the distance. The effect was atmospheric, almost lonely.

'I like this too,' Marta admitted. 'But not as much of the one of Lily. What do you think, Paul?'

'I like both.' Paul stood back and studied them for a few seconds. 'I agree with you Marta, *Wild* should be the central point of the show, but *Battered* will work alongside it. There's a fantastic mixture of styles and subjects here. Something for everyone.' Paul gazed at Josh. 'It's amazing work, you should be proud. I swear you get better every time you pick up that camera.'

Josh knocked back the rest of his whisky. 'You're only saying that to butter me up because you're worried about the best man speech.'

'I'm saying it because it's true. And for someone so determined to spend their life taking photographs, you really should learn to celebrate your talents more.' Paul sounded annoyed but Josh avoided responding because the doorbell rang again and he led Marta and Paul out of the office before locking the door to keep out prying eyes. The next time those pictures were seen by anyone would be at his show – he wanted *Wild* to be a surprise for Lily, wanted her to see how he saw her, the woman she truly was.

This time it was Ben Campbell at the door with his partner Gayle. Josh hung back at the edge of the sitting room with Paul as Emily invited them inside with a hug before taking their coats.

'Dad, this is my fiancée Paul.' Emily beamed, leading her dad through the hall to join them. Ben's expression turned icy as he took Paul's hand.

'Can I get you a pint of Castling? And Gayle, what would you like?' Josh asked, because alcohol was obviously needed.

'Castling would be great thanks,' Ben muttered.

'I'd love a glass of white wine please,' Gayle said, but instead of staying to chat, Paul headed for the kitchen looking terrified. Ben glared after him and Gayle looked embarrassed. 'I do love what you've done with this place Josh,' she murmured, her long gypsy-style skirt swishing as she moved further into the sitting room so she could admire the picture above the fireplace.

'My brother's very talented.' Paul returned with their drinks. 'Always has been. I used to be jealous when we were kids.'

Josh's brow puckered – he hadn't known that. Besides, it was almost certainly a lie. Paul had been the one celebrated, the genius of the family, and Josh had always been fine with that.

The doorbell rang again and this time Josh beat Emily to it – probably because she didn't want to leave her dad and Paul alone. A small crowd had gathered on his doorstep: his mother, Lily's dad Tom and Simon. Josh stood back again, feeling disappointed that Lily hadn't arrived too. He offered a perfunctory air-kiss or handshake as each of the guests walked inside, then took their coats and led them into the sitting room, wondering what had possessed him to host a welcome home party when he hated crowds.

Josh's mother made a beeline for Paul, Tom went for Ted and Simon did a double-take of Marta and walked towards her. Josh watched them all talking until the doorbell rang again.

'Who the hell is that?' He stomped into the hallway and yanked the door open – then his heart seemed to stop and float.

Because Lily was standing on his doorstep, covered with flakes of snow – she looked fresh-faced and beautiful and Josh had an urge to reach for his camera again.

'You're late,' he complained, as a smile crept across his face.

'I had to organise my own cover at the restaurant and Anya couldn't get there until now. Is everyone here?' Lily beamed as she stepped inside.

'I've no idea.' Josh smiled. 'Paul and Emily seem to have invited half of Castle Cove. I was thinking of packing a bag and moving out. Shall we go to yours?' He was half serious but Lily giggled as she handed him a bottle of whisky.

'I thought you'd appreciate this rather than wine.' Lily took off her coat to reveal a pair of jeans and a low-cut blue top that made her skin glow under the hall lights. 'Also, I thought I should replace what I drank the other evening.'

'Then is there a case hidden in that coat?' Josh laughed, leading her into the sitting room.

'I didn't realise my dad was coming.' Lily sounded worried.

'Oh, my dad and yours have been best friends for so long he's like family,' Emily said, launching herself at them.

'It's so good you're here Lil, I know you told me loads about the wedding plans already but I've thought of even more questions. I tried on the dress this afternoon and I love it, shoes too, but tell me more about the food – what did you guys choose? Honestly Lily, I'm so grateful to you and Josh for organising everything for us. It was really frustrating being so far away and not being able to call more and help.' Emily led Lily away, still chattering, and Josh watched them for a few moments feeling oddly content – the room had a nice buzz to it, the fire glowed and Chester had curled up in front of it and fallen asleep. A few months ago this type of domestic scene would have had him running for the hills, but today it seemed to fit.

Simon and Marta were in the kitchen scowling at each other when Josh entered. Neither of them noticed him arrive.

'Red suits you,' Simon said, filling the odd silence – he sounded irritated and scratchy and despite the kind words his mouth had set into a thin line.

'Is that a compliment? Because it's really hard to tell.' Marta's red lips stretched into a smile but Josh knew she didn't mean it – that the true sentiment underneath was either disappointment or hurt.

'I don't understand why you always doubt my motives Marta, I've not done anything to deserve it. I like the dress, it's…' Simon stopped, clearly out of his depth.

'Tarty?' Marta suggested. 'Too tight, bad taste?'

'Incredible,' Simon said, looking more confident as his eyes scanned the sexy outfit. 'You look incredible. That's what I was thinking.'

Marta picked up her wine and sipped but Josh knew she was lost for words. 'Thank you,' she whispered uncertainly.

Simon stepped closer, looking hopeful – probably because Marta hadn't snapped his head off. 'And I'm glad you've decided to have the show in the library,' he murmured. 'It's a great venue. You can hold your shows there whenever you like free of charge. I want you to know that.'

Marta stared into her wine. 'I… I don't understand – I honestly don't. Why are you doing this, what's in it for you?'

'Nothing…' Simon looked confused. 'Why does there have to be something in it for me?'

'Because there always is. People don't do anything for nothing.'

Simon's expression turned tender. 'Josh said you'd been hurt. I think I'm beginning to see how much. If you need a reason Marta, I'll say it's because I want to help. If we're digging deeper, it's because I like you…'

'You do?'

'Very much.' Josh watched as Marta looked up and her eyes met Simon's. Marta's cheeks were flushed and Josh could see she was perplexed, perhaps a little overcome.

'I… really?' Marta asked.

'Really.' Simon's tone was dry.

'Then thank you.' Her hands had turned white from gripping her glass.

'And you?' Simon tipped his head to the side. 'How do you feel about me? Because despite spending so many hours in your company, I honestly can't tell.'

'I, heavens… I don't really know,' Marta garbled. Simon stepped backwards looking wounded and she reached out to touch his arm. 'That's not true… I'm sorry, I'm not being honest. I like you too Simon – why the hell do you think I'm wearing this dress?'

'Sorry?'

'How many days have you come into my gallery and fiddled with the fuse box while you completely ignored me?' she continued. 'You say you like me, I say you've got a funny way of showing it.'

'What?'

Marta straightened her shoulders, clearly warming to the subject. 'I have no idea what's going on inside that head of yours – you've spent hours in my company without saying anything in particular unless you're bargaining for more advertising revenue. It's no wonder I'm suspecting your motives.'

Simon grinned suddenly. 'You like me?'

Marta groaned. 'Is that really all you heard?'

'That and something about what you're wearing, the rest I didn't get,' he added. 'Why are you wearing that dress?'

'To drive you crazy,' Marta growled.

Simon laughed, his grey eyes sparkling with appreciation and relief. 'You don't need a dress to drive me crazy, although I'm definitely not complaining. You've been driving me nuts since we first met.' When Marta looked taken aback Simon added, 'And I've loved every minute of it… almost. I just didn't know how to approach you, didn't know if I'd scare you off if I asked you out, so I've been working my way up to it… at least, I've been trying to.'

Simon edged closer again.

'For such a hard-nosed businessman you've been remarkably hesitant,' Marta complained.

'I prefer to think of it as taking my time, finding out what you want… strategizing.'

Marta tutted. 'That's a lot of business bullshit. Call it what it is – you've been holding out for me to do all the work.'

Simon smiled, only this time it was predatory, then he eased closer and slowly plucked the wine glass from Marta's hand. 'Maybe not all the work.' He leaned in slowly and caught her mouth with his. Marta seemed to hesitate for a beat, perhaps she was surprised? Then she reached a hand up to grab the back of his head, winding her arms around his neck and closing any distance between them.

Josh stepped back out of the kitchen doorway, suddenly aware that he'd been spying on a private moment. When he entered the sitting room, he spotted Lily talking in a group with Paul, Ben, Tom and his mother so headed for them, ready to intervene if needed.

'How's the quest for the new job?' Ben smiled at Lily, affection shining from his eyes.

'Luc's on his way back from France and he told Suze I can cook for him on the twenty-first. I'll know after that.' Lily made a face. 'I've no idea how it will go but Suze and Josh have been helping me access my inner chef.'

'I'm surprised,' his mother murmured. 'Josh has never been very domesticated.'

'I guess when you have the kind of talent he does, it's hard to focus on everyday things.' Lily's eyes shot to the picture above the fireplace but Josh's mother dismissed it with a wave of her hand.

'Paul, how soon do you plan to get back to work after the wedding?' she asked.

Paul looked for his fiancée and took her hand. 'Emily and I fancy another bout in Nepal. We're planning to go to Scotland for a week after the wedding. Emily loves it there and—'

'I took her when she was fifteen,' Ben interrupted, looking unhappy.

'I know,' Paul said quietly. 'That's why she loves it – apparently it was your last family holiday?'

Ben grunted, looking taken aback.

'It's lovely that you both want to go there and honour it,' Lily stepped in. Josh saw her hands were shaking but then Emily mouthed a silent *thank you* and she relaxed.

'It is,' Ben agreed, looking mollified. 'I'm surprised, I'll admit. Your mother would have been so happy.' As approvals went, it was lukewarm but Emily beamed and Paul's face softened.

'You did your residency in Edinburgh, didn't you Paul?' his mother boasted, changing the subject, and Josh watched his brother's shoulders tense.

'Will you be coming to Josh's show, Mum?' he asked instead of answering.

'You really should Mrs Havellin-Scott – it's going to brilliant.' Lily blushed when his mother didn't respond.

Tom stared at Lily. 'I had no idea you were into photography?'

'Josh showed me some of his work – he's going to be taking the photos at Emily's wedding.' Lily beamed. 'He's really very talented.'

Josh stared at her, lost for words.

Tom King looked thoughtful. 'Then I'll try to come along to the show.'

'That would be great.' Lily's expression lit up and Josh took a step back, feeling uncomfortable. Would Lily be embarrassed about the photograph if her dad was there to see it?

'Can I get anyone more drinks?' Josh asked, wanting to get away suddenly. Probably sensing something was off, Chester came to nudge his hand.

'Castling please.' Ben handed Josh his glass and Paul did the same.

'White wine if you have it?' Lily asked.

Josh headed for the kitchen, making plenty of noise this time so when he entered Marta and Simon had already sprung apart. He rattled around the fridge, pulling out wine and refilling glasses, wondering why the fact that Lily's dad was coming to his show and how he was going to feel about the photograph bothered him quite so much.

Chapter Thirty-Two

Lily sat on the sofa in her lounge and stared at her mobile. She had to tell Aubrey she didn't want to go along with her plans to turn her into a model. Her mother had left three messages since the night of the birthday party and she hadn't returned one of them yet. She flicked on the answerphone and put the last message on speakerphone.

'Lily, I'm not sure why you haven't called back. I expect you're busy – which I understand, a girl your age should be out having fun. But can you confirm you received my message about the shoot for the twenty-third? I've booked the photographer and the studio's in Notting Hill, I'll text you his address. I'll need you there at seven-thirty in the morning, so there's plenty of time to do make-up and hair – you'll need to get the first train. *Oh* and I've got friends coming over in the evening who I'd like you to meet; my agent's one of them. I thought we could show him some of the photos and I know he's got some ideas for work. Book the night off and stay overnight so you don't have to leave early – I'm sure your boss will understand. *Ciao* darling.'

The message ended and Lily stared at the phone, shaking her head. This was out of hand. If Josh were here, he'd tell her she had to call Aubrey and be honest with her. Lily gazed at the floor. But it wasn't as easy as that. When she was with Josh she felt wild and free – without him she didn't feel as brave. She was afraid she'd lose everything she'd built in Castle Cove, afraid that her friends and family would hate her because she'd been lying about seeing her mother.

Don't be a bloody idiot Lily, you want to be a chef not a model – tell her before you end up on the cover of Vogue.

Grabbing the mobile, Lily dialled Aubrey's number, ignoring the sick feeling in her stomach. When it went to voicemail she almost punched the air.

'Aubrey… um, Mum. I'm sorry I haven't called you, it's been busy here.' Lily stopped and looked out of the window, remembering what Josh had said – *wild, not wild, you need to be yourself Lily. You need to find out who you really are.*

'Actually, that's not true.' Lily licked her lips and straightened her shoulders. 'I'm sorry but I don't really want to be a model. I want to be a chef. I've loved cooking since I was little.' She paused. 'I have an interview. It's a real opportunity to train to be a chef, to learn how to be great. Like you…' She trailed off. 'Maybe the way I feel about cooking is the way you feel about modelling. If it is I hope you understand, and I hope you want to be part of my life because I've missed having you in it. I've dreamed of having a mother for so long… I guess I've been afraid of letting you see the real me. But I've learned recently…' Lily licked her lips, feeling more confident. 'That you have to be true to yourself, because if you aren't, you'll never be truly happy.'

When she'd finished, Lily hung up and put the mobile on the coffee table, ignoring her shaking hands, happy she'd finally been honest and embraced her true self – and knowing it was all thanks to Josh.

☆

The show had already started. Lily checked her watch again, fiddling with the belt on her dress. She'd stayed on at the teashop, helping to tidy up, and by the time she'd got home and changed she'd been late. Worse, when she'd arrived at the station car park it had been heaving so she'd driven around and around for another ten minutes before finding a space.

Lily's heels tapped as she strode up the steps to Cove Castle. There were loads of people milling about the entrance and she could see more in the grand hall. Lily walked into the entrance and saw the door to the library had been propped open. She wandered inside and got stuck behind a small crowd chatting to Marta, who was standing at the door handing out leaflets. Lily stretched her neck so she could see beyond them. The library looked different from the night of the birthday party. Simon and Marta had obviously spent hours emptying the walls and creating spaces to hang Josh's art. Tall white plinths with uplighters had been placed throughout the room so pictures could be placed on them and lit from below, while the lights in the library had been dimmed for maximum effect. In the background, Christmas music played as people mingled.

Lily craned her neck again to peer around the crowd in front of her. From this distance Lily couldn't be sure, but there seemed to be a canvas showing a trail of moonlight on the sea leading to the horizon. It was brilliant and she felt her heart lift. It could have been the one Josh had taken the night she'd arrived late back from

London after seeing Aubrey, the first incredible night when she'd allowed herself to open up and had begun to see what kind of man he really was. She'd been conflicted, she remembered, and unhappy about lying to her family about her mother.

Speaking of Aubrey, Lily hadn't heard a thing since leaving her message the day before and that was niggling her.

'Lily!' She felt a gentle tap on the shoulder and turned to find her dad and both brothers grinning at her.

'I didn't know you were all coming.' Lily gave them all a swift hug.

'I can't stay long,' Andrew admitted. 'But I wanted to see what all the fuss was about. Ted's been bending everyone's ear about your talented photographer friend.'

'It's all he could talk about the other night, and now I know you've taken such a liking to art, I thought I'd see why,' Lily's dad teased.

Scott stared at the queue in front of them. 'I hear *The Castle Cove Gazette's* coming. Your friend Josh must be good for them to take the time. Talking of Porsche drivers, I saw Rogan outside. I think he might be coming tonight as well.'

'He's probably planning on cornering Simon,' Lily said, pleased that thoughts of her ex made her feel irritated now rather than sad.

The bunch of people in front of them moved just as Scott finished his sentence and Marta came to greet them. 'I overheard you talking about Rogan. I'll warn Simon to steer clear. Let's hope the man buys something while he's here.' She handed them each a leaflet. 'You might be in for a few surprises. Just remember – Lily already knows this – but whatever you see and however you feel about it, the intentions were pure.' Marta moved so she could greet the next lot of arrivals and Lily and her family moved further into the room.

'What was that supposed to mean?' Scott asked.

'I've no idea. Josh photographed the Beast, and I'm not sure the pictures will be entirely complimentary because he was focusing on the rust – maybe Marta's referring to that?' Lily suggested.

'It looks amazing in here.' Andrew glanced at the walls. 'The contrast of books and art really works.'

They stopped in front of a picture of Cove Castle. It must have been taken recently because there was snow on the roof of the turrets and Christmas decorations outside. 'I've no idea how he manages to make something I've seen almost every day of my life look completely different,' Lily's dad murmured. 'It's like seeing a whole new world isn't it? That's a talent not everyone has.'

Lily nodded as a combination of feelings hit her – pride at Josh's incredible talents and gratitude that he'd managed to help her finally see herself and learn to be braver. 'Dad.' Lily gulped. 'There's something I need to tell you.'

As Lily turned to face him, to confess about her mother, she felt the blood drain from her face. Because Aubrey herself had just grabbed a leaflet from Marta's hands and was now heading towards them with determined look on her face, closely followed by Albert, who looked worried.

Lily's mouth opened and closed as she tried to work out what to say.

'What, love?' her dad asked, turning so he could see what she was looking at. 'Is that…?' He trailed off, his eyes widening and his smile disappearing as Aubrey joined them.

'Hello Tom.' Aubrey flicked her hair and swept her eyes across Lily's father and brothers. She was dressed to impress tonight in a calf-length fitted black dress with a white fur coat draped across her shoulders. 'Long time no see.'

'You didn't tell me you were coming,' Lily hissed. Lily's family turned to stare at her, their expressions showing a combination of confusion, anger and hurt.

Aubrey pursed her lips. 'I've been wondering what to do since picking up your message, Lily. I went to the restaurant and one of the waitresses said you were here. I thought we could talk about what you said face to face.'

'You're in touch?' Scott's eyes widened as he looked between Lily and Aubrey. 'You need to explain Lil, because if you've been seeing this woman and haven't told us I'd like to know why.'

'It's a long story.' Lily squeezed her hands into fists. This wasn't how she wanted to tell them, but it was her own fault. She should have come clean weeks ago.

Someone else tapped Lily on the shoulder – this time it was Ted. 'The story starts with me,' he said gently. 'I delivered a letter to Lily from this one.' He tipped his head in Aubrey's direction, looking annoyed. 'I should have known Lily wouldn't have been able to resist.'

'Why not?' Scott asked, sounding furious. 'This woman left when you were a baby, when you were sick. Why would you want to have anything to do with a person who treated you like that?'

'Because she's my mother!' Lily snapped as the feelings she'd been bottling up for years gushed out. 'Don't you understand?' Lily lowered her voice because she didn't want to spoil Josh's show, she didn't want to do this here, but she had no choice. 'I knew nothing about my mother, no one ever wanted to talk about her. It's like she was some kind of dirty secret. I had no idea why she left – what I'd done that was so awful that my mother would leave. When she got in touch, I tried to tell you, I tried to talk about it.' Tears welled up in Lily's eyes as she took in their hurt expressions. 'But you didn't want to hear it, you shut me down. I know it's my fault, I should have said. I've hated lying but I didn't want to hurt you.'

'She's right,' Ted agreed, his voice soothing. 'And I didn't help. I thought it would be better if Lily didn't say anything. I'm partly to blame. I'm sorry too.'

Scott's lips thinned. 'Lily knew going behind our backs was wrong.'

'I really don't see what all the fuss is about.' Aubrey jumped in, looking confused. 'I mean, she's my daughter, I have a right to see her.'

'You gave up your rights when you walked away and left her in hospital,' Lily's dad murmured.

'I left, Tom, because you told me to. You said I was no good for Lily or her brothers and you told me not to come back.'

Lily absorbed the news like a punch in the chest. Swallowing the hurt, she knew her eyes were shining and tears were about to spill. 'You did?' She turned to her dad, feeling dazed. Was it really true? Had the man she thought had spent all these years protecting her, nurturing her, actually betrayed her trust?

'Lily, that's not what happened, she's twisting it.'

Aubrey slid an arm through Lily's. 'Perhaps we could do this another time. I'm all for family reunions but this isn't the place. I came to talk about the photo shoot on the twenty-third – cancelling is nonsense. You're meant for greater things than this.' Aubrey swept an arm around the room, taking in Lily's brothers, dad and Ted. 'I understand you're scared of changing your life, but I'll be there with you every step of the way so you won't have to worry.'

'No!' Lily pulled her arm free and stepped away from all of them. They all wanted something from her, expected her to be a certain way. It wasn't their fault – she'd never been honest about who she was, had never been honest with anyone except for Josh. 'No one is going to tell me what to do. No one is going to tell me who I am or what I should think or who I can or can't see.' As Lily spoke she slowly looked each of them in the eye. 'I'm sorry I wasn't honest but you need to know this is my life. I know what I want and that includes a relationship with my mother,' she declared to her brothers and dad. 'And I want to be able to have a boyfriend without anyone interfering or checking up on me. I need to make my own mistakes without people rubbing my nose in them or telling me how I should and shouldn't feel.' Lily looked at Aubrey. 'And I don't want to be a model, I want to be a chef. It's all I've ever wanted, I've just been too afraid to go for it until now.'

Aubrey looked shocked. 'Lily, you're wasting your life staying here. Why do you think I got out of Castle Cove? Look at the life I have, look at my home – it could all be yours if you are brave enough to grab it.'

'It's not what I want,' Lily said quietly. 'A big house and lots of money is not what I need to be happy. I'm sorry I'm not the daughter you wanted and I don't measure up. I want you in my life, but this time it's got to be on my terms. Your daughter wants to be a chef – a brilliant chef – and someday I will be. I hope you can accept that and love me anyway.'

Aubrey looked angry. 'You're making a mistake, wasting that face and figure of yours. You have no idea what you're giving up.'

Lily looked around the room, at the pictures on the walls. 'I know exactly what I'm giving up and I know exactly what I have. It's your choice if you still want to see me or not.' Lily gulped down her emotions. She knew this might be the last time she saw her mother, but she didn't know what else to do. 'Now I'm going to walk around this room and look at the photos Josh has taken. This should be *his* night – he's my friend. Actually…' Lily's gaze swept over their stony expressions. She was feeling sick with emotion. 'Josh is more than a friend. I love him. He's the only person who's ever seen me as I truly am, the only person who's ever really understood me.' Feelings gushed into her chest, as the admission resonated. 'And I've never told him – so I'm going to now.'

Lily turned away from them. Her stomach felt like a dead weight. One night of being herself, embracing everything, and she'd lost almost everyone she cared about. Half stumbling, Lily headed across the library, barely registering the questioning glances of people as she went.

Lily passed the pictures Josh had taken over the last year. There was one of the castle in moonlight, a field of poppies swaying in a field, Chester playing with a stick on the beach. She walked further around the room, taking time to absorb the show, blocking out what had just happened. There was the photo of the rust from the Beast – it was an odd picture but the colours were almost magical and the details intricate like lace.

The next picture was of the log. You could see sand underneath it and the sky in the background with pinks and oranges mixed into the bluey black. Lily could almost imagine a fairy hiding underneath the wood, waiting to hop out.

Someone bumped into her. The man apologised and did a double-take before looking over his shoulder to the corner of the library where a crowd had gathered. 'It's stunning, an unexpected departure. You must be very excited to be part of it,' he murmured before moving onto the next photograph.

Confused, Lily edged towards the throng. They'd begun to scatter so she got to the front quickly – but when she looked up her heart seemed to somersault and stop. Because there, hung for everyone to see, was the photograph from Josh's kitchen – where she was half-dressed, bare of make-up and totally exposed.

Lily blinked, trying to disperse the image, praying it wasn't real. She looked again, recognising the shirt she'd been wearing, the bowl and ingredients she'd pulled from the cupboard. That was *her* collarbone, the curve of *her* chin, *her* unmade-up face and damp hair shining in the sunlight. It was all *hers* and she hadn't wanted to share any of it.

'It's beautiful isn't it?' A man beside Lily scribbled something on his leaflet. 'There's something so unreal about the colours.' Behind them someone took a photograph.

'I… I…' Lost for words, Lily stopped trying to find any. She felt someone at her shoulder.

'Well, well – and you don't want to be a model?' Aubrey sounded furious. 'At least I'd have done your make-up and put you in proper clothes.'

Lily opened her mouth again but no words came – she didn't turn around even as she felt her mother leave, too overcome to defend herself. Slowly she turned and bumped straight into Scott.

'Seriously, Lily?' Her brother's angry voice rang in her ears and then she watched him leave too, dragging Andrew, Ted and her dad along with him.

Lily ducked her head, avoiding looking at anyone as she headed towards the exit, but after just a couple of steps her eyes hit a familiar pair of shoes. 'Well that's a turn-up,' Rogan said, but Lily didn't bother to look up. Her cheeks flamed. 'You've changed more than I thought – we really should have that drink.'

Tears spilled from Lily's eyes. She needed to hide. She stumbled again, walking quickly through the crowd, trying not to look up in case anyone recognised her. Marta caught her arm at the door and tugged her to one side.

'What's wrong?' she asked as Simon joined them. 'Has something happened?'

Lily didn't answer.

'Dammit – you didn't know about the photo?' Marta guessed. 'I thought Josh had told you – at least…' She trailed off. 'Perhaps he thought you knew?'

'If Josh knew me at all, he'd know how I'd feel about this.' Lily felt the blood drain to her toes. There were so many people she knew here – Emily and Paul, Olive from the vets, Alice and Cath, Anya, Suze and Nate were coming later. How could she show her face again? She felt so embarrassed. 'I need to leave,' Lily croaked. 'I don't want to be here with all these people looking at me.'

Marta's eyes darted to the back of the room. 'Josh is here somewhere. I persuaded him to talk to a journalist which is why he's been tied up. Let me find him, I've got a few words to share with him too.'

'No,' Lily snapped, tugging her arm free and heading for the door.

Lily didn't stop, even when she heard Simon shout her name. Instead she half ran, half tripped out of the library, through the hall and out of the front door, passing people as they made their way up the stairs. She needed to get away. Needed to think. How could Josh do this to her? He knew she didn't want to be a model, knew she wasn't the type of person to draw attention to herself. Didn't he know that? Or maybe he just didn't care?

Lily heard Josh's voice behind her so as soon as she hit the pavement outside the castle, she started to run.

Chapter Thirty-Three

Josh didn't know why he was running after Lily, didn't know what the hell was wrong. Marta had dragged him away from the journalist she'd spent the whole day insisting he talk to and told him to go after Lily, who was fleeing from the castle.

'Lily, wait!' Josh increased his pace as he chased her along the pavement towards the station car park. She must have parked the Beast there. Why was she leaving? What had gone wrong? In the pit of his stomach he already knew but wasn't ready to face it – he wanted to hear the words from her mouth first.

'Dammit Lily, stop running away,' Josh half shouted as he watched her stumble as she crossed the road and reached the outside of the station. Then she stopped and turned.

Josh caught up with her in seconds. Lily looked pale and angry, her eyes were bright and he wanted to reach out to pull her to him. 'You don't like the photo?' Josh kept his voice steady because he didn't want to upset her, even though he could feel his own soul start to freeze.

'Looks like I'm the only one,' Lily said, sounding oddly calm. 'How could you do that to me?'

He shook his head, feeling the rejection, trying to stop himself from reacting to it. Normally he could shut his emotions down –

he'd had a lifetime to learn how – but they were crawling through his stomach like acid, burning into every cell.

'The camera didn't lie Lily – you look magnificent.'

'I'm half naked,' she shouted. 'I'm not wearing make-up. I look awful.' Her eyes widened as if she were seeing the picture for the first time. 'You didn't even ask!'

Josh clenched his fists. 'I don't understand, you look incredible.' He swallowed as Lily began to shake her head – how could she not see it? 'It's you. I was showing everyone the real you.' He kept his voice steady but could feel the emotion breaking underneath. He needed to hold it together, needed her to understand.

'What the hell is that supposed to mean?' Lily waved her arms around, ignoring the crowd of people walking from the car park towards the castle. They looked over so she lowered her voice. 'I remember what you said to me. I was too stupid to listen, too caught up in the man I was *falling in love with* – the man I thought you were. You told me NOTHING was more important than your photos. How could I have been so blind? You said your work came first, and tonight I guess you proved that, didn't you?' Lily raised her chin, glaring at him, and Josh felt the burn of anger low in his chest, felt her rejection right down to his toes. 'My mother left. I told her I didn't want to be a model – stood up to her like you said – and then we walked around the corner and there I was, on canvas doing exactly what I told her I didn't want to do. Did you think it was different with you, Josh? Seems to me you're just another person wanting me to be something I'm not.'

'Tonight was about showing you how I felt. If that's not good enough for you…' He trailed off. He didn't beg for love. Never had.

He straightened his shoulders, fighting the ache in his chest. He'd get over these feelings. Just because they were crucifying him now, it didn't mean he couldn't move on.

But he didn't want to.

'This isn't about something being enough, Josh – it's about you taking without asking,' Lily snapped. 'Putting your work before everything, even honesty. You had time to tell me what you were planning and didn't.'

'I didn't know myself until the other day. And I didn't ask because I wanted to surprise you – I thought… I don't know what I thought.' He pushed his hands through his hair. He was messing this up, losing her. He could see it happening and didn't know how to stop it. But how could his work be the thing that came between them? Why was it always the thing that drove people away?

'You used me, Josh.' A tear tracked down Lily's face and she brushed it aside. 'Which makes you just like Aubrey and Rogan.'

'I'm nothing like your ex or your mother.' He stepped closer, letting the anger take over and fill his chest. 'I've been encouraging you to be yourself since we met. It's a picture – an incredible picture – of you. I don't understand why that offends you so much. Unless this has more to do with how you see yourself than anything I've done?'

Josh knew he'd blown it, knew the words were wrong when Lily turned away, shaking her head. 'I don't want to do this with you.'

'What?' Josh suppressed the hurt, replacing it with anger. 'What don't you want to do – face how you feel? You said you were falling in love with me. If that really were true, could you walk away so easily now? Because that makes you no better than my parents, rejecting me because of my work.'

'It's not the same thing,' Lily howled. 'This is about honesty. Your talent is amazing. I know that, the whole sodding world knows it. But you put it before everything, even your feelings for me.'

Josh stumbled backwards. 'What's that supposed to mean?'

'You – giving me all this advice about honesty and being true to myself, yet what do you do, Josh? You push people away, pretend they don't matter even though it's very clear that they do. You tell anyone who'll listen that you're not a good man, that you live a life that's all your own and don't follow any rules – but all that means is you use your photography as an excuse not to get close to people. I think you're just too scared to see what happens if they do.'

'Perhaps this is an excellent example of why.' Josh's voice turned cold. 'My work isn't an excuse, Lily. It's me. Everything I am.' He paused, still feeling confused. 'I've always been honest about that.'

'You weren't honest tonight,' Lily snapped. 'I get it, you've been rejected just as much as me. I guess I hadn't seen that before – or seen how much it bothered you. And I'm angry so I don't want to talk about this now. But seriously Josh, stop telling everyone else how to live their lives without taking a good look at your own.'

Lily's breath hitched as she swayed and almost lost her footing before turning and breaking into a run, leaving Josh standing on the pavement looking after her, wondering what the hell had just happened.

Chapter Thirty-Four

Luc stood over Lily as she mixed the eggs in the metal bowl, adding a dash of salt. She cleared her throat – it felt dry this morning, a little sore. Probably because she'd fallen asleep last night after a bout of crying. But she wasn't going to think about that. Lily pushed the argument from her mind as she whisked the eggs, getting them to the perfect consistency.

'You are making what?' Luc asked from beside her. He'd been back from France for less than twelve hours but his whites were still starched and gleaming. It was early morning and no one else had arrived in the kitchen. All the surfaces shone and in about twenty minutes the room would be buzzing with pots and pans, knives flashing under the overhead lights as the kitchen staff began to prepare ingredients for the day.

'An omelette.' Lily put the skillet on the hob before adding a dash of butter to the pan.

'You are cooking an *omelette* to impress me?' Luc's thick black eyebrows drew together, making him look more cross than usual.

Lily turned to face him. 'It's not about the complexity of the dish, Chef – it's about the quality. That's what you've always told me; that's what your mother taught you. Or had she changed her opinion when you saw her in France?' Lily kept her chin lifted as she looked at Luc. The chef's expression didn't change but Lily thought she detected a hint of amusement in his eyes, which must have been her imagination because Luc didn't have a sense of humour.

'And like me, my mother is always right – *d'accord.*' Luc pointed at the pan. 'Continue.' He folded his arms and watched her work.

Lily added tomatoes, a smattering of onion and peppers into the pan, breathing deep as the air sizzled with the light fragrance. She loved the smell of food cooking and inhaled it, beating the eggs again. Lily knew making something so basic was a risk, but she wanted Luc to understand what food meant to her. Also, if a person couldn't create a basic dish, they were no use in the kitchen – which was another of Luc's favourite sayings.

Lily waited until the vegetables were just the right consistency before adding the eggs – she slid them across the pan, enjoying the fizz and splatter as they hit the oil. She scattered cheese on the top and watched as it was absorbed into the liquid.

'You love cooking?' Luc asked, watching Lily's expression.

'Always have.' Lily kept her voice light because she knew Luc hated emotion in the kitchen – unless he was the one having the tantrum. 'This is what I've always wanted to do.' She took a chance. 'I've just never been brave enough to say anything before.'

The omelette was perfect so Lily slid it onto the plate she's already laid ready with rocket and tomatoes for colour. She watched as Luc picked up a fork and dug in, chewing slowly. Her heart was in her mouth and she tried not to think about what Josh would say – how he'd encourage to be confident in her choice because she'd made it.

'The flavours are good.' Luc nodded, taking another slice. Did that mean he liked it? 'Good consistency.' He nodded again. 'You haven't overcooked it – most do.' He put the fork down and pushed the plate away and Lily's heart sank because he hadn't finished.

'But not good enough,' Lily said, her voice heavy.

'*Non.*' Luc waved a finger in the air. 'It was *très bon*! Brave, but the perfect choice. You proved you can cook but that you understand you are only at the start of this journey and have much to learn. This is the attitude I want in my kitchen. Lily King, you will join my kitchen as the new commis.'

'Thank you, Chef.' Lily's face exploded into a grin which dimmed when Luc frowned again.

'You will work hard, listen and keep your workstation clean. You will start on the first of January at six a.m. sharp. Speak to Rita about getting your whites,' he said sharply.

'Yes Chef,' Lily said, her smile disappearing as she realised that the only person she really wanted to celebrate with was also the man she never wanted to see again – Josh.

'I got the job,' Lily said, as she headed into the teashop twenty minutes later. Cath popped her head up from behind the counter.

'You did?' Her green eyes danced as she gave Lily a big hug. 'That's fantastic. I shouldn't be celebrating because it means you're going to leave us, but well done. I always suspected Luc was a good guy, even if he does keep it hidden most of the time.' She nudged Lily in the ribs. 'Did you tell Josh yet?'

'No.' Lily avoided Cath's eyes, letting hers slide around the teashop. It wouldn't open for another half an hour but the tables were laid ready for customers and the Christmas lights sparkled. 'He used me and I'm never speaking to him again.'

'Never is a long time Lily,' Cath said gently. 'Perhaps if you let him explain?'

'He tried that already,' Lily grumbled. 'And there's no explanation on earth to justify him using that photo.' Her heart lurched. He had put his career first and used her. Lily held back tears as she remembered her devastation at seeing the photograph on the wall of the castle. Josh was everything he'd said — a selfish rogue and a liar. He'd hurt her. And he was *nothing* like the person she'd fallen in love with – she wasn't about to forget that ever again.

Chapter Thirty-Five

'Fetch.' Josh threw another stick and watched Chester yawn before continuing to trot along the beach, stopping now and again to sniff at seaweed. It was the fourth stick he'd thrown this morning and the dog had ignored them all.

Josh sighed, contemplating the sea and sky. It would rain soon – he could already see the clouds building but didn't feel like going back to the house yet. His camera swung loosely by his side, hitting his leg. Josh picked it up and glared through it, taking in the sky and choppy sea, spanning the horizon, up to the cliffs, but there was nothing he wanted to photograph.

He'd slept badly last night and had got up early so he could walk, but after pacing the sitting room for half an hour and drinking about twelve cups of coffee he'd decided to take Chester for a walk so he didn't end up bumping into Paul or Emily. He wasn't in the mood for recriminations.

Josh looked at the sky again and saw a black cloud that for some reason reminded him of Lily and the expression on her face the night before. He squeezed his eyes shut, pushing her out of his head.

Someone shouted behind him and Josh turned to see Marta and Paul heading up the beach waving. He felt like running in the other direction but knew Marta would track him down to whatever rock he'd chosen to crawl under.

They caught up in minutes.

'You okay?' Paul tapped Josh on the shoulder, looking awkward. 'Marta called at the house and I fancied a walk,' he explained.

'Yep, great.' Josh picked up another stick and threw it, not caring where it went.

'We sold twenty-two pictures last night.' Marta studied Josh before shaking her head. 'Which, by the way, is amazing, but I'm assuming from that cloudy expression you didn't make it up with Lily?'

Josh muttered something unintelligible.

'Did you really think not telling her about the photo was the right thing to do?' Marta asked, looking frustrated.

'It was supposed to be a surprise.' Josh glanced down the beach. If he made a run for it would they be able to catch up? Because he really didn't want to have this conversation.

'I'm not sure she liked it,' Paul said, stating the obvious, but even Marta nodded.

'You think?' Josh snapped, letting the anger inside him take over, stamping down the hurt that seemed to have scorched a gaping hole in his chest.

'I was thinking if you apologised…' Marta ignored Josh's outburst and began to walk towards the sea with Paul, leaving Josh to catch up. After a few seconds he joined them. If they had it out now, at least they'd go away and leave him to stew on his own.

'I've got nothing to apologise for,' Josh grumbled, picking up another stick for Chester to ignore. He threw it into the sea before picking up another. 'She looked beautiful.'

'I don't think it was the photograph Lily didn't like. It was you not telling her about it,' Marta said.

'It was supposed to be a surprise.' Josh ignored the ache that seem to have lodged in his throat, surprised by the power of it. He didn't need Lily – didn't need anyone. He'd get over this. 'The woman has spent years hiding who she is from the world. I thought she was ready. She was ready when she was with me. You took the picture down?' he asked Marta.

'Last night. Had a few people asking if they could buy it.'

'It's not for sale,' Josh growled.

Marta's mobile rang and she pulled it from her pocket, grinning, before apologising and picking it up. 'Simon,' she answered, turning and walking away.

'This isn't about your work, you know that, right?' Paul asked quietly.

'What's that supposed to mean?' Josh stomped a little further down the beach. In a few minutes they'd hit the log – the one that *should* have been the centrepiece of his show.

'I mean you're sensitive about your photos.' Paul held up a hand as Josh tried to interrupt. 'I'm not saying you don't have a right to be. You spent years being told they weren't good enough, that you weren't good enough. It's a miracle you pursued photography at all. But you did.' Paul looked earnest. 'And you make a living at it. To be honest your work is amazing—' Paul's eyes narrowed. 'And if you repeat that in front of anyone I'll deny I ever said it. Seriously, you have a talent most of us only dream of—'

'Says the doctor,' Josh interrupted. 'The man who saves lives.'

'You're the one who captures the world on film and shows us how it really is.' Paul stopped walking and turned to face Josh, looking angry. 'It annoys me that our parents have never recognised your talent and the importance of it – but it infuriates me that you continue to deny it too. Even after all these years and all this success.'

'Deny what?' Josh felt his temper flare. 'I had a show, didn't I? I make a living, don't I? What do you think this is?' He picked up the camera and waved it between them.

'But you never talk about what you do,' Paul said sadly. 'You hate talking to journalists, and rarely show anyone your work or admit what you're up to.' When Josh frowned Paul nodded. 'Oh yes, Marta's filled me in on most of it. And now you've fallen for someone – don't bother denying it, I've never seen that look on your face. You've fallen for someone and she's angry with you. So the first thing you see is a rejection of your work?' Paul looked irritated. 'Lily's angry because you didn't share with her, because you went behind her back. Lily's reaction has nothing to do with your photography. You've got a talent you keep denying and a woman who loves you and you're letting her walk away. If I didn't know you better I'd say you were afraid.'

Out of the corner of his eye, Josh saw Marta join them as she popped the mobile back in her pocket. 'He's either afraid or stupid,' she murmured, sounding unsympathetic. 'Josh, I've known you for years. I've seen first hand the wounds you carry and how you deal with them. I'm not saying you're right or wrong, I'm just saying, isn't it time you accepted who you are and stopped caring what your parents think?'

'I *don't* care what they think.' Exasperated, Josh picked up another stick which he threw towards the waves. Chester wasn't going to chase it, but the mere act of throwing it made him feel better. 'I used to, but I don't any more. I've got people clamouring to buy my photographs. I'm everything I always wanted to be.' The words sounded hollow, even to him.

'Really?' Marta asked gently.

'Okay,' Josh sighed. 'Maybe it bothers me that even now they're offering to pay for me to train to be a doctor; that they've never accepted who I am. That I'm making a decent living but it's still not good enough.'

'And that's not right,' Paul admitted. 'But this is more to do with our mother's relationship with our grandmother than you.'

'That and the kudos that comes from having two sons who are doctors,' Josh said, as Chester came to sniff his feet.

'And you'll never change that,' Paul replied. 'God knows I've tried.'

'You have?' Josh asked, surprised.

Paul cleared his throat. 'You owe me at least one picture for those conversations – yes, I tried. At first I was jealous of you. Then I basked in the glory of their praise, then I began to see it for what it was.'

'You were jealous?' Josh asked, taken aback.

'Of your talent. Damn yes,' Paul admitted. 'Who wouldn't be? Thankfully, as I'm so much better looking than you the balance was restored, so I learned to live with it,' he joked.

'As you stuck up for me I won't give that the response it deserves.' Josh snorted, feeling both humbled and grateful. 'Thank you for trying, I appreciate it. I certainly never knew or I wouldn't have kept trying to steal your girlfriends.'

Paul flashed a grin. 'Lucky for me you never succeeded. But jokes aside, what our parents think doesn't matter. You're successful – enjoy it, see it as karma. They might come around one day, see you for what and who you are, be as proud as they should be. And they might never understand or appreciate your work because they're too caught up in what they think is right – in what they need. Whatever they decide, don't screw your life up because of it. Find Lily and apologise. You'll regret it if you don't.'

'Maybe.' Josh looked up the beach, trying to push Lily from his mind. 'Or maybe I need to walk away.'

'Don't push love away,' Marta said, pressing a gentle hand on Josh's shoulder. 'Especially for all the wrong reasons. You'll regret it if you do.'

But would Josh regret it more if he let Lily into his heart again?

Chapter Thirty-Six

'I can't believe you're leaving after Christmas, Lily,' Cath declared as Lily polished one of the tables in the teashop. It had been busy all afternoon and they were enjoying a short lull that was due to end soon. A coach-load of visitors who'd arrived earlier were making their way around the castle ready for a well-earned slice of cake.

'I'll miss you.' Lily gave Cath and Alice a quick hug before polishing the table again. 'But I can't wait to get started working in the kitchen, and I'll still see you all.'

'You look tired.' Cath studied her. 'Still no word from Josh or your family?'

Tears threatened to spill. 'It's been two days – and I don't want to hear from Josh.' Lily thought about the photograph in the library and her eyes welled up.

'The picture's been taken down if that's what you're worried about,' Alice said. 'I went to take a look this morning and there's a canvas of a log in its place.'

'Marta probably sold it,' Cath guessed and Lily marched to another table so she could wipe it down. A complete stranger might be gazing at her image even now.

The bell at the front of the teashop dinged but Lily didn't bother to turn around. It was only when Cath called her that she looked.

Lily's dad, Scott and Andrew were stood at the doorway. 'If you're here to tell me off again you can just go away,' Lily complained, intending to shoo them out. 'I'm sorry I didn't tell you about Aubrey but you didn't make it easy, to be honest.'

She was almost at the door, ready to make them leave when Scott held up a hand, looking sheepish. 'We know, Lily. That's why we're here and Dad's got something to say.'

'Shall I get you all drinks and cake while you chat?' Cath's sing-song voice seemed out of place in the charged atmosphere but Lily's dad and brothers agreed, sitting at an empty table. 'Give them a chance,' Cath whispered. 'Maybe they want to apologise?'

Lily joined her family and sat, folding her arms, feeling a painful mix of anger and hurt fill her chest.

'I am sorry,' Tom began, his voice raw. 'I talked with your brothers and we realise we weren't fair to you.'

Cath put a hot chocolate in front of Lily along with a slice of cake and served the others. Lily wrapped her hands around the steaming mug as her heart ached.

'We heard you got the job at the restaurant,' Scott mumbled. 'Well done.'

Lily ignored him and glared at her dad. 'Aubrey said you told her to leave when I was in the hospital?'

'That's not what happened but there is some truth in it,' he admitted sadly.

'What truth?'

Her dad looked uncomfortable. 'It's a long story.'

'One I deserve to hear,' Lily said bravely. She wasn't going to let them avoid it any longer.

Tom picked up his mug of hot chocolate and put it down again as he considered the question. 'I'm afraid you won't forgive me Lily…' His forehead creased as he wrestled with the words and Lily could hear the emotion in his voice as he began to talk, had to stop herself from reaching for him. She had to know the truth, even if it broke her.

'I fell head over heels in love with Aubrey. It was sudden and there are probably a lot of reasons for that. I'd been recently widowed and was raising your brothers alone. My life was a mess.' Her dad's voice cracked. 'Then this beautiful woman showed an interest in me and, I've got to admit, I was flattered. We fell in love – at least I did, I'm not sure about Aubrey. We got married and she moved in. When we had you, a beautiful daughter, I thought life couldn't be more complete. But your mother never took to our life. She hated Castle Cove and wanted to move to London.' He grimaced. 'I had the brewery so moving was out of the question. Aubrey found parenting difficult and struggled looking after you. The boys were pretty self-sufficient but you can't exactly leave a newborn to it.' He looked distressed. 'It didn't get better when you grew older. Aubrey kept disappearing into London to interviews   at least that's what she called them, I never really knew what they were. The real reason you got pneumonia is because she left you in your pushchair without a blanket one afternoon while she disappeared.'

'Left me?' Lily asked, shocked. 'For how long?'

'Almost an hour. I know because Olive found you. Apparently your mum had been making a call.'

'That's… awful.' The news shocked her, and Lily took a moment to process it. How a mother could leave her baby out in the cold alone was beyond her.

'You picked up a nasty cold and it got worse from there… but Aubrey never took responsibility for it. Everything was always someone else's fault… if you were hungry it was because you hadn't eaten enough, or the supermarket sold the wrong food. If you cried it was because you were a fussy baby.'

'So she was an irresponsible mother,' Lily confirmed gently, ignoring the sick feeling in her chest. 'I'd still like to know why you made her leave for good, why she never got in touch. People change – she might have – especially as they get older.'

'It doesn't explain it,' her dad agreed. 'Perhaps I thought you deserved better. You were such a pretty baby, so good, you never fussed. I could take you to work and you never got in my way – only wanted to help.' His eyes shone with love and then his face darkened. 'Aubrey would get annoyed with you over the slightest thing and it began to bother me. You seemed anxious when you were around her. When you got sick and were admitted into the hospital, she didn't want to visit, said she hated hospitals. Your brothers and even Ted wanted to be there round the clock, but she went shopping in Portsmouth. I lost my temper.'

'And?' Lily asked, finding it hard to imagine a mother shopping while her baby daughter lay in hospital, fighting for her life. She was beginning to understand her father's reservations.

'I told her that unless she was willing to take on the responsibility of being your parent, you'd be better off without her and that she should leave.' Her dad paled. 'I think I expected her to realise you deserved better and to rush to the hospital to see you.'

'What did happen?'

'Aubrey went home and packed her bags. She told me she wasn't cut out for motherhood, and perhaps I was right.' His shoulders slumped. 'I felt guilty about that. I didn't intend to drive her away.'

'But she couldn't wait to go,' Scott snapped, his expression murderous. 'Aubrey didn't even stop by at the hospital to say goodbye.'

'Oh…' Lily trailed off, speechless. In her wildest dreams, she wouldn't have imagined that level of callousness.

'The boys weren't even upset when she went.' Her dad looked devastated. 'That's when I realised how little she cared. She'd been too busy pursuing her modelling dream.'

'In short, we didn't matter,' Andrew finished, his voice matter-of-fact. 'You can't blame Dad because Aubrey left. The woman made a grave mistake, then had one conversation she didn't like, walked away and never came back. It's like she'd been waiting for it – and already knew it would be the final straw. You were distraught at first. I still remember. You were eighteen months old and wanted your mummy. Only Mummy had disappeared to London. You cried every day for three weeks. Aubrey never got in touch, never bothered to call. For all she knew, you'd died. I've got no idea what her reasons are for getting in touch now, but I will say I doubt it's got anything to do with you. We're your family, Lily.' Andrew reached out a rough hand, placing it over hers. 'We love you, always have. Dad sat by your bed day and night when you were sick; we had a party when you came home. We've not been perfect, but we've always loved you.'

'If you want to have a relationship with your mother now though Lily, that's your right. We just ask that you're careful. I'm concerned she might break your heart all over again,' her dad pleaded. 'It was hard enough when you were too young to understand what was happening, now I'm afraid she'll destroy you.'

'Oh Dad,' Lily started, finding it hard to talk because she felt so emotional. 'Aubrey wants me to be a model, but I don't want that,' she admitted, feeling her anger evaporate. 'Perhaps you are right and she does want to use me, I've thought the same… but I'd like to find out for sure. She called this morning and wants to meet and talk. I'll do it, because she just might have changed enough to let me be her daughter without expecting anything back. I'm willing to listen and in my heart I don't believe she's that callous. But whatever happens, she can't destroy me because I have all of you. You're my real family because you love me just as I am and you've always been there for me.' A tear slid down Lily's cheek as her brothers and dad each lay a hand over hers and squeezed.

'Enough of the soppy stuff.' Scott snatched his hand back suddenly and picked up his drink, looking awkward. 'When do you start work in the restaurant?'

Lily wiped the tears from her face and grinned, feeling better than she had in days. 'In the new year.'

'You don't look very happy considering it's your dream,' Andrew pointed out.

'I don't know…' Lily trailed off. 'Things haven't worked out the way I planned.'

'The photograph?' her dad asked.

'I didn't know Josh was going to put it in the show.' Lily's cheeks burned.

'It was a pretty picture,' Scott admitted. 'It made me mad at first but you looked… content, I think is the word I'm after. You have that expression you get sometimes, when you're thinking, or cooking. Josh caught it perfectly.'

'Apparently it's already been sold.' Lily scowled.

'It hasn't,' Tom said.

'Cath said it's been taken out of the library, that there's another picture in its place.'

'It wasn't for sale. I know because I asked if I could buy it.' Lily's dad looked sheepish. 'I was taken aback, but I went to look at it again and you looked so happy. I thought I'd get it – to remind you that you can feel like that whenever you want to. When I talked to Marta she said Josh refused to sell it and wanted it taken down. I guess he's got it now.'

Lily ran a hand across her forehead, confused.

'Maybe he saw you were upset and wanted to make it better?' Andrew suggested.

'I was horrible to him.' Lily chewed her thumbnail, remembering the awful things she'd said.

'I'm guessing he'll forgive you,' Scott murmured. 'He has that look when he's with you.'

'What look?'

'The look of a man who's in love. My guess is he wanted to impress you with the photo and was trying to show you how he felt,' Scott said.

'He didn't tell me,' Lily grumbled. 'He lied.'

'I think he wanted to surprise you,' Cath said softly, standing over them holding a brown paper bag.

'I hadn't thought about it like that before. But he should have asked,' Lily said, uncertain now.

'Perhaps.' Cath looked thoughtful. 'And you'd have said no, which would have been a shame because that was one awesome photo. But are you going to punish him forever? Let this thing between you go because he made a mistake?'

'I… I don't know,' Lily murmured. All Josh had ever done was support her. It was the only reason she'd got the job with Luc and the only reason she'd found the courage to be honest with her family now. Perhaps the picture had been him showing her who she'd become? He'd said as much but she'd shouted him down. He'd been wrong, but she hadn't listened when he'd tried to explain.

'I'm not one for romantic declarations, but I'm guessing your Josh might need one.' Lily's dad suggested.

'Jeez!' Scott and Andrew looked disgusted.

'I *am* one for romantic declarations,' Cath murmured. 'And that man deserves one, maybe even a slice of Death by Chocolate.' Cath handed Lily the brown bag. A quick look inside confirmed it was filled with cake. 'You can take off now. Alice and I will finish up.'

'I've got three more hours to work,' Lily gasped as butterflies filled her stomach.

'You've got something far more important to do instead,' Cath said. 'Be brave, Lily King. You've got the job you always wanted – now it's time to get your man.'

Chapter Thirty-Seven

Josh wasn't on the beach, he wasn't at home or in Picture Perfect – Lily had checked there first and had found the lights off and the entrance locked. She'd called his mobile about a million times but it had gone to answerphone. Even Emily and Paul didn't know where Josh had gone. His car was missing, so was Chester and so was the framed canvas of her that Marta had removed from the show. Lily knew that because Emily had said it was resting beside the fireplace in Josh's sitting room in the early hours of this morning, before disappearing along with a ton of other photos.

Lily drove the Beast along Charles Street heading out of Castle Cove. The air was cold but the sky looked blue and clear and Lily knew Josh sometimes headed for the cliffs to walk Chester if the weather was decent. If he wasn't there he might have decided to head for the airfield again so he could put his foot down. If he wasn't there either, Lily didn't know where to look and she *had* to find him.

Lily drove along the coast, searching the roads for Josh's Porsche. Was he leaving, perhaps heading for London – surely he wouldn't miss the wedding?

Lily's heart ached as she thought about the awful things she'd said on the night of the show. She turned a sharp corner and as she did, the Beast slipped over the white lines in the centre and almost collided with a car coming in the other direction. She slammed on her brakes and swerved back on the right side of the road again. At the same time, the car she'd almost collided with swerved in the other direction and glided off the tarmac with a long screech before coming to a standstill in a grassy ditch on the other side of the road.

'Oh no.' Feeling wobbly and guilt-ridden, Lily drew the Beast to a stop and got out before sprinting towards the car she'd run off the road in a panic. She felt terrible. What if she'd hurt the driver because she hadn't been paying attention? She'd never forgive herself.

Then Lily's heart raced even more, because she recognised the black Porsche immediately and the man emerging from the driver's side.

Lily headed towards Josh, her mouth gaping as she tried to think of what to say. Sorry didn't seem sufficient – even if it did sum up her feelings.

As Josh spotted her he came to a standstill. 'I know you loathed the photo, but isn't this a little extreme?' He looked at the flat tyre on the front of his car. 'Or is it just the Porsche you dislike?'

'It's not that.' Lily's heart fluttered. Josh looked tired and unhappy, and she had an irresistible urge to hurl herself at him. 'I mean, it was an accident.'

Josh looked at her blankly.

'I wanted to apologise,' Lily blurted.

'By running me off the road?'

'I was trying to find you. I wanted to say sorry for losing my temper at your show, for saying you put your work first. I was so angry I didn't see what you were trying to do.'

A deep groove appeared in Josh's forehead. 'No. It was my fault. I've done a lot of thinking since my brother and Marta gave me a good talking to yesterday. A man can only be told he's an idiot so many times before he realises it's true. I just went for a drive to clear my head and was heading back to Castle Cove to find you and apologise. I've got all the canvases of you in the boot.' Josh tipped his head towards the Porsche. 'I thought we could have a bonfire on the beach, maybe cook marshmallows?'

'I don't want a bonfire.' Lily edged closer to him, feeling her heart fill. 'I can't believe you'd burn your work for me.'

'I think I've finally realised they're just photos,' Josh said softly.

'They're a lot more than that – and I don't want to burn them. I won't say no to the marshmallows though, we trainee chefs don't have to worry about our figures.'

'You got the job?' Josh's expression lit up and he stepped closer to Lily. They were standing in the middle of the road now so Josh took her hand and led her to the safety of the bank.

'I did. But you were the only person I wanted to tell. I'm pretty sure I couldn't have done it without you.'

'You would have.' Josh put a palm against her cheek. 'I have a feeling you could do anything you set your mind to.'

'Perhaps.' Lily leaned into his hand. 'But only because you helped set the real me free. I'm sorry. For doubting your motives, for pushing you away – I'm not sure why I did it.'

'I do.' Josh's expression softened. 'You were afraid of being hurt. I know because I felt the same. Perhaps that's why I didn't tell you about the photograph.'

'Or perhaps you wanted to surprise me?' Lily suggested. 'I should have given you credit and understood.'

'I was trying to tell you I love you, my wild Lily King. Whatever you're wearing, whatever you're doing – I love the real woman behind those smiles. I know this isn't the best place to say it.' Josh looked at the Beast on the other side of the road, at his Porsche in the ditch. 'I've spent years putting my work first, rejecting love and relationships – searching for life through my lens, perhaps hiding behind my photographs. Then you came along and suddenly none of that mattered.'

Lily grinned. 'You know I'm going to ask you to repeat that when we're somewhere more romantic, don't you? Perhaps with marshmallows? And I've got cake in the car.'

Josh laughed. 'I might need a glass of whisky too.'

'Done.' Lily looked up, suddenly serious. 'I love you too, Josh Havellin-Scott. For your talent and honesty, for seeing me as I truly am. I'm grateful for that lens of yours, proud of the man you are, and I'm so sorry I doubted you.'

Josh leaned down for a long slow kiss. 'I'm just glad we found our way back to each other.'

Chapter Thirty-Eight

The grand entrance to Cove Castle had high vaulted ceilings of exposed brick lined with dark oak beams decorated with sparkling white Christmas lights. A star hung above the crowd gathered below, who were sipping a combination of champagne, Suze's special Poinsetta punch and Castling from sparkling glasses. Waiters dressed in black and white circled the room carrying silver trays piled high with canapes.

'You look beautiful.' Josh swiped a fig and goat's cheese puff from a tray, swallowed it and took a quick snap of Lily before stepping backwards. He wore the dark suit and shiny black and red shoes they'd chosen in Happily Ever After and looked handsome and relaxed. 'The blue bridesmaid dress suits you. I almost prefer it to the wedding gown, although nothing will beat my shirt,' Josh joked, his brown eyes warm.

'Just wait until you see Emily,' Lily beamed, as Ted and Olive came to join them. Ted wore his red fleece but had dressed up in suit trousers especially. Olive wore a huge yellow tent dress.

'Where is Emily?' Ted looked around the room. 'Is she waiting to make an entrance? Should we all be seated?' He pointed to the chapel where Josh's parents were busy chatting with Anya and Pat.

'No,' Paul replied, arriving to join them. He was dressed in the same dark suit as Josh and they both wore a red rose with silver beads and sparkle in their buttonholes. Lily smiled, remembering choosing the flowers. 'Enjoy your drinks first, and the canapes. Emily is with Ben. She wanted to arrive in the Rolls Royce with her dad.' Paul grinned at Josh. 'I'm looking forward to driving Simon's Mercedes later.'

'The seats are very comfortable.' Lily caught Josh's eye and giggled. 'Are you nervous?'

'No.' Paul's eyes darted towards the chapel. 'Not in the least. I can't wait to get married.' His expression turned sly. 'I'm pretty sure more people should try it.'

'They take a lot of organising.' Josh smiled.

'You two are old hands.'

'It's all about the cake,' Josh murmured, taking Lily's hand as her dad, Andrew and Scott wandered over, holding matching glasses of Castling.

'Don't forget the shoes.' Lily grinned at Josh.

'The car's outside.' Scott ushered them towards the chapel. 'Emily asked you to join her, Lily. I think she wants someone to hold the train. Aren't you meant to be taking photographs instead of ogling my sister?' he joked.

Josh held the camera up to his face again to take one last shot before Lily headed for the entrance. 'I'll see you in a sec,' he promised. 'I just want a picture of my brother waiting in the chapel looking terrified. Tell Emily I said good luck.'

As Lily got to the entrance Simon and Marta walked through it holding hands.

'Emily's just arrived.' Marta smiled.

'Are Paul and Josh's parents over there?' Simon asked, without taking his eyes off Marta.

'They've only come for the ceremony,' Lily confessed. 'They can't stay for the rest apparently, because their dad has to work.' Or maybe it was just an excuse to avoid any more difficult conversations with their sons? Especially now they knew Josh would never be a doctor and Paul agreed with him. Perhaps it was for the best. Sometimes you had to be prepared to walk away from people if they weren't able to accept you.

'I'll see you in the chapel.' Lily kissed them both.

On the way outside, Lily paused by the Christmas tree to the right of the entrance. Rita had redecorated it this morning with tiny brides and grooms which hung like baubles along with red roses that matched the bridal flowers. On the top a fairy resembling the one in the restaurant sparkled and Lily grinned, remembering her argument with Josh when he'd helped her decorate the tree weeks earlier. Thanks to him her light now shone for everyone to see.

When Lily got outside, she found Ben standing beside the shiny cream and black vintage Rolls Royce that had been dressed with a huge red ribbon. He opened the door and Emily got out. Lily picked up the silky train so it didn't drag on the floor. She'd helped her friend get ready earlier but seeing the beautiful white dress with the diamanté belt sparkling in the winter sunshine brought tears to her eyes.

'You look gorgeous Em – Paul's going to fall in love with you all over again.' Lily blushed, remembering Josh's reaction when she'd worn it in the changing room at Happily Ever After.

'You did good work.' Emily gave Lily a quick hug, taking care not to crush the bouquet of red roses in her hand. 'Are Paul's parents here?' Emily's eyes darted towards the castle.

'Yes, and they're behaving. Paul had a word. Today is going to be perfect, Em.'

Emily nodded. 'I know, I just love the dress, and these are exactly what I wanted.' She kicked her foot from underneath her skirt, flashing her sparkling shoes. 'Come this evening, we'll have the top down on the Mercedes and I'll be flaunting these babies to anyone who cares to look.'

Beside her, Ben rolled his eyes, looking embarrassed. 'Shall we head inside? It's taken me a while to come around to your choice, Emily. But I'll admit you've made a good one, so let's get on with it before he changes his mind.'

They began to head up the stairway, past the large sparkling Christmas candles that ran along the edges of the stairs. As they did, Josh walked down, making Lily's heart spin. He turned to Ben and Emily. 'If you stand halfway up, I'll get a shot of you both with the castle in the background. You look gorgeous Emily, my brother's a lucky man. I'm not sure he deserves you.'

'He'd better or I'll be coming after you,' Ben joked, following his daughter up the steps, leaving Josh and Lily standing at the bottom.

After Josh took pictures they walked into the grand entrance together. It was empty now as the guests had been seated in the chapel minutes earlier. Lily absorbed the sparkling white and silver lights, the candles burning on the mantlepiece next to china bride and groom ornaments, the fire underneath which had been lit this morning specially. Someone had even placed a mixture of dried lavender and spices between the logs and the room smelled delicious.

'Can we take a quick look at the cake before we go in?' Emily asked, looking towards the restaurant. 'I want to see it again and I'm sure the bride should always be late.'

'Definitely,' Josh laughed. 'Paul's used to getting what he wants – I recommend you start as you mean to go on and keep him on his toes.'

Two three-tiered cakes sat side by side on a table covered with a white starched tablecloth sprinkled with silver and red confetti. The cakes were the same size and shape and each had a bride and groom on top, but the resemblance ended there. The Fruit Cake looked elegant with traditional white icing and silver baubles interlaced between piped royal icing. Beside it, Josh's choice was an explosion of colour – each tier a rainbow of pinks, purples, greens and yellows dotted with chocolate buttons, Smarties, Maltesers and an array of multi-coloured sweets.

'Eye-catching,' Emily laughed as she approached the table. 'I love them, but I'm not sure whether to eat the Fruit Cake or sweet shop first.'

'I'd go with the fruit,' Josh said, smiling as he took a couple of shots. 'Leave more of the interesting one for me.'

'Here you are,' Rita shrieked from the restaurant door. 'Your groom is expecting you Emily, and unless I'm mistaken he's developed a few grey hairs in the last ten minutes wondering if you're going to turn up. Don't you want to get married?'

'I do. Of course I do,' Emily exclaimed, heading towards the chapel, quickly followed by Ben, Lily and Josh.

'He'll wait,' Josh soothed. 'Give me a second to join him and I'll get some photos of you walking down the aisle.'

The wedding march began as Josh disappeared into the chapel leaving Emily, Ben and Lily waiting patiently outside.

'Nervous?' Lily asked Emily.

'Excited.' Emily beamed as Ben took her arm. Lily picked up the train on Emily's dress and they walked slowly into the chapel. Lily's breath caught as she took in the vaulted ceilings lined with white and silver lights. Someone had placed hundreds of white candles in tall silver candelabras along each wall and the effect was both Christmassy and romantic, almost magical.

The chairs were packed on both sides of the aisle. Even Luc and Suze had taken a short break from preparing the wedding breakfast to watch the ceremony.

The music continued and Lily's heart swelled as they passed Cath, Shaun, Alice, Jay, Ted, Olive, Anya, Nate, Gayle, Pat from Patty Cakes, Julie from Happily Ever After, Scott, Andrew and her dad who wiped a tear from his eye as she glided down the aisle past them all.

Paul looked stunned as Emily drew closer and Lily was sure his eyes filled with tears. Then his face broke out into a huge grin and he winked at Emily before they both turned to face the vicar. Lily kept her face fixed forwards throughout the ceremony, watching her friend, but her eyes crept to Josh a couple of times before the end.

Afterwards Josh fell into line next to her as they followed the bride and groom out of the chapel towards the grand hall where Josh planned to take photos.

As they drew towards the crowd and Josh readied his camera, Lily leaned over to murmur in his ear. 'Thank you for doing the photos. I know you don't do people.'

Josh pointed the camera at her and took a quick photo. 'I do now, thanks to you giving me a second chance.' He edged closer to kiss her gently on the lips and whispered, 'Wild Lily King, you blew into my life, turned it upside down and showed me what I've always needed. Do you think you could spend the rest of your life with a recovering Porsche driver and rebellious photographer who loves you?' He leaned in again and took the kiss deeper, drawing Lily to him as the crowds of people milled around them, their voices buzzing, until someone coughed and laughed and Josh drew back to look into Lily's face. 'Well?'

Lily grinned as her heart filled. 'I do.'

A Letter from Donna

I want to say a huge thank you for choosing to read *The Little Christmas Teashop of Second Chances*. If you enjoyed it (I do hope you did) and want to keep up to date with all my latest releases, just sign up at the following link. Your email address will never be shared and you can unsubscribe at any time.

www.bookouture.com/donna-ashcroft

I had such a good time writing *The Little Christmas Teashop of Second Chances* – the characters constantly made me laugh, doing all kinds of things I wasn't expecting, and I'm so delighted to be sharing it with you. Did you love Josh and his rebel ways as much as I did? Were you rooting for Lily to finally let go and be herself? I hope the romance between them left you feeling warm and Christmassy. If so, it would be wonderful if you could please leave a short review. Not only do I want to know what you thought, it might encourage a new reader to pick up my book for the first time.

I really love hearing from my readers – so please say hi on my Facebook page, through Twitter, or on my website.

Thanks,
Donna Ashcroft

DonnaAshcroftAuthor

@Donnashc

www.donna-writes.co.uk

donnaashcroftauthor/

Acknowledgements

Writing a book is a little like being pregnant. Some days you feel like it's never going to end, on others you're filled with a glowing sense of achievement. And whether things are going badly or well, you've got your friends, colleagues, family and even strangers, cheering you on, helping you to the end – without them all, you'd never get to the good bit.

So, thank you… to my romantic hero Chris, and gorgeous kids Erren and Charlie, for putting up with my moods, for all those squillions of cups of coffee and tea, and for the gin and tonic lollies. You've kept me sane and you got me here.

To Natasha Harding for your magical editing, advice and assistance in directing my wayward creative brain. To Kim Nash and the rest of the Bookouture team for the support, fantastic covers, blurbs, social media support and everything else you've done.

To Connor McKinney, Head Chef at the Akeman in Tring, for sharing your knowledge of working in a restaurant – all mistakes and misinterpretations are my own. To Tara Grey, for the insight into being a photographer. Josh was a hot mess before you.

To Jules Wake for the constant encouragement, brainstorming and write-in Fridays that I look forward to every week. To Katy

Walker for the weekend in France where I wrote my first two chapters – they wouldn't have happened without you, the red wine or cheese.

To Guy Caplin for the incredible marketing gif – I've loved seeing my book come to life!

To Bernadette O'Dwyer – my Katie Fforde Bursary twin – for the support, emails and fabulous review. I do appreciate it.

To Jackie Campbell and Julie Anderson, for your encouragement, listening and drinking skills – I can't (and wouldn't want to) remember my life before you came into it.

To Kirsty Egan-Carter, Paul Campbell, Daniel Munday, Hester Thorp and Sue Moseley for the support and Chris Conrad for all those retweets. To the Thursday night mums Amanda, Caroline, Sarah, Liz, Guilia and Claire, for cheering me on. To Mrs Beryl Dale who taught me many things over the years, not least to never give up – you may be gone but you'll never be forgotten.

To Ben, my boss, who let me work four days a week, giving me time to write and to my colleagues Gemma, Kay, Masha, Olga and Alasdair for the good work days.

Last but not least, to Mum, Dad, Tanya, Peter, Philip, Christelle, Sonia, Auntie Gillian, Uncle Ian, Auntie Rita, Louis and Lynda – thanks for making every single relative, friend and neighbour buy my first book. Now please can you do it again?

Printed in Great Britain
by Amazon